THE YEAR'S
BEST

MYSTERY AND SUSPENSE
STORIES

1992

Other Books by Edward D. Hoch

THE YEAR'S BEST

MYSTERY AND SUSPENSE STORIES

1992

Edited by Edward D. Hoch

WALKER AND COMPANY
NEW YORK

First published in the United States of America in 1992
by Walker Publishing Company, Inc.

Published simultaneously in Canada by Thomas Allen & Son
Canada, Limited, Markham, Ontario

Library of Congress Cataloging-in-Publication Card Number
83-646567

Printed in the United States of America

2   4   6   8   10   9   7   5   3   1

For Mike Nevins

CONTENTS

Introduction

The year 1991 was one of major changes for the mystery-suspense short story. The most important change was a sad one—the death of Eleanor Sullivan, who had worked closely with Fred Dannay on *Ellery Queen's Mystery Magazine* from 1970 to 1982 and guided its editorial direction in the years since his death. Uppermost in Eleanor's mind during the nine years of her editorship was what Fred would have wanted, what he would have done in various circumstances. She'll be missed, and fondly remembered, by everyone who knew her.

Although Eleanor Sullivan died in July, she had completed purchases of virtually all stories through the 1991 issues. The editorship of *EQMM* has now passed to Janet Hutchings, and the first few issues of the new year show every sign of continuing the magazine's high level of achievement.

The other major change last year was really a continuation of a trend we had noted previously—the increasing importance of anthologies of original mystery and suspense stories. For the first time in this year's volume, half of the twelve stories I selected are from original anthologies or collections. Part of the reason for this was a drop in the number of new stories published by mystery magazines. *EQMM* used only ninety-two new stories, reprinting numerous earlier tales as part of its fiftieth anniversary celebration.

But in America, Great Britain, and Canada, original anthologies and anthology series continued to proliferate. This past year we had *Cold Blood III, Dark Crimes, The Fourth Woman-sleuth Anthology, Sisters in Crime 4, New Crimes 3, Crime Waves 1, Winter's Crimes 23,* and *Midwinter Mysteries 1.* All are annuals using all or some new fiction. In addition to these, the bibliography at the back of this book lists several other one-shot anthologies, often devoted to a particular subject like Christmas or cats—the two favorites in recent years. Other anthologies, published as new collections of horror or fantasy, were often found to contain a few crime or mystery tales.

The year was not a particularly strong one for series sleuths in the short-story length, although Bill Pronzini's "Nameless" and my own Dr. Sam Hawthorne are both present here. Also appearing is Stuart M. Kaminsky's imaginative resurrection of Inspector Porfiry Petrovich from Dostoevsky's classic *Crime and Punishment.* And we can hope that we might be seeing more of Carolyn Wheat's troubled New York transit police Sergeant Maureen Gallagher.

Here too is the MWA Edgar Award–winner by Wendy Hornsby, two Edgar nominees, Doug Allyn and Lawrence Block, an award-winning story from Canada by Peter Robinson, and an *EQMM* Reader's Award–winner by Peter Lovesey. Completing this year's volume are three fine stories by Brendan DuBois, Barry N. Malzberg, and Ruth Rendell.

My special thanks to John F. Suter, Douglas G. Greene, and my wife, Patricia, who helped in immeasurable ways with this year's volume.

A late note: On January 24, 1992, it was announced that the Dell Magazines division of the Bantam Doubleday Dell publishing group had acquired *Ellery Queen's Mystery Magazine, Alfred Hitchcock's Mystery Magazine, Analog Science Fiction and Fact,* and *Isaac Asimov's Science Fiction Magazine* from Davis Publications. The news was certain to signal further changes for the future.

—*Edward D. Hoch*

THE YEAR'S BEST

BEST

MYSTERY AND SUSPENSE STORIES

1992

DOUG ALLYN
SLEEPER

In 1985 the Mystery Writers of America presented Doug Allyn with its Robert L. Fish Memorial Award for his first mystery short story. Since that time Allyn has become a regular in the mystery magazines, often with gripping tales that read like novels in miniature. Such a tale is "Sleeper," a memorable novelette that earned him his third MWA Edgar nomination and marks his third appearance in this series.

Cass shot the street sign first, held it in close-up for five seconds to give the location, then two seconds longer to give viewers time to cope with the Polish name. Kosciusko Street. He softened the focus on the sign a bit, bringing in the maple leaves above it, gray-green in the August heat, then panned the minicam slowly to the tickytack split-level tract house midway up the block. The house was a white clapboard box with *faux*-brick facing exactly like its neighbors, a row of baby boomers fading quietly into middle age. A white picket fence minus a slat here and there encircled the front yard, sorry as a gap-toothed grin.

Cass walked cautiously up the driveway, filming all the way, the shoulder-held Panasonic Steadycam smoothing his movements. Keeping the waning afternoon light at his back so he wouldn't need a sun gun, he zoomed through the open garage door, did a swooping pass over the battered old Chevy four-door parked inside, panned down to the hydraulic jack jammed under the front wheel hub, then followed the rusty rocker panels to the splayed, denim-clad legs protruding from beneath the car.

He zoomed a little closer, focusing the shot the way a human eye would see it but without blinking. He slid down the legs, tracing the pant seams past the frayed knees to the scuffed

1

brown work shoes, then pulled the shot in even tighter, dropping it to the trickle of blood crawling away from the body,
inching along a wayward crack down the concrete driveway.
Beautiful.

Great stuff. He felt his breathing go shallow, the familiar
sensual tightness in his chest, as he tracked the blood trail all
the way out to the street. The blood gleamed black as oil in the
Steadycam's viewfinder, but it would glow bright crimson on
the "Six O'Clock News." Lingering on it would crowd the
borderline of airtime standards-and-practices guidelines for
early evening, but he didn't give a damn. It was dynamite film.
Still, in TV news there's no such thing as too much footage, so
he reshot the car and the legs beneath it from three more
perspectives, shifting the shot every five to fifteen seconds,
attention span of Mr. and Mrs. Average American tube spud.

He was filming the house from the driveway when the front
door opened and Stephanie Hawkins came out with a stunned,
chubby blonde in nurse's whites. The widow? Definitely was if
she was married to the poor sonovabitch pancaked under the
car. He shifted the lens back toward the garage, watching Hawk
out of the corner of his eye for a signal that the woman had
given permission to film, sure she'd get it. She nearly always
did. Sympathy, empathy, anger, whatever it took, Hawk had it.
She was the best newswoman Cass had worked with since he
came back to Motown from the Coast, possibly the best in the
Metro Detroit media market. Tall, slender, articulate, clear cafe-
au-lait skin, great cheekbones, cool under fire. Too good, really,
to stay at WVLT much longer. A pity. Welcome to show biz,
check your heart at the door. Hawk tapped the side of her purse
as she took out her portable recorder mike. Okay to shoot.

Cass casually swung the Steadycam lens, following the neatly
trimmed hedge to the small front porch, keeping his distance
to avoid spooking the woman. No need to move closer, Hawk
had positioned herself in good light, he could shoot them from
the driveway. He zoomed in, centering the shot on Hawk first,
then widening to the woman, trembling, haggard—Sweet Jesus!

The pallid, tear-streaked face in the viewfinder flashed from
black-and-white to color, filling the lens. Sonya! It was Sonya!

And the guy under the car. Stan? It must've been! Holy Mary Mother of God— The lens started to blur.

Shoot it. It's not real, damn it, it's just TV. A photo op. Shoot it. Get the footage. His mouth was cotton-dry, blood pounding at his temples. But the lens never wavered, never blinked. And gradually Sonya's face reverted to being another image in the viewfinder again, losing her color, her reality, fading to black-and-white. She was mumbling responses to Stephanie Hawkins's professionally empathetic questions, but Cass could see she was in shock, out on her feet, dabbing helplessly at her streaming eyes, some snot on her upper lip. Running on empty. He kept shooting her, following the conversation with the camera's eye, hearing sirens in the distance now.

Hawk heard them, too, switched off her mike, said something to Sonya, and helped her stumble back inside, leaving the front door ajar for Cass. He finished the shot, hesitated, wondering whether he should go into the garage to check the body. No— whoever was under that car was dead. No question. And he already had all the footage he needed. He trotted up the sidewalk to the porch.

The living room was cramped and dim after the afternoon glare, too much stuff in it, a worn turquoise Sears sofa and matching easy chairs, sagging Lazyboy in front of the tube, knickknacks, figurines cluttering the end tables, cheap reproductions and family photos on the walls. He'd never been here, but the room was familiar, like the home he'd grown up in, or his friends' houses.

His friend. Stan. He didn't have to ask. A wedding picture of Stan and Sonya on the coffee table told him more than he wanted to know. Cass stood silent, invisible as his own ghost in an old friend's home. Half hiding behind his Minicam, feeling the subsonic vibration of its gyro against his cheek, the comforting heartbeat hum of the machine. Not shooting, just . . . watching. Cool, detached, untouched. Until he noticed the car.

He'd been idly scanning the junk on the mantel over the gas-log fireplace: postcards, a bowling trophy, a framed snapshot of Stan, Sonya, and her younger brother—what was his name? Billy? No, Bobby. That was it. Twelve or thirteen when Cass last saw him, early twenties in the picture. The car was half hidden behind the snapshot. A plastic-and-steel model of a '57 Ford Skyliner hardtop convertible. My God.

He walked to the mantel, picked up the car, half hearing Sonya tell Hawk how she'd come home from work, found Stan in the garage, called 911. Mint condition. The Ford's wheels still spun, perfectly balanced. The headlights worked. The hard-top retracted invisibly into the trunk better than the original ever had, thanks to Stan.

Months. He and Stan had handcrafted every single part of the little Ford in high school machine shop. After school, between classes, whenever. Copped second prize at the Michigan State Fair. A phony silver cup and a fifty-buck savings bond. Cass had long since lost the cup somewhere. But Stan had kept—

"Cass?" He glanced up. Both Sonya and Hawk were staring at him. Sonya looked bloodless, ready to fall. "Cass? I don't under-stand. How did you get here? How did you know?"

"Sonya, I—didn't know. I'm a cameraman, WVLT News. We monitor police and EMS bands; we just heard the call. I'm sorry, I can't tell you how sorry I am—"

An EMS van howled to a halt in the driveway, doors slam-ming, men charging into the garage.

"Oh," Sonya said, "seeing you there I thought I must be asleep, that— Oh, God. Stan—" Sonya lost it, broke down completely, dropped her face to her knees, wailing, covering her head with her forearms like a child trying to avoid a beating.

"Mrs. Sliwa? Sonya?" One of the EMS attendants rapped on the door once, stepped in without waiting, knelt awkwardly beside her, took her hand. "Sonya? You okay?" He was tall, rangy, with reddish thinning hair, freckled face, thick wrists. He kept swallowing hard, eyes misty, struggling to keep himself together. He glanced vaguely at Hawk, blinking in confusion as he tried to place her. And he noticed Cass. And the WVLT logo on the minicam.

"Hey, what the hell is this?" he said slowly, rising. "What are you people doing in here?"

"Mrs. Sliwa invited us in. I'm Stephanie Hawkins—"

"I know who you are. I asked what the hell you're doing here. Christ, the cops aren't even here yet and you're already tryna get a goddamn interview? You get the hell outa here, the botha ya!"

"Charlie, please," Sonya quavered, "it's all right. I—"

"No, it ain't all right! Goddamn vultures! Damn it, clear out, lady, now, or I'll kick your black ass all the way back to Motown where you belong. Now move it!"

"Hey," Cass said, setting the camera aside, "just cool down, buddy, that's enough!"

"It's all right, Cass," Stephanie said, rising. "The gentleman's upset and it's time to go, anyway. Mrs. Sliwa, I'm very sorry about your loss—"

"Keep your sympathy, lady," Charlie said. "Stan was nothin' to you but a couple minutes on TV. G'wan, get outa here."

"Okay, okay," Cass said, shouldering the camera, opening the front door. "Miss Hawkins, ma'am?"

Hawk hesitated, standing her ground in front of Mister Charlie for a moment, then stalked out past Cass without a word.

"Sonya?" Cass said. "I'm sorry as hell, you know that. I'll call you later." He glanced back from the doorway. Charlie was on his knees again, holding Sonya's hands. He wasn't crying, but he wasn't far from it.

A blue-and-white patrol car, flashers on, pulled in and parked beside the EMS van. Local Warsaw Heights cops. A salt-and-pepper team, Misiak and Jackson. Big and Bigger. Cass knew them from other crime scenes in the Heights—a shooting, a dope bust.

"*Jak sie mas, bracia*, Meesh," Cass said. "How you doin'?"

"Don't gimme that homeboy stuff, Novak," Misiak said, "I only speak Polish to my mother. You guys already interview the lady who called?"

"Afraid so."

"Damn it, Novak, you know you people been warned about doin' interviews at a crime scene before the police—"

"No offense, officer," Hawk interrupted coldly, "but it's not our fault you can get a pizza delivered in this town faster than you can get a cop. This isn't a crime scene until you tie it off, and we're accredited members of the press with First Amendment rights. If you've got a problem with that, I'd love to hear it. On camera, of course. You feel like an interview?"

Misiak glared at her a moment, then shrugged. "Nah, just lemme do my job, stay outa the way, okay?"

"And is harassing the press part of your job?"

"No, ma'am," Misiak said. "Mostly we just hang out at Dunkin' Donuts and snooze in the booths. In between gang fights and drive-by shootin's. 'Scuse me, I got next of kin to talk to, assumin' she feels like talkin' to anybody *else*." Misiak stamped off toward the front door. His partner, Walker Jackson, finished talking to the EMS medic in the garage and wandered over.

"Nice work, Miss Hawkins, ma'am," he drawled softly. "'Nother milestone in police/press relations. What's the problem?"

"No problem," Hawk said, "it's just—hell, it's not your fault. Is this situation pretty much how it looks?"

"I'd say so," Jackson nodded. "Guy working under his car, the jack lets go, weight of the car suffocates him. We get two or three a summer. What'd the wife say?"

"That she came home from work, found him like that. They've had some junkie burglaries in the neighborhood, always keep the house locked. Guy was a wonderful husband, everybody liked him. Like that."

"Lady seem straight to you?"

"Absolutely. She's a basket case about it. Cass knows them, though. Anything to add, Novak?"

"No," Cass said. "Straight people. Good people." He coughed, his eyes stinging.

"Right," Jackson nodded. "Well, I guess that covers it. Buy you a drink after work, *Miz* Hawkins?"

"In your dreams, Jackson," Hawk said. But she smiled a little as he sauntered back into the garage.

"Cass," she said carefully, "you *did* know this guy, right? A friend?"

"Yeah, a friend. A good friend. In high school. About a thousand years ago."

"Well, no offense to your friend, but all we've got here is local interest, two minutes tops, C-bag."

"Maybe not that much. The story'll probably get bumped

altogether if anything happens in the Middle East. You want me to try for a better shot when they remove the body?"

"That won't be necessary," Hawk said, eyeing him oddly.

"Look, don't worry about me—you want the footage of the body, I'll get it."

"I believe you. We just don't need it, okay? Let's shoot a stand-up in front of the house and that'll cover it. You ready?"

"Sure." He backed off a few feet and got Hawk focused while she checked her makeup in a hand mirror. She took out her handmike, nodded.

"Take one, Sliwa accident. A tragedy today, a fatal accident in—" She stopped, startled, glancing skyward as a sheet of raindrops suddenly splattered. No, not rain. Somebody was spraying them with a garden hose from behind the garage. Cass had an idea who.

"This is Stephanie Hawkins, WVLT-TV," Hawk continued coolly into the camera, ignoring her wilting hair, the water dripping down her face, "signing off from soggy, scenic Warsaw Heights and getting my butt back to Motown where I belong."

Novak went straight to the fridge when he got back to his apartment, rescued a couple of joints from his stash in a box of frozen waffles. He went into the living room, shucked his shoes, and eased down crosslegged on a futon in front of the tube. Left it dark. Turned himself on instead. Fired up the first doobie, sucked the Lebanese smoke deep into his lungs, holding it, feeling the buzz spread out from his chest, mellowing him out. Better. Not good, but better. By the time Hawk wandered in half an hour later, he was medium-mellow, cloud seven, maybe seven and a half.

"What's going on?" Hawk said. She stepped out of her heels at the door, set her briefcase on the dining-room table, then sat on the couch, folding her legs under her.

"Nothing's going on. Bad day."

"I had most of the same day, plus a staff meeting at the end of it. Which you skipped."

"I wasn't in the mood. Anybody notice?"

"Only the assignment editor. I told him you were drunk in a

ditch. Seems I wasn't far off. I thought we agreed you were through smoking dope in the apartment."

"Stefania, dark goddess of my soul, you know I would gladly lay me down and die for you," he said, taking another hit, holding the smoke, "but don't get in my face. Please."

"I'll get out of your goddamn life you don't tell me what's up in about thirty seconds, Novak. Make up your mind, while I've still got time to meet Jackson for a drink."

"Since you put it so tactfully. You remember me talking about a friend from high school, the guy who introduced me to the sacred logic of machines, got me my first job on a newspaper?"

"Nope, afraid not."

"That was him today—Stan Sliwa. Under that car."

"I see," she said slowly. "I'm sorry. Wait a minute—best friend? The one who married your high-school sweetheart? Her father was a big shot on the paper or something?"

"He owned the paper, but it was no big deal since it was only a Polish-language weekly. And how come you don't remember Stan but you remember who he married?"

"I am woman, hear me roar. Only, if this guy was such a good friend, why haven't you seen him since you came back? Warsaw Heights is only what—fifteen, twenty minutes out of Motown?"

"Twenty minutes, a dozen years. I guess I should have called him. But you can't go home again, or so I've heard. Maybe I was afraid to find out if it's true."

"Or maybe you were afraid to see the best friend's wife. Old flames burn the brightest, they say."

"Who says? Smokey Robinson?"

"I think it was Waylon Jennings," she said, picking up the remote control, flicking on the tube and the VCR. "Time for the news."

"I'm not sure I want to see this."

"Tough. If you're too stoned to take a walk, close your eyes. *I* want to see it. Strictly business, okay?"

A-bag, the first segment of the broadcast, was a tenement blaze in Dearborn.

"Damn," Hawk said. "I was hoping the drive-by shooting we covered would cop the first slot."

"Nah, the burn has better footage. Nice lookin' fire. Good color."

The Detroit drive-by was next. Two corpses, one a small boy in a Pistons T-shirt, were sprawled in a doorway off the corridor while Hawk did the stand-up in front of the crack house. "Damn it, Cass, what the hell is on my face? I look like I've got leprosy."

"Shadows, darlin'—you were standing near a tree. Don't worry, it makes you look even more interesting. It's a good shot."

"For an art gallery, maybe. I'm not a model, Cass, I'm a reporter, and I'll never make anchor looking like Typhoid Mary."

B-bag was a millage vote, a Greek festival in Hart Plaza. Lame stuff. C-bag was a fluff piece on the U of D mascot. And then Stan. Cass sucked down the last of the joint, ground out the roach. Street sign, street, garage, car, body. Hawk talking to Sonya on the porch.

"All due respect, your long-lost love could lose a few pounds," Hawk said.

"So could Liz Taylor. Roll that back, show me the garage. I screwed it up somehow."

"It looks all right to me. Mmm, good shot of the blood. Looks alive."

"No, before that. Hell, take it from the top." Street sign, street, garage— "Freeze it. Right there. The car."

"What about it?"

"I don't know, but something—"

"I don't see anything. It's just a car. Pretty ordinary."

"Yeah, it is, isn't it?" he said, blinking, trying to clear away the fog. "Old Chevy four-door, Michigan cancer holes in the rocker panels. A junker. So what was Stan doing under it?"

"Fixing it. What else?"

"Yeah . . ." Cass nodded slowly. "Only, why bother? It's a ten-year-old beater. Stan wasn't just a putzer, he was a master mechanic—hell, he was state certified when he was sixteen. I'm damn handy with machinery, but Stan was an artist. So why is he working on a piece of crap like that? It'd cost more for parts than it's worth. The tires alone are probably worth more than—That's what's wrong with the shot."

"What, the tires? What's wrong with them?"

"Nothing, they look new. And they're not stock, either. Footprint's too wide. Racing tires. Exhaust could be oversize, too."

"Maybe he was turning it into a hot rod or something."

"Not that car. Wrong type. It's a four-door—more weight, weaker frame. Any two-door would be better."

"But don't guys sometimes soup up ordinary-looking cars for street racing?"

"A sleeper, you mean?"

"A what?"

"They're called sleepers. A car that looks normal on the outside but it's tricked out under the hood. Same problem. Wrong type of car."

"Even so, what difference does it make now?"

"None," Cass said, flicking off the tube, easing to his feet. "But it bothers me. I, ah, I think I'll go over there."

"To see the car?" Hawk said evenly. "Or to comfort the grieving widow?"

"Look, the guy was a friend, okay? They both were. If you're worried, you're welcome to come along."

"No, thanks, I've seen as much of Polish Harlem as I care to for one day. Weather's too damp there. The only thing that worries me is that you've burned a couple of joints and it's bad for your short-term memory."

"What's that supposed to mean?"

"Nothing heavy. Only, while you're checking out this— sleeper of yours, try to remember where *you* sleep, okay?"

"Darlin'," he said, slipping on his sportcoat, "when our thing crashes, you'll be the one who walks away, not me. Anyway, not to worry. You're right—the lady could stand to lose a few pounds."

"Not so many," Hawk said. "She still looked pretty good."

"Yeah . . ." He nodded. "She did, didn't she?"

A half dozen cars were parked in Stan's driveway when Cass pulled up in the WVLT minivan. Charlie Bennett, the angry EMS attendant, answered the door. He'd traded his uniform for civvies, a dark ready-to-wear suit that looked a size too small for his large frame. "Well, well, if it isn't the rainmaker," Cass said. "You here on a house call?"

"I'm a friend of the family," Bennett said. "Look, about this afternoon—I was upset, I didn't realize you were a buddy of Stan's. I called over to the station there to apologize but you'd already gone. I was outa line, I'm sorry. Fair enough?" He offered his hand.

"I guess so," Cass said, accepting it. "It was a lousy situation, anyway. How's Sonya holding up?"

"Not too bad, considering. It probably hasn't sunk all the way in yet." Bennett stood aside, ushering Cass in. "A few friends and neighbors came over to sit with her, brought a ton of food, some beer. Everybody's down in the family room."

Cass followed him through the cramped living room to the foyer, where the split level divided. A young guy in ragged jeans and a grimy T-shirt was coming down the stairway from the upstairs bedrooms carrying suitcases. He was almost concentration-camp gaunt with the same vacant stare, spiky hair the color of moldy hay, ragged stubble of beard. And vaguely familiar.

"Bobby?" Cass said, but the boy ignored him, brushed past, headed for the front door.

"That *was* Sonya's little brother, right?" Cass asked Bennett. "God, he was just a kid the last time I saw him. I guess he didn't remember me."

"Don't feel bad, he doesn't remember his own name half the time," Bennett shrugged.

"He moving out?"

"I wouldn't know," Bennett said, and his tone made it clear he didn't care. Cass followed him downstairs into the family room. And twenty years back in time.

The "family room" was a recycled basement, plastic oak-paneling, cheap carpet, Sears washer and drier at one end. A few dozen people were standing around, groups of older men in shirtsleeves, dark slacks, conversing in lowered tones. Housewives in plain print dresses were clustered near a Ping-Pong table laden with enough food for a Polish division, the air delicious with aroma of duck's blood soup, *golumpki*, cabbage rolls, *budyn z szykni*, steaming ham pudding. Two heavyset older women were filling plates, passing them out. As Cass

scanned the room looking for Sonya, he noticed he was catching a lot of stares, a few frowns, and realized he was the only
person in the room not dressed somberly. In his white Armani
sportcoat, peach shirt, faded jeans, he was a flamingo in a flock
of starlings. Terrific. He spotted Sonya in the corner of the room
with a few women friends and started over.

"Kazu? Is that you?" An ancient gnome of a man in a rumpled
black suit levered himself up from a metal chair against the wall
and hobbled toward him, leaning on an aluminum cane. Ignace
Filipiak, Sonya's father.

"Mr. Filipiak, how are you?" Cass said, embracing the old man
gently, afraid he might shatter him. "You look good."

"I look like a stomped pissant." The old man smiled. "But
you, you look good, Kazu. Well and prosperous. Sonya tells me
you're working for the TV now."

"That's right. I was here, ah, this afternoon. I'm very sorry
about Stan, Mr. Filipiak, he was a good man."

"He was, he was." The old man nodded. "It's a terrible thing
what happened. Funny—putting out the paper over the years,
you see so many things you think it makes your soul as dried
out as leather, tough, invulnerable. Then a thing like this . . ."
His eyes were swimming, but he swallowed the pain, shrugged
it off. "It must be hard for you, too, Kazu. You and Stanley were
good friends, back when you worked for me."

"Yes, sir, we were."

"But you don't see him since you come back to town. You
don't come around the old neighborhood. You ashamed of us,
Kazu?"

"No, sir, of course not. But my folks are gone now . . . you
lose touch, you know?"

"Yah, I know. The Heights isn't like it used to be, anyway, so
many plants closing, no work. White Harlem they call it now,
people on the welfare or moving away or mixed up in the
holjeda."

"The *holjeda?* The plague? I don't understand."

"You know—the drugs, the crack. It's here, too, like everywhere else where people lose heart. In the war, the Nazis took
young people for the slave-labor camps. This crack *holjeda* is

like that, except the young people volunteer to die. I don't understand it, Kazu. Maybe I'm just too old."

"I don't think anybody understands it, Mr. Filipiak. And you don't seem older to me."

"I am, though," the old man sighed. "I feel like I'll be two hundred my next birthday, maybe more. And I talk too much. You go talk to Sonya, Kazu. She needs her friends now. If this TV job doesn't work out, you come see me. You can have your old job on *Populsku Warsaw Heights* anytime."

"You're still publishing the paper?" Cass asked, surprised.

"Of course. It's only biweekly now, not so many people read Polish in the Heights any more, but I'm still in the same building, still spend more time in the coffee shop downstairs than at work. Come by, see me sometime, we'll talk like the old days."

"I will, Mr. Filipiak—soon, I promise."

"You're a good boy, Kazu Novak, you always were. You and Stanley were . . ." He winced, blinking rapidly, then turned and hobbled back to his chair against the wall. And suddenly the room seemed too close, filled with too many people, memories. Cass forced himself to glance around, bleeding the color out of the picture, seeing everything in black-and-white now, mentally filming the scene, the people. Sonya was surrounded by friends, looking lost, dazed. A pity he didn't have a camera. It would have made a great shot.

He turned away, went back upstairs, through the kitchen to the garage. He switched on the lights and stepped out on the small landing, took a deep, ragged breath, glanced around.

In the cold glare of the overhead fluorescents, the garage seemed doubly empty. No car, no jack. The tools had been returned neatly to the racks above the workbench, the bloodstains washed away. As though nothing had happened here. Nothing.

"What are you doing out here?" Charlie Bennett said, stepping out onto the landing.

"I wanted to see something. What happened to the car?"

"The police took it. The car and the jack both. For testing, I guess."

"I can see why they might want to test the jack, but why take the car?"

"How the hell would I know? I thought you came here to see Sonya, but instead you're out here snoopin' around. What's the matter, you didn't get enough pictures today? Maybe you just better take a hike, mister *news*man."

Cass glanced up at him. A big guy, Bennett, half a head taller, forty pounds heavier. Angry. And pushy. But standing with his back to the landing stairs, four steps down to a cement floor. Cass could see himself giving Bennett a stiff jab to the belly, dumping his big ass down the stairs, see how pushy he felt when he got up. If he got up. But the moment passed. Wrong time, wrong place. Or at least that's what Cass told himself, walking out to his car.

The Warsaw Heights police station was nearly new, brick fronted, white-tile floors, built a dozen years ago when G.M. bought the old station and half the downtown area to build a new auto plant, which closed eight years later. Cass inquired at the front desk and was directed to a corner office, glass walled, overlooking the brightly lit parking lot.

"Have a seat, Mr. Novak, what can I do for you?" Lieutenant Gil Delacruz was balding, moon-faced. Brown suit, black bow-tie. His desk was piled with paperwork and the remains of a Chinese takeout supper. He looked like a history teacher from a small college.

"You're the officer in charge of the Sliwa case?" Cass said, easing down on the metal folding chair facing. "I thought you worked narcotics."

"Do I know you?"

"I'm a cameraman for WVLT. I've filmed you at crime scenes a couple of times."

"I see." Delacruz nodded, munching the last of an eggroll. "I thought you looked familiar. Anyway, here in the Heights, the department's not divided quite as neatly as in Metro Detroit. The Sliwa death happened on my shift, so I caught it. But there's no case, it's already closed, accidental death. Unless you've got information to volunteer?"

"No, just a couple of questions. Like, what happened?"

"The jack apparently let go, the decedent suffocated."

"Apparently?"

"We've impounded it, it'll be shipped to the police lab at Lansing and checked out in case there's a product-liability civil suit, but most likely Mr. Sliwa just mis-set the jack and it slipped."

"Stan was a licensed master mechanic. It's hard for me to believe he'd make a mistake with something as basic as a jack."

"There were a few empties near the body, and I expect the autopsy will show the decedent killed a couple beers, screwed up. Why the interest? I thought you people ran your story on the 'Six O'Clock News.'"

"It's personal. Stan was a friend."

"I see. Well, there's not much more I can tell you. The widow said the house was locked, no sign anyone else had been there. Sliwa died around two, while she was still at work. I checked."

"I saw her brother, Bobby Filipiak, tonight. He seemed to be moving out."

"From what I understand, Bobby Flip and his brother-in-law got along fine. You have any reason to think otherwise?"

"No, I just—"

"I didn't think so. Look, Mr. Novak, I cut you some slack because I figure you're upset over the death of a friend, but you're a little out of line here. Your friend had too many beers, made a mental error—end of story. We don't have the manpower or the high-tech goodies in the Heights that Detroit Metro has, but we're not incompetent."

"I didn't say you were."

"No, but you must think so. Otherwise why would you walk into my office with reefer smoke on your clothes and think I wouldn't notice? I'll tell you something, Novak—I don't like newspeople much—they get underfoot, interview witnesses before I get to them, and generally make my job tougher—and I especially don't like yuppie potheads because you contribute to the cash flow of scumbags who are screwin' up the world. Any other questions before you go?"

"Just one," Cass said, rising warily. "Do you know what Stan was doing to the car?"

"No. What difference does it make?"

"Probably none. I just wondered. Can I see it?"

"The car? I guess you can try."

"What does that mean?"

"We don't have it. I just had it towed away as a courtesy to the widow. Rostenkowski's Scrapyard took it. I imagine it's the size of a suitcase by now. Anything else, Novak, or should I ask the desk sergeant to shake down your car for your stash?"

"No," Cass said, "don't bother. I'll see myself out."

And that was it. Cass went to Stan's funeral stoned to the bone, overdosed on vodka and memories at the wake afterward, lost his lunch out in the alley behind Dom Polski Hall. A few weeks later, he also lost Hawk. She got a promotion to "Morning News" anchor and moved back to her own place. They promised to remain friends, to stay in touch, then avoided each other like death. He got a new partner, an earnest kid fresh out of CMU named Metcalf. Cass nicknamed him Cowbell but worked hard at showing him the ropes. It seemed to help. The pain of loss faded as the weeks passed, and after a month he only thought of Hawk once or twice an hour, and Stan hardly at all. Until Sonya called, said she'd sold the house, thought he might like some of Stan's tools.

He almost didn't go.

It was seven when he arrived. The garage door was closed, a Century 21 "sold" sign stood in the overgrown front yard, but otherwise things looked much the same as that first terrible day. He rang the doorbell. Sonya answered, and for a moment neither of them spoke, eyeing each other through the screen door. Across half a lifetime.

"So," he managed at last, "how are you doin'?"

"Better than you were the last time I saw you. Come on in."

"You look terrific," he said, following her in, and she really did. She'd dropped a dozen pounds and seemingly a dozen years. In designer jeans, a T-shirt, and running shoes, her figure firm, her hair lightened and tousled, she looked more like the girl from Pulaski High than the shattered widow of a few months ago. "I called you a couple of times, never caught you."

"I've—been gone a lot," she said, opening the door to the garage and stepping out on the landing. "I didn't want to be here while they were showing the place, you know? As far as I know, everything's the way Stan left it. Take whatever you like."

"Are you sure? Some of these tools are expensive."

"It's all right, I have no use for them, and Charlie—" She coughed. "Anyway, Stan would want you to have them."

"Charlie?" Cass said, walking down the steps to the workbench, pointedly avoiding her eyes. "You and Charlie an item now?"

"I know it might seem like I'm rushing things a little,," she said, sitting down on the steps, watching him, "but I'm not. I won't lie to you, Cass, I've been seeing Charlie for—a while."

"I see," he said, sliding open a drawer. Vise grips, a complete set, arranged by size, each one lightly oiled.

"I doubt that you do. You've been away a long time, Cass, people change. God knows I loved Stan, but he wasn't the easiest guy in the world to live with. He was—dull. Maybe not to you; you two could always talk about cars, or cameras, or some damned helicopter motor you read about in *Popular Mechanics*, but what do you think *we* talked about? Machinery was all he really cared about."

"You're wrong. He cared about you." He opened another drawer. Allen wrenches, standard, metric—

"I suppose he cared about me as much as he cared about anything that wasn't gear-driven," she conceded. "Maybe if we'd had kids it would've been different."

"Why didn't you?"

"I can't have children," she said simply. "Ever. And Stan would have made a wonderful father. Maybe that's why he stayed so distant. Because I was broken and he couldn't order a part or tune me up to solve the problem."

"You know he didn't feel like that."

"No, the truth is I don't know how he *really* felt about anything. When things got tense between us, he'd just come out here and crawl under a car, or bury his nose in a manual. The funny thing was, I thought Bobby might help. What a joke."

"How so?"

"Have you seen Bobby lately?"

"I saw him here the, ah, the night of Stan's accident. He was carrying a couple of suitcases."

"Right," she said bitterly. "Know what was in them? Our silverware, a couple of Stan's handguns, anything he could pawn

for a few bucks. A real prize, my little brother. Killed our
mother being born and he's gone straight downhill ever since,
in and out of jail—you name it, he's done it. He's just a damned
junkie now, steals to support his habit. The last time he got out
of detox my father wouldn't have him in the house, couldn't
handle him anymore, so Stan and I took him in."

"But it didn't work out?" Another drawer, chromed-steel
socket sets, ratchet arms, extensions, silent, gleaming.

"It almost did." She leaned on the rail, resting her chin on
her palm. "They spent a lot of time together. Stan taught Bobby
about tools, thought if he put a wrench in his hand it might
straighten him out. They completely rebuilt Bobby's car, and
for a while it seemed to be working. Stan was sure it was—I
mean, how could anybody who understands the guts of an
engine do dope?"

"What happened?" Cass opened a storage cabinet stacked
with large boxes and peered in to read the labels. Street
Dominator intake manifolds for big block Chevys, six sets of
them. Six Holley dualfeed carburetors to match.

"Bobby drove it around till the kick of having the fastest
wheels on the street wore off, then he traded it for dope money,
got so trashed he almost died, wound up in the hospital, and
then in jail. And when he got out, Stan let him come back. Just
didn't believe there was anything he couldn't fix. What's
wrong?"

Cass didn't answer for a moment, trying to make sense of
what he was seeing, then realized Sonya was eyeing him,
shaking her head. "Sorry," he said. "Where were we?"

"I was talking about Bobby—I don't know where you were.
Stan used to do that to me all the time, drift away. I'd be talking
to him and realize he wasn't hearing a word, he was off inside a
transmission or something. I forgot how much alike you two
were."

"Yeah, well maybe he wasn't perfect, who is? But not many
guys would've bothered trying to straighten Bobby out. I
wouldn't have. I doubt Charlie would, either. Are you, ah, sure
you're doing the right thing, being involved with him so soon?"

"Hell no, I'm not sure," she snapped, "how could be? I've
never been in this situation. I think I would have left Stan

eventually, but"—she swallowed hard, blinking back tears—
"but not before we'd fought it out, gotten things straight
between us. Not like this," she said, rising suddenly, her eyes
streaming. "Not like this." She turned and walked back into the
house, slammed the door.

Cass thought about following her, but couldn't think of a
damn thing to say. Maybe she was right, he and Stan were too
much alike, better with machinery than people. He began
opening the boxes in the closet. Four of the Holley dual-feed-
carburetor boxes contained used carbs off older cars. What the
hell?

"What's goin' on out here?" Charlie Bennett said. "Soni came
in bawling her eyes out. What did you say to her?"

"It was a private conversation," Cass said, opening one of the
Street Dominator boxes. "If you want to know, you'll have to
ask her."

"I asked you, Novak, or Polack, whatever your name is, but I
don't much care. I didn't like you from day one. I want you
outa here."

"Sonya invited me here and I'm not quite finished," Cass said,
replacing the last Dominator box, "so why don't you cool down
a little and back off."

"That's the trouble with you TV guys," Bennett said, stalking
angrily down the steps, slamming the cabinet door in Cass's
face, "you're outa touch with reality. Like a guy your size tellin'
a guy my size to back off. I told you to get steppin', mister. I
mean right now."

"You know, Stan Sliwa was a friend of mine once," Cass said,
rising, glancing idly around the garage. "Sonya thinks we're a
lot alike." He took a twenty-inch crescent wrench out of its
drawer, hefted it, checking the balance. "For instance, Stan
thought you can fix damn near anything, you use the right tool.
How about it, Charlie? You see anything out here needs fixing?"

Bennett hesitated, glancing at the wrench, then at Cass, then
the wrench again. "Maybe not now," he said evenly. "No need
to disturb the lady."

"Good point," Cass nodded. "Now why don't you just go
back in the house? I'd like to be alone."

"I'll let it pass this time, Novak," Bennett said from the safety of the landing, "but when you leave, you'd better not come back."

"Not to worry," Cass said, taking a last look around the empty, immaculate garage, "nobody lives here anymore."

The Jury's Inn was busy and dim, the usual mix of cops, bailiffs, and bondsmen from the Heights Hall of Justice down the street. The air was thick with smoke and the din of a dozen simultaneous conversations, dishes clattering, a jukebox thumping Motown goodies against one wall. Cass found Lieutenant Gil Delacruz sitting alone at a corner table cluttered with empty beer mugs, an overflowing ashtray.

"They told me at the desk you might be over here. Got a minute?" Cass asked. "It's important."

Delacruz frowned up at him blearily, trying to place the face. "Hey, I know you," he said at last. "Novak the pothead cameraman, right? Hate to be rude, but since I'm off duty, whyn't you just go away, okay?"

"Thanks, I appreciate it," Cass said, pulling up a chair facing Delacruz. "You remember the Stan Sliwa case?"

"I vaguely remember a Sliwa accident," Delacruz slurred. "The case of the Polish pancake, no?" He grinned, then sobered a little as his eyes met Cass's. "Sorry, forgot he was a friend of yours. Okay, what about it?"

"I was in Stan's garage earlier tonight, and I came across something odd. I found sixty-grand worth of bolt-on racing gear for Chevy engines there—enough equipment to trick out a half dozen cars like the one that killed him."

"So I guess your buddy was heavy into hot rods, so what?"

"Damn it, Delacruz, I said sixty thousand dollars' worth of equipment. Stan was a blue-collar guy, he didn't have that kind of money. And nobody builds six cars at once."

"Did I miss somethin' here? I thought you just said that's what he was doin'. What's your point?"

"It's one that I don't like much," Cass said, taking a deep breath. "You allowed you know Bobby Filipiak, Stan's brother-in-law. A while back Stan tried to straighten Bobby out, built a car for him. Bobby dumped it for dope money, wound up back in jail."

"Sounds like Bobby. So?"

"So I think maybe that car impressed some of the people Bobby did business with. And they did a deal with Bobby or Stan to build a half dozen more just like it. But not just hot rods, sleepers."

"You're saying your buddy Sliwa was buildin' fast cars for the drug trade, that it? Nice guy, your friend."

"He was, but—damn it, he was having trouble in his marriage, maybe he needed money, I just don't know. From the spare parts I found, I'd guess Stan had already built at least three cars, was working on the fourth. If you can find the cars—"

"Catch 22," Delacruz grinned, finishing off a beer.

"What?"

"Catch 22. Even if your buddy was buildin' sleepers, we can't prove it because we can"t find 'em. 'Cause they're sleepers. Catch 22. Get it?"

"Jesus," Cass sighed, slumping back in his chair, "what I get is you're about half in the bag. Maybe I'd better try you another time."

"Nah, let's settle this now. Look, you're buggin' me because you want me to do something, right? Okay, like what? Let's say I could find the cars your buddy built. Then what? It's not illegal to own a fast car, even if you're a dope dealer. Way I see it, *if* he was building hot cars for the dope trade and one of 'em fell on him, I got no problem with it. Poetic justice, no?"

"The problem is that I don't think the car did just fall on him."

"No? Why not?"

"It's hard to explain, but being in Stan's workshop tonight, seeing the way he kept his tools, those old carbs cleaned up and reboxed even though they were almost worthless. I could set a jack wrong, or you could. But not Stan. He just couldn't make a dumbass mistake like that. I think maybe somebody dropped that car on him."

"'No kidding? And who do you figure did the taxpayers this favor?"

"Maybe the dopers he was working for. Maybe Bobby. Hell, maybe his wife's new boyfriend, I don't know. But neither do you, and you should. It's your job to know, or to find out."

"My job?" Delacruz said, flushing dangerously. "You come in here gettin' in my face after I put in a sixteen-hour day, and now you wanna gimme a lecture on how to do my damn *job?*"

"Look, all I'm saying is I think—"

"I don't give a damn what you think!" Delacruz roared, staggering to his feet, weaving. "I listened to your sad story, now you listen to mine! I'll try to explain it so even a punkass yuppie pothead can understand." He cleared the table with his forearm, trashing the beer mugs and the ashtray on the hardwood floor, then jerked a handgun out of a shoulder holster and leaned unsteadily on the table, holding the muzzle an inch from the tip of Novak's nose.

"Jesus Christ, Delacruz," somebody said, but otherwise the room fell absolutely silent. Only the jukebox kept pumping. The Temptations. "My Girl."

"You know what this is, Novak?" Delacruz said, blinking, trying to focus. "It's a piece of machinery, a nine-millimeter Taurus Model 92 automatic. It's brand new, but it's not all that complicated. For instance"—he cocked the hammer with an audible snick—"you just pull the trigger, it'll fire sixteen rounds *boom boom boom* fast as you can squeeze 'em off. Twin safeties, safe as houses, you know? But last year a state police firing-range officer, a twenty-year man who handles guns for his damn living, shot himself in the foot out in Highland Park. We don't know how it happened. Hell, *he* don't know what happened, it just happened. That's why they call 'em accidents. Like what happened to your buddy. Like what could happen to you if you don't get outa my face. Get the picture?"

"I think so," Cass managed.

"Good," Delacruz nodded. "One other thing about this piece of machinery. It locks open automatically"—he jerked the slide back with his left hand, locking it—"when it's empty. See?" His face split in a grin and he dropped back into his chair as the room erupted into a roar of laughter. Cass glanced around, shaken. The other cops were grinning—they'd known all along. Delacruz laid the pistol on the table as an anorexic waitress brought him a fresh beer, bitching him out about the mess on the floor.

"Do you mind?" Cass said, picking up the gun, not waiting for an answer. He touched the magazine release, popping out the clip, then thumbed the slide latch and removed the slide and barrel assembly. "You know about guns, right?" he said. "You must, considering the business you're in." He depressed the spring guide, stripped out the recoil spring. "Did you know the action of your brand-new pistol was designed over a hundred years ago? Guy from Utah named Browning invented it. I don't know the exact date, but Stan would have. Probably could've told you the patent number." He separated the barrel assembly from the slide.

"Hey," Delacruz said, "what the hell are you doing?"

"Same thing you just did," Cass said, "making a point." The gun was now in a half dozen pieces neatly arranged on the table. "Okay, let's say you're in a tight spot in a dark alley. You fall down, get mud in your piece. Can you field-strip it, clean it, and reassemble it in the dark? Stan could. Machinery talked to him. It was all he was good at, all he really cared about. He was too good to screw up with a damn jack. And he didn't. Which you'd know if you'd made any kind of a competent investigation."

"You've made your point, Novak," Delacruz said. "Now take a walk, okay? *After* you put that piece back together."

"Nah," Cass said, rising, "a punk like me might blow it. If I were you, I'd get somebody like Stan to fix it for you, so it'll be done right."

"Yeah? You know that alley you mentioned, smartass? I wouldn't take time to clean my gun. No *competent* cop would. I'd just use my backup." He reached down and pulled a fist-sized automatic out of an ankle holster, displaying it on his palm. "You don't have to be a goddamn gunsmith to be a good cop."

"What would you know about being a good cop?" Cass said, turning away.

"Hey, Novak?" Delacruz called, pointing a wobbly index finger at him. "Boom, boom, boom! Gotcha."

"I've never had to cover the death of a friend," Stephanie Hawkins said carefully, avoiding Cass's eyes. "I'm not sure I could." She was behind her desk in her new office in the newsroom the next morning. Nicer than her old one—award plaques on the wall, autographed celebrity 8 × 10s. She was wearing her navy-blue WVLT anchor blazer and looked even better than Cass remembered. It was the first time they'd been alone together since the split.

"I take it that's your tactful way of saying you think I'm off base?" Cass said.

"I don't know. Look, we're both pros, Novak, let's do this thing by the numbers. One, you think Sliwa was building fast cars—what did you call them?"

"Sleepers."

"Right, sleepers, for the drug trade. And, two, you think he may have been murdered. By who? The dopers?"

"I don't know. Possibly."

"But you said he had enough equipment to build six cars." She checked the notes she'd made as he'd explained. "He'd apparently delivered three and was working on the fourth, correct? So why would they kill him?"

"Maybe to avoid paying him."

"But they'd probably already given him a down payment to buy the equipment, right? So even if they intended to kill him, wouldn't they wait until he'd delivered all six cars to get their money's worth?"

"Maybe it wasn't over money."

"But would your friend have been under the car if someone he distrusted was there, near the jack?"

"No," Cass conceded, "I suppose not."

"All right then, I think we can eliminate the wife, because she apparently cared for the guy even if she was going to leave him. And the boyfriend had no motive. Why buy a cow if the milk is free?"

"Very delicately put," Cass sighed.

"Sorry," Hawk said, "but I call 'em like I see 'em. Okay, who's left? The junkie brother-in-law? Again, what motive? Your friend treated him very well."

"Who can say what's in a doper's head?"

"You might be able to make a better guess than most," Hawk said sweetly, "but let's move on. Okay, I'll grant you it bothers me that Bobby Flip dropped out of sight, and it seems awfully convenient that the car disappeared the way it did. But those are just feelings, Cass, and here's a fact. The Warsaw Heights chief of police called the station manager this morning, complaining that you were harrassing his officers."

"Maybe he's worried about something."

"Or maybe he's just annoyed. Look, Cass, we've both worked a lot of stations in a lot of towns. Do you really think the Warsaw Heights force is corrupt? That they'd cover up a murder?"

"No," he said slowly, "I guess not."

"Good, neither do I. And, anyway, why would they bother? Their crime rate isn't as high as Detroit's yet, but the way the crack trade's developing out there an unsolved homicide is no big deal. So let's cut to chase. You asked me what I think—here it is. One, I don't know if your friend was murdered or not, but I'm inclined to agree with the police that it was an accident. Two, even if it wasn't, I don't see what we can do about it. We're not detectives, we're in TV news and there's nothing to shoot here. What would the pictures be of? An empty garage? A jack? Some boxes of used car parts? Bottom line is, no pictures, no story. I'll tell you what: if the brother-in-law turns up, we can try talking to him on our own time, but that's the best I can do. And that's the news as it looks from here. Sorry."

"Don't be sorry," Cass sighed. "I asked for your opinion, and the truth is, that's about how I figured it myself. I just needed to hear it from somebody I respect. Helluva thing, isn't it? A guy's life, start to finish, is only worth two minutes of airtime?"

"Or less," Hawk said. "We aren't here to change the world, Novak, just report it. And speaking of reporting, how are you and your new partner getting on?"

"His lips aren't as sweet as yours, darlin', but at least he doesn't snore."

"Good God. What did I ever see in you?"

"A Polish Prince Charming. Wit, charisma."

"That must've been it," she said. "It certainly wasn't your kielbasa, my prince."

"Damn," he winced, rising, "you know, I'd forgotten what a surly bitch you are in the morning. Rest of the day, too, for that matter. I, ah, I miss you."

"I miss you, too," she said. "A lot."

"But not enough?"

She shrugged, a five-page letter in the slightest movement of a shoulder. "Are you going to let this Sliwa thing go?" she asked.

"Yeah," he said, "I think so."

And he did.

For the next few weeks, Cass disappeared back into his life, hiding in the whirlwind, an endless reel of crime scenes, fires, strikes, shooting Metcalf talking to stunned victims, witnesses, exhausted firemen, angry strikers. No two days alike, yet as similar as frames on a roll. Same movie, different faces. Motown news.

Then they hit an ugly accident scene just off the Chrysler Freeway. State Police had high-speed-chased a drug suspect from downtown Woodward all the way out into the Heights. Edgy scene—three prowl cars, one with its grill caved in, had the road blocked, gumball lights flashing, police-line tapes strung around. The car they'd chased had skidded broadside into the back of a moving van, smashing up both vehicles, the two of them welded together like modernist sculpture. A half dozen Early American sofas from the van strewn around the road added to the surreality.

Two state troopers were leading the ashen van driver away from his truck, dazed, shaken. The runner in the car had been thrown out by the impact, was dead or dying on a stretcher on the ground, one EMS attendant giving him mouth-to-mouth, another coolly rigging an IV bottle to the stretcher. Cass filmed them from behind the police tapes, zooming in slowly, gradually tightening the shot, focusing in on the three faces, the desperate urgency of the attendant giving mouth-to-mouth, his buddy's empty expression, knowing it was useless, his eyes as lifeless as the victim's. Good footage, even better when the victim convulsed, breathed on his own for a moment, the two attendants feverishly jacking up the stretcher, rushing it to the EMS van.

Cass filmed them until the doors slammed and the van gunned away, rubber howling, lights and sirens. Somebody jostled him, running, shouting. The truck was on fire, diesel fuel trickling down from the rear tanks, pooling out, flames spreading, panicky gawkers stampeding away from the coming explosion. Novak was getting footage, two state troopers trying to control the blaze with handheld extinguishers, losing the fight, the rear of the van alight now, paint peeling, flames engulfing the car.

The car. A nondescript Chevy junker, rusty, battered. But wearing new rubber. Racing tires. Cass vaulted the police line and sprinted to the car. The hood was sprung half open from the impact. He got his shoulder under it and thrust it farther up, buckling it, metal shrieking. He focused the minicam into the yawning darkness under the hood. Too dim, damn it! He tightened the shot, getting more light from the flicker of the flames. A tricked-out engine, Cyclone headers, Street Dominator manifolds, Holley—

"Get outa here, goddamnit!" one of the troopers screamed at him. "It's goin' up!" Cass ignored him, filming, shifting his position to be sure he got the—

"You crazy sonovabitch!" One of the cops hit him shoulder high, knocking him back. Another grabbed his arms, dragging him away from the car. The Chevy's trunk was engulfed, the fire billowing to a thundering inferno, flames towering into the sky. Cass clutched the camera close, struggling to pull away, stumbling to one knee, then getting flattened, hammered down by the fireblast of heated air as the car's tank blew with the deep metallic *whoomp* of a naval gun.

Cass staggered to his feet. The cop who'd been dragging him was down, stunned, hat blown off, his face a bloody mask from a gash in his scalp. His buddy was leaning over him, trying to get him up, away from the fire. Cass turned, reeled toward the WVLT minivan. Caught a glimpse of Delacruz coming on the run, two uniforms with him. Tried to run, but his legs went rubbery and he fell, hitting the gravel hard but protecting the steadycam.

"Get him up!" Delacruz snapped. "Somebody read him his damn rights, he's under arrest!" The two cops hauled him like a sack of potatoes to a Heights patrol car. One of them tried to pull the camera away from him, but he folded over it, hanging on with all he had left.

"Leave it," Delacruz said, "just get him in the car!"

They pushed him into the back seat still clutching the camera, slammed the door. He sat up slowly—dazed, deafened, head ringing in the sudden silence. Metcalf was arguing with a stonefaced trooper a few yards away, getting no place. Delacruz climbed into the front seat, closed the door, and swiveled to face him.

"You stupid bastard," he said coldly. "You coulda gotten killed, or gotten my people killed. Well, welcome to shit city, Novak, you're in it up to your eyeballs, crossing a police line, reckless endangerment, interfering with officers in the performance, and a whole lot more. You're gonna do some slam time, my friend, maybe a year. How's that grab ya?"

"It was one of Stan's cars," Cass said numbly.

"Think so?" Delacruz said, glancing back at the wreck. "Kinda hard to tell now, almost nothing left of it."

"I got it on film."

"Hope that's a comfort to you in the joint. Give me the camera."

"No."

"You want me to have it taken from you? I can, you know."

"It won't matter," Cass said, blinking. "It won't work. You bust me and I'll be news, Delacruz, heavy press coverage. And I'll talk to anybody who'll listen. You can't cover this up."

"No," Delacruz said, eyeing him, reading the set of his mouth, "maybe I can't. So I guess you'll have to cover it up."

"What are you talking about?"

"You were half right," Delacruz said simply. "Your buddy Sliwa was workin' for dopers, a Jamaican named Johnno, moved his operation into the Heights about six months ago. Bobby Flip traded the car Stan built for him to one of Johnno's people, he liked it, did a deal with Stan for six more—seventy grand in front, fifty more on delivery."

"My God," Cass said.

"Lotta money," Delacruz nodded. "More'n he'd made at the plant in five years. Which is why I was kinda surprised when Sliwa contacted me, told me about the deal, and offered to build a special long-wave beeper into each car so we could track 'em."

"And you went along with it?"

"You're damn right, it was like a gift from God."

"Except that Stan was no good with people, only machinery. And the Jamaican smelled something wrong and stomped him like a cockroach. Damn it, you should have guessed it would happen, you bastard!"

"No, you're wrong. The Jamaican didn't tumble to anything or he wouldn't still be using the cars. And he is. In the last six weeks or so we've tracked down his whole network, plus his contacts in Detroit. Believe me, Johnno doesn't know. Nobody knew but Stan and me. And now you."

"Not Bobby?"

"Get real, Novak, I wouldn't piss on Bobby Flip if he was on fire. I didn't tell him anything, and I doubt like hell that Stan did, either."

"But you don't believe Stan's death was an accident, do you?"

"I honestly don't know yet. Hell, I didn't like the coincidence any better'n you, but everybody checked out. Johnno had no reason to do it, and the wife and her boyfriend both have solid alibis."

"But you didn't talk to Bobby, did you?"

"No," Delacruz admitted, "I couldn't. He dropped out of sight right after and I was afraid if we beat the bushes for him we'd spook the Jamaican. Besides, he had no reason to do it. Stan loved the kid, God knows why. Hell, Bobby's the reason he came to me in the first place. After seein' what crack had done to him, he wanted to do something."

"And you let him. And now he's dead. And Bobby's still walking around free as the air."

"For now. But as soon as we bust the Jamaican's ring, I'll find Bobby and lean on him, I give you my word. So how about it, you gonna give me the film?"

"No," Cass said, "no chance."

"But damn it—"

"If Metcalf sees me turn over the film he'll know something's up. I'll keep the film, but I promise not to use it until after you bust the Jamaican. Word of honor."

"All right . . ." Delacruz nodded slowly. "I guess the word of a guy who's willing to risk burnin' to death for a goddamn picture has to be worth somethin'. But you cross me, Novak, I swear to God I'll stick you in a hole so deep you'll have to phone out for sunshine."

"I believe you. Can I go now?"

"Yeah, get out of here," Delacruz said, hitting the release on the dash, opening the rear door. "Just remember, not a word about this until after you hear from me. And stay the hell out of my way."

"Funny," Cass said, climbing stiffly out, "I don't remember promising that."

A sunny fall afternoon. Cass was wearing a sleeveless MSU sweatshirt, jeans, tennies, and he was sixteen again. Or could have been. Things hadn't changed much in the Heights. The cars were different, there was a "for lease" sign in Woolworth's empty window now, Zerwinski's hardware had gone Ace, but otherwise the street looked much the same as a dozen years ago. When Cass had worked for *Populsku Warsaw Heights*, and most afternoons Ignace Filipiak would be in the window booth of Klima's Coffee Shop.

"Kazu, *jak sie mas*," the old man said, his face lighting up like a winter sunrise, "sit, sit. Zosia, bring *kawa* for my young friend. You want some *babka* rolls, Kazu? Fresh made this morning?"

"No, thank you, coffee will be fine. How are you, Mr. Filipiak?"

"How am I? I sit in the sun in a room breathing the scent of *chelba* bread baking, a well-fed woman to bring coffee, a friend stops by to talk. Heaven will be many fine days like this."

"I doubt I'll ever find out," Cass said.

"Nor I," the old man smiled. "So, what business brings you home, Kazu?"

"Business?" Cass said, accepting a mug of steaming coffee from a large, bell-shaped woman.

"Kazu, my legs are bent, not my head. I'm here almost every day since you left, so I know you didn't come just to see me. It's okay, we'll talk, have coffee, but first the business, so I don't sour the cream wondering."

"You haven't changed a damn bit, Ignace, you know that?"

"*You* have. You're more polite now, and your eyesight's failing. So, how can I help you?"

"I, ah, I need to get in touch with Bobby. Do you know where he is?"

"I can probably guess," the old man said, "but I'm not sure I should tell you. He is hiding, Kazu, seeing ghosts. He has one of Stanley's guns. He's very dangerous now."

"It's important."

"To you, maybe, Kazu, but nothing is important to Bobby but the cocaine. There's nothing left of him. He's lost, a victim of the *boljeda*, the plague. He still walks, but he's dead. If you talk to him, only the drug will answer."

"I still need to see him."

The old man looked away, idly stirring his coffee. "Tell me, Kazu, why you want to see Bobby. Does this have to do with your work on the TV?"

"Yes, sir, in a way."

Filipiak glanced at him curiously, then shrugged. "You've changed more than I thought. You never used to lie to me, Kazu Novak. You shouldn't try. You have no talent for it. It only makes me wonder what you're trying to hide. And I think it must be that you've learned about Bobby and Stanley and those damned cars. Is that it?"

"You know about it?"

"I still have the newspaper, Kazu. People talk to me. And I'm not blind, just old. Do you think my son and my son-in-law could hide such a thing from me? Let it be, please. Sonya is all that matters now. If it comes out what her husband was doing—" The old man seized Novak's wrist with a palsied hand. His grip had no more strength than a child's, but his eyes were alight, like staring into a flame. "Let it go, Kazu. Stanley is dead. Bobby and I will join him in hell soon and it will be over—for us and for Sonya, too."

"What do you mean you'll join Stanley in hell? Why? Why should you?"

"It isn't the gun that makes Bobby dangerous, Kazu, it's the *boljeda*. The evil is contagious. Bobby's heart is long dead. But Stanley. To know what happened to my son, then to work for the *psiakref* dogs who poisoned him for *money!* He was even worse than the animals who sell the drugs. He sold his soul. But he paid for it. I hope the bastard is still paying."

"My God, Mr. Filipiak—Stanley?"

"Not the Stanley you knew, Kazu. He was contaminated by the *holjeda*. I did what I had to do. God forgive me, I would do it again."

Cass couldn't speak, could barely breathe, a fist clamped around his heart so tightly he thought he would die. He slid out of the booth and stood staring down at the old man. He seemed so much smaller than he remembered, and he realized he was shrinking, receding, fading to black-and-white. To a still life, an old man dreaming in the afternoon sun. He tried to think of something to say. Nothing came. Mr. Filipiak was a man people talk to. He would learn soon enough.

Outside, the street had changed, too. It wasn't a dozen years ago. The haze had burned away. A few blocks down, a kid was lounging on a corner, scouting traffic, open for business. Bobby? Too far away to tell. Then his eyes misted and he couldn't see the boy anymore. He walked to his van, groped blindly under the dash, and pulled out a small cellophane baggie. Five joints. A hundred and fifty bucks' worth. He tore them to pieces and threw them in the gutter. It didn't help. It didn't help a damn bit.

It's true. You can't ever go home again. But sweet Jesus, you can never truly leave it behind, either.

The old man blinked up at him as he slid back into the booth.

"I didn't finish my coffee," Cass said, "and we never did talk about the old times."

"No," the old man said, "we didn't."

LAWRENCE BLOCK

A BLOW FOR FREEDOM

A regular in The Year's Best series since 1975, Lawrence Block is one of today's leading mystery writers, perhaps best known for his darkly realistic novels about unlicensed private eye Matt Scudder. In his award-winning short stories he has often explored other directions—as he does in "A Blow For Freedom," another of this year's Edgar nominees.

The gun was smaller than Elliott remembered. At Kennedy, waiting for his bag to come up on the carrousel, he'd been irritated with himself for buying the damned thing. For years now, ever since Pan Am had stranded him in Milan with the clothes he was wearing, he'd made an absolute point of never checking luggage. He'd flown to Miami with his favorite carry-on bag; returning, he'd checked the same bag, all because it now contained a Smith & Wesson revolver and a box of fifty .38-caliber shells.

At least he hadn't had to take a train. "Oh, for Christ's sake," he'd told Huebner, after they'd bought the gun together, "I'll have to take the train back, won't I? I can't get on the plane with a gun in my pocket."

"It's not recommended," Huebner had said. "But all you have to do is check your bag with the gun and shells in it."

"Isn't there a regulation against it?"

"Probably. There's rules against everything. All I know is, I do it all the time, and I never heard of anyone getting into any trouble over it. They scope the checked bags, or at least they're supposed to, but they're looking for bombs. There's nothing very dangerous about a gun locked away in the baggage compartment."

"Couldn't the shells explode?"

"In a fire, possibly. If the plane goes down in flames, the bullets may go off and put a hole in the side of your suitcase."

"I guess I'm being silly."

"Well, you're a New Yorker. You don't know a whole lot about guns."

"No." He'd hesitated. "Maybe I should have bought one of those plastic ones."

"The Glock?" Huebner smiled. "It's a nice weapon, and it's probably the one I'll buy next. But you couldn't carry it on a plane."

"But I thought—"

"You thought it would fool the scanners and metal detectors at airport security. It won't. That's hardly the point of it, a big gun like that. No, they replaced a lot of the metal with high-impact plastic to reduce the weight. It's supposed to lessen recoil slightly, too, but I don't know if it does. Personally, I like the looks of it. But it'll show up fine on a scanner if you put it in a carry-on bag, and it'll set off alarms if you walk it through a metal detector." He snorted. "Of course, that didn't keep some idiots from introducing bills banning it in the U.S. Nobody in politics likes to let a fact stand in the way of a grandstand play."

His bag was one of the last ones up. Waiting for it, he worried that there was going to be trouble about the gun. When it came, he had to resist the urge to open the bag immediately and make sure the gun was still there. The bag felt light, and he decided some baggage handler had detected it and appropriated it for his own use.

Nervous, he thought. Scared it's there, scared it's not.

He took a cab home to his Manhattan apartment and left the bag unopened while he made himself a drink. Then he unpacked, and the gun was smaller than he remembered it. He picked it up and felt its weight, and that was greater than he recalled. And it was empty. It would be even heavier fully loaded.

After Huebner had helped him pick out the gun, they'd driven way out on Route 27, where treeless swamps extended for miles in every direction. Huebner pulled off the road a few yards from a wrecked car, its tires missing and most of its window glass gone.

"There's our target," he said. "You find a lot of cars abandoned along this stretch, but you don't want to start shooting up the newer ones."

"Because someone might come back for them?"

Huebner shook his head. "Because there might be a body in the trunk. This is where the drug dealers tend to drop off the unsuccessful competition, but no self-respecting drug dealer would be caught dead in a wreck like this one. You figure it'll be a big enough target for you?"

Embarrassingly enough, he missed the car altogether with his first shot. "You pulled up on it," Huebner told him. "Probably anticipating the recoil. Don't waste time worrying where the bullets are going yet. Just get used to pointing and firing."

And he got used to it. The recoil was considerable and so was the weight of the gun, but he did get used to both and began to be able to make the shots go where he wanted them to go. After Elliott had used up a full box of shells, Huebner got a pistol of his own from the glove compartment and put a few rounds into the fender of the ruined automobile. Huebner's gun was a nine-millimeter automatic with a clip that held twelve cartridges. It was much larger, noisier and heavier than the .38, and it did far more damage to the target.

"Got a whole lot of stopping power," Huebner said. "Hit a man in the arm with this, you're likely to take him down. Here, try it. Strike a blow for freedom."

The recoil was greater than the .38's, but less so than he would have guessed. Elliott fired off several rounds, enjoying the sense of power. He returned the gun to Huebner, who emptied the clip into the old car.

Driving back, Elliott said, "A phrase you used: 'Strike a blow for freedom.' "

"Oh, you never heard that? I had an uncle used that expression every time he took a drink. They used to say that during Prohibition. You hoisted a few then in defiance of the law, you were striking a blow for freedom."

The gun, the first article Elliott unpacked, was the last he put away.

He couldn't think of what to do with it. Its purchase had seemed appropriate in Florida, where they seemed to have gun shops everywhere. You walked into one and walked out owning a weapon. There was even a town in central Georgia where they'd passed their own local version of gun control, an ordinance requiring the adult population to go about armed. There had never been any question of enforcing the law, he knew; it had been passed as a statement of local sentiment.

Here in New York, guns were less appropriate. They were illegal, to begin with. You could apply for a carry permit, but unless there was some genuine reason connected with your occupation, your application was virtually certain to be denied. Elliott worked in an office and never carried anything to it or from it but a briefcase filled with papers, nor did his work take him down streets any meaner than the one he lived on. As far as the law was concerned, he had no need for a gun.

Yet he owned one, legally or not. Its possession was at once unsettling and thrilling, like the occasional ounce or so of marijuana secreted in his various living quarters during his twenties. There was something exciting, something curiously estimable, about having that which was prohibited, and at the same time, there was a certain amount of danger connected with its possession.

There ought to be security as well, he thought. He'd bought the gun for his protection in a city that increasingly seemed incapable of protecting its own inhabitants. He turned the gun over, let the empty cylinder swing out, accustomed his fingers to the cool metal.

His apartment was on the twelfth floor of a prewar building. Three shifts of doormen guarded the lobby. No other building afforded access to any of his windows, and those near the fire escape were protected by locked window gates, the key to which hung out of reach on a nail. The door to the hallway had two dead-bolt locks, each with its cylinder secured by an escutcheon plate. The door had a steel core and was further reinforced by a Fox police lock.

Elliott had never felt insecure in his apartment, nor were its security measures the result of his own paranoia. They had all been in place when he moved in. And they were standard for the building and the neighborhood.

He passed the gun from hand to hand, at once glad to have it and, like an impulse shopper, wondering why he'd bought it.

Where should he keep it?

The drawer of the night stand suggested itself. He put the gun and the box of shells in it, closed the drawer, and went to take a shower.

It was almost a week before he looked at the gun again. He didn't mention it and rarely thought about it. News items would bring it to mind. A hardware-store owner in Rego Park killed his wife and small daughter with an unregistered handgun, then turned the weapon on himself; reading about it in the paper, Elliott thought of the revolver in his night-stand drawer. An honor student was slain in his bedroom by a stray shot from a high-powered assault rifle, and Elliott, watching TV, thought again of his gun.

On the Friday after his return, some item about the shooting of a drug dealer again directed his thoughts to the gun, and it occurred to him that he ought at least to load it. Suppose someone came crashing through his door or used some advance in criminal technology to cut the gates on his windows. If he were reaching hurriedly for a gun, it should be loaded.

He loaded all six chambers. He seemed to remember that you were supposed to leave one chamber empty as a safety measure. Otherwise, the gun might discharge if dropped. Cocking the weapon would presumably rotate the cylinder and ready it for shooting. Still, it wasn't going to fire itself just sitting in his night-stand drawer, was it, now? And if he reached for it, if he needed it in a hurry, he'd want it fully loaded.

If you had to shoot at someone, you didn't want to shoot once or twice and then stop. You wanted to empty the gun.

Had Huebner told him that? Or had someone said it in a movie or on television? It didn't matter, he decided. Either way, it was sound advice.

A few days later, he saw a movie in which the hero, a renegade cop up against an entrenched drug mob, slept with a gun under his pillow. It was a much larger gun than Elliott's, something like Huebner's big automatic.

"More gun than you really need in your situation," Huebner had told him. "And it's too big and too heavy. You want something you can slip into a pocket. A cannon like this, you'd need a whole shoulder rig or it'd pull at your suit coat something awful."

Not that he'd ever carry it.

That night, he got the gun out of the drawer and put it under his pillow. He thought of the princess who couldn't sleep with a pea under her mattress. He felt a little silly, and he felt, too, some of what he had felt playing with toy guns as a child.

He got the gun from under his pillow and put it back in the drawer, where it belonged. He lay for a long time, inhaling the smell of the gun, metal and machine oil, interesting and not unpleasant.

A masculine scent, he thought. Blend in a little leather and tobacco, maybe a little horse shit, and you've got something to slap on after a shave. Win the respect of your fellows and drive the women wild.

He never put the gun under his pillow again. But the linen held the scent of the gun, and even after he'd changed the sheets and pillowcases, he could detect the smell on the pillow.

It was not until the incident with the panhandler that he ever carried the gun outside the apartment.

There were panhandlers all over the place, had been for several years now. It seemed to Elliott that there were more of them every year, but he wasn't sure if that was really the case. They were of either sex and of every age and color, some of them proclaiming well-rehearsed speeches on subway cars, some standing mute in doorways and extending paper cups, some asking generally for spare change or specifically for money for food or for shelter or for wine.

Some of them, he knew, were homeless people, ground down by the system. Some belonged in mental institutions. Some were addicted to crack. Some were lay-abouts, earning more this way than they could at a menial job. Elliott couldn't tell which was which and wasn't sure how he felt about them, his emotions ranging from sympathy to irritation, depending on circumstances. Sometimes he gave money, sometimes he didn't.

He had given up trying to devise a consistent policy and simply
followed his impulse of the moment.

One evening, walking home from the bus stop, he encountered a panhandler who demanded money. "Come on," the
man said. "Gimme a dollar."

Elliott started to walk past him, but the man moved to block
his path. He was taller and heavier than Elliott, wearing a dirty
Army jacket, his face partly hidden behind a dense black beard.
His eyes, slightly exophthalmic, were fierce.

"Didn't you hear me? Gimme a fuckin' dollar!"

Elliott reached into his pocket, came out with a handful of
change. The man made a face at the coins Elliott placed in his
hand, then evidently decided the donation was acceptable.

"Thank you kindly," he said. "Have a nice day."

Have a nice day, indeed. Elliott walked on home, nodded to
the doorman, let himself into his apartment. It wasn't until he
had engaged the locks that he realized his heart was pounding
and his hands trembling.

He poured himself a drink. It helped, but it didn't change
anything.

Had he been mugged? There was a thin line, he realized, and
he wasn't sure if the man had crossed it. He had not been asking
for money, he had been demanding it, and the absence of a
specific threat did not mean there was no menace in the
demand. Elliott, certainly, had given him money out of fear.
He'd been intimidated. Unwilling to display his wallet, he'd
fished out a batch of coins, including a couple of quarters and a
subway token, currently valued at $1.15.

A small enough price, but that wasn't the point. The point
was that he'd been made to pay it. *Stand and deliver*, the man
might as well have said. Elliott had stood and delivered.

A block from his own door, for God's sake. A good street in a
good neighborhood. Broad daylight.

And you couldn't even report it. Not that anyone reported
anything anymore. A friend at work had reported a burglary
only because you had to in order to collect on your insurance.
The police, he'd said, had taken the report over the phone. "I'll
send somebody if you want," the cop had said, "but I've got to
tell you, it's a waste of your time and ours." Someone else had

been robbed of his watch and wallet at gunpoint and had not bothered reporting the incident. "What's the point?" he'd said.

But even if there were a point, Elliott had nothing to report. A man had asked for money and he'd given it to him. They had a right to ask for money, some judge had ruled. They were exercising their First Amendment right of free speech. Never mind that there had been an unvoiced threat, that Elliott had paid the money out of intimidation. Never mind that it damn well felt like a mugging.

First Amendment rights. Maybe he ought to exercise his own rights under the Second Amendment—the right to bear arms.

That same evening he took the gun from the drawer and tried it in various pockets. Unloaded now, he tried tucking it into his belt, first in front, then behind, in the small of his back. He practiced reaching for it, drawing it. He felt foolish, and it was uncomfortable walking around with the gun in his belt like that.

It was comfortable in his right-hand jacket pocket, but the weight of it spoiled the line of the jacket. The pants pocket on the same side was better. He had reached into that pocket to produce the handful of change that had mollified the panhandler. Suppose he had come out with a gun instead?

"Thank you kindly. Have a nice day."

Later, after he'd eaten, he went to the video store on the next block to rent a movie for the evening. He was out the door before he realized he still had the gun in his pocket. It was still unloaded, the six shells lying where he had spilled them on his bed. He had reached for the keys to lock up and there was the gun.

He got the keys, locked up, and went out with the gun in his pocket.

The sensation of being on the street with a gun in his pocket was an interesting one. He felt as though he were keeping a secret from everyone he met, and that the secret empowered him. He spent longer than usual in the video store. Two fantasies came and went. In one, he held up the clerk, brandishing his empty gun and walking out with all the money in the register. In the other, someone else attempted to rob the place and Elliott drew his weapon and foiled the holdup.

Back home, he watched the movie, but his mind insisted on replaying the second fantasy. In one version, the holdup man spun toward him, gun in hand, and Elliott had to face him with an unloaded revolver.

When the movie ended, he reloaded the gun and put it back in the drawer.

The following evening, he carried the gun, loaded this time. The night after that was a Friday, and when he got home from the office, he put the gun in his pocket almost without thinking about it. He went out for a bite of dinner, then played cards at a friend's apartment a dozen blocks away. They played, as always, for low stakes, but Elliott was the big winner. Another player joked that he had better take a cab home.

"No need," he said. "I'm armed and dangerous."

He walked home, and on the way, he stopped at a bar and had a couple of beers. Some people at a table near where he stood were talking about a recent outrage, a young advertising executive in Greenwich Village shot dead while using a pay phone around the corner from his apartment. "I'll tell you something," one of the party said. "I'm about ready to start carrying a gun."

"You can't, legally," someone said.

"Screw legally."

"So a guy tries something and you shoot him and you're the one winds up in trouble."

"I'll tell you something," the man said. "I'd rather be judged by twelve than carried by six."

He carried the gun the whole weekend. It never left his pocket. He was at home much of the time, watching a ball game on television, catching up with his bookkeeping, but he left the house several times each day and always had the gun on his person.

He never drew it, but sometimes he would put his hand in his pocket and let his fingers curl around the butt of it. He found its presence increasingly reassuring. If anything happened, he was ready.

And he didn't have to worry about an accidental discharge.

The chamber under the hammer was unloaded. He had worked all that out. If he dropped the gun, it wouldn't go off. But if he cocked it and worked the trigger, it would fire.

When he took his hand from his pocket and held it to his face, he could smell the odor of the gun on his fingers. He liked that.

By Monday morning, he had grown used to the gun. It seemed perfectly natural to carry it to the office.

On the way home, not that night but the following night, the same aggressive panhandler accosted him. His routine had not changed. "Come on," he said. "Gimme a dollar."

Elliott's hand was in his pocket, his fingers touching the cold metal.

"Not tonight," he said.

Maybe something showed in his eyes.

"Hey, that's cool," the panhandler said. "You have a good day just the same." And stepped out of his path.

A week or so after that, he was riding the subway, coming home late after dinner with married friends in Forest Hills. He had a paperback with him, but he couldn't concentrate on it, and he realized that the two young men across the car from him were looking him over, sizing him up. They were wearing untied basketball sneakers and warm-up jackets and looked street smart, and dangerous. He was wearing the suit he'd worn to the office and had a briefcase beside him; he looked prosperous and vulnerable.

The car was almost empty. There was a derelict sleeping a few yards away, a woman with a small child all the way down at the other end. One of the pair nudged the other, then turned his eyes toward Elliott again.

Elliott took the gun out of his pocket. He held it on his lap and let them see it, then put it back in his pocket.

The two of them got off at the next station, leaving Elliott to ride home alone.

When he got home, he took the gun from his pocket and set it on the night stand. (He no longer bothered tucking it in the drawer.) He went into the bathroom and looked at himself in the mirror.

"Fucking thing saved my life," he said.

One night, he took a woman friend to dinner. Afterward, they went back to her place and wound up in bed. At one point, she got up to use the bathroom, and while she was up, she hung up her own clothing and went to put his pants on a hanger.

"These weigh a ton," she said, "What have you got in here?"

"See for yourself," he said. "But be careful."

"My God. Is it loaded?"

"They're not much good if they're not."

"My God."

He told her how he'd bought it in Florida, how it had now become second nature for him to carry it. "I'd feel naked without it," he said.

"Aren't you afraid you'll get into trouble?"

"I look at it this way," he told her. "I'd rather be judged by twelve than carried by six."

One night, two men cut across the avenue toward him while he was walking home from his Friday card game. Without hesitation, he drew the gun.

"Whoa!" the nearer of the two sang out. "Hey, it's cool, man. Thought you were somebody else is all."

They veered off, gave him a wide berth.

Thought I was somebody else, he thought. Thought I was a victim, is what you thought.

There were stores around the city that sold police equipment. Books to study for the sergeant's exam. Copies of the latest revised penal code. A T-shirt that read, N.Y.P.D. HOMICIDE SQUAD. OUR DAY BEGINS WHEN YOUR DAY ENDS.

He stopped in and didn't buy anything, then returned for a kit to clean his gun. He hadn't fired it yet, except in Florida, but it seemed as though he ought to clean it from time to time, anyway. He took the kit home and unloaded the gun and cleaned it, working an oiled patch of cloth through the short barrel. When he was finished, he put everything away and reloaded the gun.

He liked the way it smelled, freshly cleaned with gun oil.

A week later, he returned and bought a bulletproof vest. They had two types, one significantly more expensive than the other. Both were made of Kevlar, whatever that was.

"Your more expensive one provides you with a little more protection," the proprietor explained. "Neither one's gonna stop a shot from an assault rifle. The real high-powered rounds, concrete don't stop 'em. This here, though, it provides the most protection available, plus it provides protection against a knife thrust. Neither one's a sure thing to stop a knife, but this here's reinforced."

He bought the better vest.

One night, lonely and sad, he unloaded the gun and put the barrel to his temple. His finger was inside the trigger guard, curled around the trigger.

You weren't supposed to dry-fire the gun. It was bad for the firing pin to squeeze off a shot when there was no cartridge in the chamber.

Quit fooling around, he told himself.

He cocked the gun, then took it away from his temple. He uncocked it, put the barrel in his mouth. That was how cops did it when they couldn't take it anymore. Eating your gun, they called it.

He didn't like the taste, the metal, the gun oil. Liked the smell but not the taste.

He loaded the gun and quit fooling around.

A little later, he went out. It was late, but he didn't feel like sitting around the apartment, and he knew he wouldn't be able to sleep. He wore the Kevlar vest—he wore it all the time lately—and, of course, he had the gun in his pocket.

He walked around, with no destination in mind. He stopped for a beer but drank only a few sips of it, then headed out to the street again. The moon came into view, and he wasn't surprised to note that it was full.

He had his hand in his pocket, touching the gun. When he breathed deeply, he could feel the vest drawn tight around his chest. He liked the sensation.

When he reached the park, he hesitated. Years ago, back when the city was safe, you knew not to walk in the park at night. It was dangerous even then. It could hardly be otherwise now, when every neighborhood was a jungle.

So? If anything happened, if anybody tried anything, he was ready.

BRENDAN DUBOIS

MY BROTHER'S NIGHT

*Brendan DuBois makes his third appearance in this series
with the sort of hard-hitting yet compassionate story he
does so well. His first novel,* Dead Sand, *will be published
in hardcover by Pocket Books early in 1993, with a sequel
to follow.*

After the fight with my wife, Denise, I am in no mood to worry
about parking spaces, but worry I do, and I spend almost a half
hour going around the blocks until I find a space near the hotel.
It seems like my car is the only one on the street that has been
washed in months. I make sure twice that I lock both doors to
my BMW, and I feel a tingling at my back as I get out to the
sidewalk. The hotel is a block away, and near me is a liquor
store with barred display windows and a church mission with
empty wine and beer bottles scattered along its front sidewalk.
It seems convenient to have both of them within walking
distance.

The trash is piled so high in the cracked cement gutters that
I have to almost jump to get onto the sidewalk, which is fairly
difficult considering I'm carrying a bag of groceries.

Then the whispers start, of trouble afoot, and I look around
at the people going by, and the men sitting on the tenement
stoops, sipping from bottles wrapped in a paper bag. I always
listen to the whispers. They had gotten me far, from a vo-tech
high school and not much else to managing one of the three
biggest car dealerships in this part of the state, and now they
are telling me to get moving. I'm not too worried about the
car—it has the latest alarm system and the insurance is paid up.
But I worry about me, about slouching through these dark
streets, carrying a brown paper bag of groceries and with a six-
hundred-dollar suit flapping in the warm summer breeze.

I walk fast, feeling little glass vials crack under my feet. The smell around me is awful, like an open sewer or the breath of some beast, sighing and heaving along the dark alleyways.

At the hotel two of the five letters on the sign are burned out and flicker dimly against the darkening sky. I go through the open doors of the lobby and avoid the elevator and run up the two flights of stairs. On the landing a man wrapped in cardboard and newspaper snuffles and growls at me. I go along the hallway, which smells of old socks and urine, and I knock at a door marked 23 in dull gray numerals, waiting for a stranger with the same last name as me to answer the door, wanting to make sure he is alive.

Three hours ago Denise was in the kitchen, arms folded, a gin and tonic in one hand. Her brown hair, shoulder length, is streaked with gray. She wears a simple flowered dress whose cost years ago would have fed my parents and my brother for a week, and her light blue eyes are not happy.

"I don't see why you have to go, Owen," she says, leaning against the counter that contains the espresso machine and the microwave. "What do you owe him?"

Memories tug at me, and I focus on what is in the refrigerator. The double doors are open and I'm trying to remember someone else's tastes. It's hard to do. I start removing bottles and packages almost at random and begin filling up an empty brown bag on the spotless floor.

"I owe him a lot," I say.

"Hmph." She sips from her drink. "He won't take money. He won't take a job from you at the dealership. What makes you think he'll take our food?"

"On occasion, he's been practical," I say. Ketchup, I remember. Ketchup on everything, including scrambled eggs at breakfast. Lord, how that had sickened Father.

"Practical," Denise says. "What has he done for you or your family lately? Can you answer me that? Why do you owe him?"

My hands suddenly feel greasy and cold, and I almost drop the half-full bottle of ketchup.

I can't look at my wife. "Sometimes you can owe a person, even when he doesn't know it."

*　　*　　*

After the third knock there is a muffled grunt and the clicking sound of locks being undone, and I walk into the small room and immediately begin breathing through my mouth. The stench is terrific. The room is small, with a bed on one side and a small metal table on the other with two mismatched chairs. The floor is covered with cracked and chipped flowered linoleum, with two or three gray throw rugs scattered about, like rags too worthless to be saved. There is a counter near the single window, and on the counter is a minifridge and a single hotplate. Clothes are grouped in piles in the corner, and there are yellowed stacks of newspapers and paperback novels with their covers ripped away scattered on the table. There is another chair by the window, and the window is open, and the breeze does little to blow away the smell. A man is sitting on the chair, having returned there after unlocking the door.

And as before, I feel a little part of me die and wither away inside at the sight of my older brother. Our birth certificates say we're seven years apart, but on this night, it looks more like seventeen. His black hair is slicked back and shot through with gray, and above his greasy forehead there's a prominent widow's peak. This time around he has grown a mustache, and both ends are long and straggly. His face is puffy and red, and he looks at me with watery blue eyes as I come through the room. In the heat and stench he is wearing only a tattered pair of dungaree shorts. He has an enormous beer gut, and there are two furrowed scars across the dimpled flesh. On both thick forearms are black ink tattoos of skulls and daggers, the kind you get from amateurs in the state prison who don't care about disinfectant or AIDS. And his right arm is heavily scarred and slightly twisted, and it moves slowly. The arm had been scarred a very long time.

"Owen," he says, his voice raspy. "Come to rescue me again?"

"Hardly, James," I reply. "I gave up on that a long time ago," and an old memory and guilt scrape at me, like a razor being used that has grown rusty and scaling.

He coughs. "Put 'em down and have a seat."

I put the groceries down on the table and pull up the chair, and we sit silent for a while, and he looks at my suit and says, "Business doing well?"

"Pretty good." I was too smart to offer him a job. That has never worked, and we made a truce some years ago, between his stints up in Concord, that I would never speak of his working for me again.

"Good enough that you still keep that piece in your bedroom?" he says, smirking, and I blush for a moment, as one would do when caught at something by his older brother.

"That piece is a 9 mm Beretta," I say, remembering the time last year when a series of break-ins were plaguing our neighborhood and I had briefly talked to James from Concord. "You should know. You recommended it to me last year."

He smirks. "Shouldn't have listened to me, little bro. You should have picked yourself up a 12-gauge shotgun. More effective in a house. Especially a house like yours, such a nice neighborhood." He looks around the room and smiles and says, "Think you can put me up at your place for a few weeks, while I job hunt? My parole officer would love that, getting me into a stable home life and all that crap."

I'm sure that my mouth is hanging open and I'm running forth some answers in my mind, all the while thinking, Denise, my God, what would she say, when James laughs and says, "Chill, my little brother, chill. I was just goofing you—wanted to see you get a little excited. Tell you the truth, if I move in your house, I'm not sure if either Denise or I would last the first evening."

He coughs and strokes at his mustache and looks out the window. Across the way is a darkened office building and, beyond, the bright lights of downtown.

He says, still staring out at the darkness and lights, "In the joint you miss a lot of things, you know, from your favorite ice cream to clean sheets to women. The difference is, it's easier to remember some things than others. It's easy to remember the smell of a clean sheet and how it feels on your skin, the first night you sleep on it. It's easy to remember the taste of chocolate ice cream, and how cold and sweet it is, resting in your mouth, before you swallow it."

He turns to me, his eyes still watery. "I don't know, but in the joint, it don't work for women. You can't remember a damn thing. Oh, you know what you've done and with who and the number of times, but the smell, the feel, the touch. All gone. You can't remember that."

My brother gestures to the window with his good arm. "All those women out there, Owen, and I don't know the first thing about them." He scratches his hairy chest and tries to laugh. "Not that any of them would have anything to do with me, a guy that looks like this. You and Denise getting along still?"

I nod.

"That we are."

"Children?"

"Not yet," and I look away from him.

He chuckles. "You two been together almost seven years. Children not ever, I'd guess. The few things I remember about Denise, I remember well, little brother. She likes things just the way they are. She likes herself, and I don't think she's gonna like seeing her belly bloom up and get saggy and wrinkly. Maybe you two ought to think of adoption or something."

I rub my hands against my pants and try to ignore what he's saying, and I say, "Your parole officer have something lined up?"

He rubs his right arm, the scarred one. The scar tissue is pale pink and ropy against the white skin.

"Yep. Night work. But not the type of night work I'm used to. Of course, I can't do that type of night work anymore. Cons can't buy guns. This work, though. Frying doughnuts." He looks at me, almost in disbelief. "Frying doughnuts. Some career move for a college grad, eh?"

I look around the room and see two brown insects move against the greasy wall. I try to think of what to say and I remember old arguments, and I try again.

"You don't have to stay here, you know," I say.

He rests a chin in his hand.

"Oh, yes, I do," he says. "Yes, I do."

That evening I'm in bed, resting, one arm across my forehead. I'm covered by a flowered sheet, and I remember what my brother said earlier, about remembering clean sheets. On the far walnut counter a candle flickers and sputters, and from the open bathroom door I hear the shower slowly being turned off. No matter the time, no matter how long and wonderfully it goes on, Denise always takes a shower afterward. I try not to think, and I find it very hard.

My hands feel cold and clumsy. Next to me, less than a foot away, is a nightstand with a darkened lamp, and in that nightstand is an unread Bible and the 9 mm Beretta. I look about the room, feeling out of place, out of sorts.

Denise comes out wearing a light pink robe, toweling down her hair. She sits at the edge of the bed and leans toward me, as if wanting to be touched or caressed, and I lie still.

She says, "So. How's he doing, his first week out?"

"He's alive."

She has a look that's almost a sneer, and it saddens me. "That's an accomplishment?"

I close my eyes, remembering. "For my brother James it is. He's kept himself alive through a lot. When he was in college, he was in army ROTC, and he wanted to be a helicopter pilot and go to Vietnam in the worst way. Think of that, and the survival rates of pilots back then, and what his odds of survival were. But a couple of weeks before he was due to report, he was in a bad car accident. Almost got killed and ruined his right arm. The army wouldn't have him. And while in the hospital he was depressed and got hooked on pain medication. That monkey rode his back for a long time and rode him into prison. I'm pretty sure he's off of everything now, but I don't think it makes much of a difference to him. He's a stubborn man. He sees himself as a con, no matter the circumstances, no matter what's ahead."

"So he's alive," my wife sniffs. "Some life."

Waiting for a moment for a touch that never comes, she gets up and goes into the bathroom without looking back, and I roll over on my side and wonder why my hands are so cold.

And I remember:

Fourteen years old, with a brother that was bigger and better and a guy I could depend on. A guy who would give you a better description of the mysteries of women than Mother or Father. A guy who would buy you beer for those warm summer nights when you camped out in the backyard with your buddies. And one who was always there to listen, to advise, to argue.

In his bedroom, me sitting on his bed, looking over at him as he gets dressed in his ROTC uniform. His hair is full and dark and he is clean-shaven, and his blue eyes glitter as if smiling continuously at everything about him, finding humor there. He tugs at the uniform, looking slightly self-consciously in the closet mirror. He has a small pudginess around his waist that exercises and diets refuse to melt away.

On one wall of the bedroom is a poster of John Wayne, from his Green Berets movie. The war in Vietnam has been lost for some time, I know, but my brother doesn't care. ROTC has paid for his college, and he wants to be a helicopter pilot, and he wants to go overseas. Mother and Father are unsure of it all, at one moment being fiercely proud of him and passing around wallet-sized photos of James in his uniform, and in other moments, sitting quietly out in the backyard, holding hands, the smoke from Father's cigarette eddying up slowly from his other hand.

I have no doubt. I watch the evening news, of the body counts and the atrocities, of the villages destroyed and the protests in the streets. I clip out photographs from *Newsweek* and *Time* and *Life*, and every time I see a photo of a burned and crashed Huey helicopter, my heart seems to slow down and ooze away.

He turns and smiles. "Pretty sharp, right? Amanda thinks so, and let me tell you, little brother, there are still some women out there that get turned on by a man in uniform."

In a month he will graduate from college. And some months after that, he will be going thousands of miles away to a strange land, and I know, and I hear the whispers that tell me that he will be killed this summer. I don't want to lose him, and I can't say this to him, and afraid of crying, I only smile and nod fiercely.

I sit in my office at the dealership, the door shut, just looking out the window. It's a sunny day and a stiff wind is flapping the pennants and banners strung up across the building and light posts. People are moving through the rows and rows of cars.

The customers are the ones who move slowly, going from car to car, deep in thought, whispering at each other, nodding or shaking their heads. My salesmen and saleswomen are the confident ones, the ones who move quickly and to the point or who rest against a polished fender, smiling and just waiting.

Cars. To everyone out there those are wonderful vehicles, the latest from Detroit or Japan, shiny and ready to fulfill everyone's dream, everyone's fantasy.

To me, they are just hunks of iron, and my job is to get them off the lot as fast as possible. The more iron that rests and rusts there, the more money it costs me.

Cars. I feel sorry for the kids now who were like me in high school, not too bright when it came to math or English but who knew how to change a car's oil when they were twelve and who could do a tune-up when they were fourteen. Cars in my youth were simpler and had hardly changed much from Father's time. But now they have all this electronic gadgetry and computer diagnosis crap, well, you almost need a college education to work on a car these days.

I lift my feet up against the low windowsill, admiring my two-hundred-dollar Italian shoes. How our parents would shake their heads at that expense, and how they would shake their heads at the novelty of it all, of me doing well, and of James going sour. Back then it was, Owen, look up to James. James is going places. James has gone to college and has a service career ahead of him. And what about you? Going to change spark plugs for the rest of your life?

On my walls are my trophies and certificates and photos of triumph. Chamber of Commerce awards. Recognition for cash volume and car sales. And one photo, taken at some political function where I shook this senator's hand, and a year later he was elected president. I look at them and they seem covered with dust, as if they didn't belong to me, and had never belonged. I feel like I am an impostor, sitting in someone's office, and that in a moment I'll be discovered and tossed out into the parking lot.

The sun reflecting on the cars outside is very bright and makes my head ache, and for a moment I think if I had my pistol right here, right now, I'd shoot out every goddamn windshield.

I clasp my hands together and wait.

Another memory:

In the courtyard the grass is scuffed and brown and the stiff plastic badge clipped to my jacket flips back and forth in the breeze. I sit down at one of the dirty concrete tables in the yard and look around me, at the groups of men working out among clanging and heavy weights, at the others playing basketball with shouts and expressions that make no sense to me, and the other men, hunched over and walking alone, staring at the yellow grass, their fists clenched inside their pants pockets. Those were the ones who scared me the most.

From one group he approaches, nodding a bit, his gait sure and cocky, as if he were there not because of some offense or penalty but because he wanted to prove to anyone who cared that he had what it took to make it in such a world, where every man was an enemy, every corner a potential ambush. His black hair is combed straight back and his skin is pasty white. His right arm hangs stiffly at one side, and he wears light denim pants and shirt.

He sits down across from me, saying, "Dutiful Owen. If Mother and Father were still alive, they'd be proud of you."

I try to smile and fail, since it seems impossible to smile inside such a place, with the glistening coils of razor wire about the yard, and the uniformed deputies who walk two abreast, their heads and eyes constantly moving around. From an inside pocket I take out four packs of Marlboros, which I slip across the table to him. They have been opened and examined not more than five minutes ago, and James nods and tucks the packs into his shirt pockets.

"Thanks for the cash," he says, wrinkling his old eyes at me. "It'll help a lot. There's a scam going on, you see, where I was getting squeezed to do some servicing for these Nazi types, over on the east wing. Water boys. That's what they call 'em, but you do more than just errands. You sit there and you do. So. A couple a packs a week to these other boys and I've got my protection. A little weight on my side and they don't bother me."

James moves his right arm. "Arm like this makes me very attractive." He pats his shirt pockets, as if afraid the cigarettes are already gone. "You seem all right, Owen. You doing all right?"

"I'm doing okay." I look around at the wires and the muttering men, walking by at such a slow pace, and I say, "What does your lawyer think?"

"My lawyer?" He rubs at his jaw with his left hand. "My lawyer spends most of his time telling me how stupid I am."

"Do you think he has a point?"

James smiles. "Getting testy, younger one?"

"James, you knew you were violating parole the minute you got the gun."

He shrugs. "And robbing the store was extra, as was taking the shot at the clerk. So what."

I stare over his shoulder, at the concrete buildings. "Why?"

"Why?" James asks. "You mean, why am I here, or why did I take a shot at the clerk? The answer's connected, you know. I'm here because of the clerk, and I shot at the clerk because I didn't want to come back here."

"If money was—"

"Yeah," he interrupts. "A problem, always a problem, but what I need you can't provide. A feeling of doing something on my own, something I know I can do. And no matter how successful you are or how many cars you sell, Owen, and what you might want to plan for me, that's something I have to do by myself. And stealing things is what I'm good at. I was out of that store, a good haul, I could feel the weight in the bag, and I saw the clerk go up to the alarm. Right there in a second, I saw it all, him doing that and the cops coming and me back here, wondering who's going to try to make me his new boyfriend. So I took a shot at him. He should have stayed on the floor."

"He's still in the hospital."

James grunts. "He should have stayed on the floor. He made his choice."

Choices, I think.

*   *   *

It's a warm night. I park across the street from the doughnut shop in a red BMW I had borrowed that day from my lot, having left my blue one behind. I don't want to be made. Even so I am still uncomfortable, as if expecting some police officer to charge me with stealing this car. I park so I can see the kitchen area, where the doors are open to allow some breezes in. I can make out James, working stolidly and silently, his arms pasty white, up to the elbows in flour. His hair looks odd, and I figure he's wearing a hairnet. He moves slowly, wearing black shoes, white pants, and a white shirt that seems to strain from the weight of his belly.

I watch for long minutes, resting my head on my cold left hand. James's life has always revolved around uniforms. His whole life, his whole progression: the blue uniform of the Cub Scouts, the khaki of the Boy Scouts, the dark green of ROTC, the light green of the hospital clothes, the denim of the prisons, and now the clear white of his doughnut shop.

For so long I prayed to God not to let James die. And after that last whole summer of his, at the time of his accident, was when I stopped going to church.

And it was then, that night:

James was to report to the army in two weeks, and every day, the news from Vietnam seemed to get worse and worse. The television images play themselves in my mind again, over and over. Soldiers in rice paddies. Villages being burned. And the *slap-slap* sound of the helicopters, scurrying above the smoke and the bullets and noise like giant locusts, and the twisted and black and green wreckage of the helicopters whenever they crashed.

I lie awake in bed, waiting. James is out, visiting some friends, and when he left he was singing some army song, going out to his '68 Chevy Impala, parked in the darkened backyard. My room is right across from his, and many times he would come in to see me. The Christmas Eve night, years ago, when he deftly shook a burned-out lightbulb and told me that the light and airy tinkling sound was Santa's sleigh, coming to our house. A summer evening when he sat on the edge of my bed and told me stories of the times he had struck out in Little League. And the cold winter mornings when he would come in and pull off the blankets, and get me up for school.

From downstairs the phone rings, its noise shrill and loud. I lie there, still, my fists clenched. I hear Father answer and make a low shout, and then Mother starts sobbing. I roll off the bed and put my head next to the heat register, and that's when I learn of James's accident.

A month or two later. I visit James in his hospital room, and his right arm is still hanging above him, held up by plaster and wires and pulleys. His hair is quite long, and he is growing a mustache. I go into the sour-smelling room and James is sitting up, and sitting by him is a guy about his age, and I feel myself clench up. Hippie. Long hair, odd-colored T-shirt, patched jeans, and sandals. He has a thick and wiry beard and is wearing round glasses, and I don't know why this man is here. James is loud in a lot of ways, and he has always been loud in his dislike of the hippies.

I look at James and feel scared. His eyes are funny, swollen and small at the same time, and they are rolling around some, like they can't focus.

"Owen," he says, his voice slurring. "Meet my new buddy George. Ol' George here is my own private pharmacist. Man, the pain here gets so bad only George can help."

I say, "Your arm still hurts?"

George giggles and James looks over at me again, and I know I will only stay for a few seconds more.

"Who said anything about my arm?" James asks.

In my rear yard Denise sits on the grass while I rest in a redwood lounge chair. She leans her head against my thigh. She wears acid-washed designer jeans and one of my Oxford shirts, the sleeves rolled up to expose her tanned arms. She is barefoot and holds a drink in her hands. Tonight I'm wearing my own suburban uniform: light blue polo shirt and tan shorts. I look at her and the yard and the house behind us, filled with expensive gadgetry, and I think, iron. Iron got me all of this. Years before, I had hired the woman who became my wife as a bookkeeper at one of my dealerships. Now she is an independent accounting consultant, and I think she is mine. But I'm not sure. I don't feel like I belong. I don't feel that either she or the house is mine, but I do feel like a trespasser.

She flexes her toes in the grass and says, "Your brother?"

"He's staying alive," I say, wondering about the lie I just uttered. I've had too many drinks myself, and it's a struggle to keep still in the chair.

Denise looks into her glass and says, "You ever feel vindicated, Owen?"

"What do you mean?"

She stretches one foot out.

"I think you would," she says. "After all, from what you told me, growing up wasn't that great for you. Your older brother was always held up as an example of success, and your parents always gave you a hard time about school and what you wanted from life. Right? They were sure that James was going to have a wonderful career in the army and that you were going to be a gas jockey. But it didn't quite work out that way, did it? Then again, nothing ever does. Your older brother gets into a bad car accident, turns into a junkie and a criminal, and you become a pretty damn good businessman."

A robin prances along the lawn, cocking its head back and forth, back and forth.

I say, "You know, Mother could never bring herself to say what you just did, about James. She would only say that James was in his own dark night, and that one day things would get light for him. I tried to believe that, as much as I looked up to him."

The robin snaps forward and rears back, a worm squirming in its harsh beak. It flies off and I turn my head, trying to see where it goes.

"You said you looked up to James. Weren't you ever jealous of all the attention he got?"

"No, never," I say, not quite looking at her.

She asks, "How did that car accident happen, Owen?"

"Went off the road and into a tree," I say. "No one knows why."

She sighs and in a bit rubs her lips against my leg, and gently nibbles at the skin there, and I am too ashamed to respond, being the liar that I am.

I visit him once again, and he is resting on his sagging bed, slightly drunk. His white clothes from the doughnut shop are stained and crusty, and there is a sickly-sweet smell that I can taste in my mouth. His feet are bare and dirty, and I notice that his little toe on his left foot has been cut off. I wonder what awful thing happened to have caused that.

"It's like this, Owen," he says, and his voice is unsteady. "Suppose the car accident never happened. Or suppose it was just a little one, not enough to keep me out of the army. Man, it would have been something else. I knew I had the talent, knew I could fly helicopters, Owen. Sure, it was dangerous, but I knew I could make it. And when it was over I'd either stay with the army or become one of those corporate pilots, fly a helicopter anywhere in the world. Man, that would have been something. Money. Women. Travel. Keep myself slim and in good shape. But my damn luck . . . And even if I bought it in Vietnam, Owen, it would have been better than this crap. If I could trade my name and put it on that wall in Washington and take it off all of those police and parole reports, I'd do it in a second."

I don't know what to say. He closes his eyes. I take out my wallet and remove two twenty-dollars bills, and I stuff them in his pants pocket, hoping that he won't remember how he got them in the morning.

At night I wake up and sit against the bed. Denise sighs and stirs against me, and murmurs, "You awake?"

"Yes," I say, looking out the fine bedroom windows of what is supposedly my house to the well-groomed yard. "Yes, I am. Thinking of James."

She moves against me and she is too warm, making me feel nervous, like I don't belong. "That's all you've been thinking about, the past couple of weeks."

Denise yawns and rolls over. Her naked back is tan and smooth in the light from the rising moon.

She says, "Don't hate me for this, Owen, but I wish he was back in prison. At least you could sleep at night."

I think of what she says for a long time.

It didn't take much and yet I'm here, in the stinking room that belongs to James, thinking, thinking of what might have been. If the car accident had never happened, and everything he had planned, had dreamed and worked for, had come true.

So. My brother's room, which is empty. A half hour ago Denise had called me at the dealership, saying that someone had broken into our house, breaking through the rear door's lock. The police told my wife that it had been a professional job, and they thought it was a professional, save for one puzzling fact. Nothing had been taken from the house, except for one thing.

Of course. My 9 mm Beretta.

The night air is hot and seems to seize my chest, and I look out the tiny window and out at the lights of the city.

Choices.

Tonight my brother has made his choice, one he has continued to make ever since that day I saw him in the hospital, his eyes glittering at all that was around him. Tonight, with weapon in hand, he was roaming out there, looking for cash, of course, but looking for something he could call his own, something he has never grasped before. And I get very small consolation that in this instance he has chosen to take something from me, even though I had never offered it.

Choices.

I breathe deeply, wishing for one horrible moment that some carcinogen in the air would strike me down at this instant. And here I am, waiting, wondering if I will ever talk to him again, wondering about the cops out there who might catch him, who might not make him live, and for a moment I think of going to the police, giving them his description, plead with them to pick him up, for violating his parole means he'll go back to prison, but at least he'll live.

I shake my head. It would be no use, whatever I did with James. I learned that so many years ago, the night I went out to the dark night and disabled the brakes on his car, the night of his accident.

I wanted him to live. I wanted him to be hurt, not badly, just enough so he would stay home that summer.

So he would live.

And, of course, everything I had touched had become a failure, for my brother is dead, has been for years, and I had killed him.

I wonder about his dying tonight. I wonder if I will ever tell him.

I wait. And I hear steps approaching. The door opens. And:

James stands there, a half-smile on his face, carrying a paper bag under one arm. He is wearing jeans and a creased brown-leather jacket. His hair is down his back in a greasy ponytail. And I stare at him for so long that I can no longer smell the decay in the room.

"Surprised?" he says as he closes the door behind him.

I can't think of what to say for what seems hours, until I say, "No. Just disappointed, James."

He smiles again, and drops the bag. It makes a solid noise when it lands on the table, and there's a slight metallic sound and I know where my Beretta is.

"Disappointment. Very original."

I take a deep breath and say, "James, you've had a lot of opportunities, a lot of times along the way when you could have done something different. A lot of opportunities."

"Maybe I don't want them."

"For Christ's sake, why?" and I hear my voice rise.

"Maybe I have my own reasons. My own little joys of life. Maybe I enjoy seeing my little professional brother get so uptight and bothered. Maybe I like that."

I try to think, then, of how he looked before the accident, the slightly overweight but determined brother who was going to go far in his life, and all I see is this creature before me. I wonder how it's possible that we come from the same parents.

"Maybe I should leave," I say.

"Maybe you should," he agrees. I go past him and open the door and I say, "So. How long do you intend to keep on doing this?"

He shrugs. "Until I get caught. Or blown away. Or score so well I can stop."

"Some profession," I say. I go through the open door and stand in the hallway and look back at him.

He smiles again, a disturbing look. "A profession you should be familiar with, little brother. We're both thieves. I'm just more current in my thievery. What you stole, you stole about twenty years ago. From me."

At that, he slowly closes the door in my face.

I close my eyes. Take a deep shuddering breath. Open them and look at the greasy door and the trash-cluttered hallway, and I listen to the murmurs and shouts and the distant wail of sirens, and I smell the ever-present scent of things gone terribly wrong, and out of everything I feel, I feel like I finally belong.

EDWARD D. HOCH

THE PROBLEM OF THE GRANGE HALL

A big band plays a gig in a small New England town in the late 1930s, in another locked-room puzzle for Dr. Sam Hawthorne.

Dr. Lincoln Jones, Northmont's first black physician, joined the staff of Pilgrim Memorial Hospital in March of 1929 [Dr. Sam Hawthorne reminisced as he poured two glasses of wine]. The hospital opened that month, and I've already told you about the Pilgrims Windmill affair and the trouble we had at the time with ghostly figures, a terrible fire, and threats from the Ku Klux Klan.

Happily for us all, the next eight years passed uneventfully for Lincoln Jones—if you can call marriage and the birth of two children uneventful. I wasn't on the hospital staff myself, but my office was in the physicians' wing of the building and I usually saw Linc a couple of times a week. He was a tall, handsome man on the verge of forty like myself, specializing in children's illnesses. In the city he would have been called a pediatrician, but in Northmont we weren't nearly so fancy.

It was decided that the hospital would celebrate its eighth anniversary that March with a community dinner and a dance at the Grange Hall. Eighth anniversaries aren't usually worth noting, but the Depression had been hard on Pilgrim Memorial along with every other facet of American life. The hospital needed money for new equipment, and the celebration was a perfect opportunity to raise some of it. The committee was bringing in a big New York band, Sweeney Lamb and his All-Stars, for the dance.

"Are you and your wife going to the dance on Saturday?" I asked Linc Jones one day when I encountered him in the hospital corridor.

"Do we have any choice?" he answered with a grin. It had been made clear that all of the staff physicians and doctors with offices in the building were expected to purchase a pair of tickets. "Who are you taking?"

"My nurse Mary Best," I told him. "She deserves a treat for putting up with me."

"Well, it should be fun. I went to high school with Sweeney Lamb's trumpet player, a fellow named Bix Blake. Haven't seen him in years."

The Grange Hall was out beyond the hospital, almost to the edge of town. I felt a bit like a high school kid myself on Friday night, calling for Mary Best at the small house she rented, going up to the door with a corsage to go with her dress.

"How nice of you, Sam!" she told me as she pinned it on. "This is just like a date." She may have been gently mocking my bachelor status, but I couldn't be sure.

"It's not every week we have a dance with a big-city orchestra here in Northmont."

The month of March had started out cold that year, but there'd been very little snow. By the weekend of the dance it was feeling almost like spring. As I parked my car and helped Mary out, taking care that her long gown didn't drag on the ground, the first arrivals we saw were Sheriff Lens and his wife. We exchanged warm greetings and walked into the hall together. The sheriff and I had worn blue suits, and I was surprised to see some of the hospital and town officials in tuxedos. "It's sure a big night," the sheriff said. We went in and found a table together, with me sitting between Vera Lens and Mary.

"A little excitement in this town at last!" Vera Lens said. She was younger than the sheriff and they'd been married about ten years. "I hope it'll liven thing up. We haven't even had a good murder since last summer."

"And let's hope we *don't* have one," the sheriff told her, "at least not tonight."

I spotted Linc Jones and his wife, Charlene, at another table. "Let's go say hello," I suggested to Mary.

The tables were arranged in a horseshoe shape around the dance floor, with the bandstand at the front of the hall. Linc and his wife were opposite us, on the other side of the horseshoe. "Well, Sam! Good to see you here. You remember my wife, Charlene, don't you?"

"I certainly do!" She'd be hard to forget, a lovely dark-skinned woman who knew how to use just the right amount of make-up. It had been the talk of Pilgrim Memorial when he returned from vacation that first year with a new wife.

"Hello, Sam," she said with a smile. "Good to see you again. You too, Mary."

Sweeney Lamb's musicians were beginning to take the stage. Until then I hadn't thought much about Linc's high school chum, and the fact that the Sweeney Lamb orchestra had always been white. There was an audible murmur from a few tables as two black musicians joined the fifteen others on stage. One of them carried a trumpet and Linc Jones waved to him.

"That's my old buddy," he said. "Come on up, Sam, and I'll introduce you."

Bix Blake was darker than Linc, with a pushed-in nose that may have been broken at one time. I saw him frown as we approached, and his eyes seemed to go beyond our heads to the table where we'd been seated. "Lincoln Jones," he said with a trace of resignation. "I forgot this was your town."

"It's not really mine, Bix. This here's Sam Hawthorne, one of the doctors I work with."

I held out my hand. "How are you, Bix? Welcome to Northmont. We've all been looking forward to this affair."

Blake's handshake was firm. "It's a bit different from playin' in New York."

"Can we get together after?" Linc asked. "We've got a lot of catching up to do."

Bix Blake worked the valves of his trumpet. "Our bus is leavin' right after the show, but I'll be back in that little dressing room during the break, after the first hour. Come back then."

"I'll do that."

Sweeney Lamb himself had appeared by that time, fronting the band as he murmured instructions to some of his people. He was fairly well known and I recognized him at once from his pictures—handsome, broad-shouldered, with traces of gray in his hair. In person his eyeglasses were thicker than I'd expected, but otherwise he was just like his photographs. "Nice to meet you, Mr. Lamb," I said. "I'm Dr. Sam Hawthorne from the hospital. Dr. Jones here went to school with your trumpeter."

He glanced at Linc, and then over at Bix. "Nice town you got here," he said, not offering to shake either of our hands. He started adjusting the microphone, and we took the hint that the music was about to begin.

Back at the table Charlene asked, "Did he remember you?"

"Oh, sure," Linc answered. "We're getting together during the break."

"Did he ask about me?"

"No."

I glanced from one to the other. "You knew him too, Charlene?"

She glanced down without replying and Linc answered for her. "They were engaged once, briefly, but that was a long time ago."

"Bix said I picked Linc instead of him because I wanted to marry a doctor and have lots of money."

Mary Best placed her hand on Charlene's and tried to say something comforting, but just then Sweeney Lamb's voice boomed through the Grange Hall.

"Good evening, ladies and gentlemen! It's a pleasure to be here in Northmont to help you folks celebrate the eighth anniversary of Pilgrim Memorial Hospital. I'm Sweeney Lamb, but I guess you all knew that." He paused for the applause and then continued, "Before we strike up the band for an evening of fabulous music, we're going to hear just a few words from the director of Pilgrim Memorial, Dr. Robert Yale."

Bob Yale had been part of Pilgrim Memorial since its beginning, and when the previous director retired he'd been the logical successor. He was bright, articulate, and willing to try new things. "I won't keep you long," he told the audience. "I know we're all anxious to get out on the dance floor. Just remember why we're here. Pilgrim Memorial needs your help. We need money. Northmont may be a small community, but the hospital is known and respected in this state. I want it to stay that way. I want us to grow as the community grows, to be ready for tomorrow's challenges. The medical problems of today, whether TB or polio or cancer, cannot be met with yesterday's equipment. You know our goal—help us to reach it! And now, without further ado, it's back to Sweeney Lamb and his All-Stars!"

Lamb's band opened with a jazzy theme and then switched to something slower for dancing. *Pennies from Heaven* and *Red Sails in the Sunset* had even some of the older townspeople out on the floor. "Your friend Bix is mighty good with that trumpet," I told Lincoln Jones.

"I'm glad to see some black faces up there. It's been a big problem, especially for a band that tours. In most cities the Negro musicians have to stay at separate hotels. But some of the big New York bands are starting to integrate their players now."

After another jazz tune Sweeney Lamb took the microphone to announce, "Now, as a special treat, the song stylings of Miss Helen McDonald, with Spider Downs on saxophone."

A blond young woman in a long pink dress came on stage and bowed, then started a dreamy rendition of *It's a Sin to Tell a Lie*. Mary stirred and stood up. "Aren't you ever going to ask me to dance, Sam?"

"Sorry," I said, perhaps blushing a bit. I'd been enjoying the music so much that I'd almost forgotten she was my date for the evening. I certainly owed her a dance or two. Linc and Charlene quickly joined us to cover my awkwardness.

"She's good," Mary Best decided, fitting comfortably into my arms. "I think I've heard her on the radio."

Helen McDonald was indeed good. There was a swinging beat to the way she delivered the lyrics that really put them across. On the next number, *The Way You Look Tonight*, Bix Blake contributed a trumpet bit and then Spider Downs, the other black musician, did a saxophone solo. Sweeney passed around some sheet music for the next selection. Helen and Spider Downs each took one. She folded hers and passed it on to Bix, then stood on the sidelines while the band played an instrumental version of *I'm Putting All My Eggs in One Basket*. After that they took a break.

I stopped to say a few words to Bob Yale, the hospital

director. "Great evening, Bob! This should encourage a few donations."

"I certainly hope so."

Linc Jones had walked on ahead, crossing the dance floor to intercept Bix. Watching them from a distance, I wondered just how friendly they were. Bix's face, at that moment, was twisted into an expression like pain or anger. I walked close enough to hear Linc compliment him on his playing, and Bix reply, "I'll be better next set." Bix led the way to a door behind the stage, apparently the dressing room he'd mentioned earlier.

I saw that Mary was at the table alone. "Where's Charlene?"

"Ladies' room. I didn't feel like battling the crowd."

I kept an eye on the dressing room door as we spoke. After several minutes, they still hadn't emerged and, feeling a concern I couldn't quite express, I headed back in that direction. Sweeney Lamb appeared at that moment, glancing around the floor. "Seen Bix?" he asked me.

"I believe he's in there, chatting with an old high school friend."

Lamb walked to the door I'd indicated, and the other black musician, Spider Downs, joined us. The bandleader knocked and tried the knob. "It's locked."

I tried knocking and called out, "Linc! It's Sam Hawthorne. Open up!"

A voice beyond the door distinctly said, "Sam!" I didn't know whether it was a cry for help or only one of recognition, but I felt I had to get in there. I rattled the knob uselessly. "Who's got the key to this?"

"No key," Lamb said. "There's a bolt on the other side. We used it as a dressing room earlier."

"Help me with this," I said to the black musician. We hit the door together with our shoulders and the bolt pulled from the wooden frame. The door sprang open.

Lincoln Jones was kneeling next to the body of his old school chum. In one hand he held a hypodermic needle. "What's happened here, Linc?"

"I—I don't know."

I knelt on the other side of Bix Blake and felt for a pulse.

Behind me I heard the voice of Sheriff Lens. "What's goin' on here? Let me through, please. I'm the sheriff. What is it, Doc?"

I looked up at him. "Bix Blake. He's dead."

Sheriff Lens took in the rest of the scene in an instant. He wasn't the smartest man in the world, but he knew his job. "Doc Jones," he said, reaching out his hand, "you'd best give me that hypodermic."

Word of the tragedy spread quickly through the large room, becoming as distorted as one might expect under the tense circumstances. As I headed back to the table to tell Mary, the first person I encountered was Charlene Jones. "What in God's name has happened?" she demanded, close to hysteria. "Someone just told me Linc stabbed a man!"

"Nothing like that," I assured her. "Bix Blake is dead and no one knows what happened. There was no knife. Linc had a hypodermic needle—"

"What for? What does it mean?"

"He may have been trying to save Bix's life. We don't know yet."

"I have to see Linc," she insisted, pushing past me toward the crowded doorway.

Finally I reached our table and told Mary Best what had happened. "Do you think Linc killed him?" she asked, getting right to the point.

"I don't know. We have to find out what killed him first."

Dr. Bob Yale came hurrying over. "What do you know about this, Sam?"

"Very little. One of the black musicians, the trumpet player, is dead. Linc Jones was with him when he died."

"My God! Does this mean they won't be finishing the dance?"

"You'll have to ask Sweeney Lamb that." At the moment a man's death seemed more important to me.

But Bob Yale did get to Lamb, and I saw the two of them off in a corner a few minutes later. When Yale returned to me he was all smiles. "They don't have another job for three nights. He's willing to stay in Northmont and do the whole thing again tomorrow night. How does that sound?"

"For the same price?" I asked skeptically.

"He's donating it. Do you think everyone will come back, Sam?"

"Bix Blake won't."

I walked away from him as an ambulance arrived from Pilgrim Memorial. The person I really wanted to see was Sheriff Lens, but it was another half-hour before I found him alone, looking decidedly unhappy. By that time the word had spread that the dance had been postponed until the following night, and some people were beginning to depart.

"How does it look, Sheriff?"

"Not good for Lincoln Jones, Doc. I want you to sit in while I go over his story in detail."

"Glad to. Want to do it now?"

"I'm just waiting for a preliminary report from the hospital. There's a slight chance it was a natural death, but I doubt it. Looks to me like he was injected with some fast-acting poison."

"Surely not by Linc!"

"I don't know, Doc. The room has no windows and the only door was bolted from inside. No one else was in there."

"Can I take a look at it? I just had a glimpse when we broke in."

He led the way to the broken door, which he'd secured with a length of twine. I entered behind him and stared at the walls. Its main function was obviously as a storeroom, and cardboard boxes were stacked along the left wall. I looked inside one and found extra tablecloths, apparently on loan for tonight's function. The room was about fifteen feet square, with a line of mirrors fastened to the wall opposite the door. Chairs and small tables were placed in front of the mirrors, the best the Grange could offer in the way of dressing room facilities. Along the right wall was a pipe with wooden coathangers holding the band members' outerwear, a variety of coats and jackets.

"Someone could have been hiding behind these coats," I suggested.

"That's pretty doubtful, Doc, but let's see what Jones has to say."

They were beginning to clear the tables in the hall now, and Sweeney Lamb was standing with the girl singer, Helen McDonald. Both of them seemed to be in a daze.

"He was such a nice man," the blond girl said. I doubted if she was much over twenty. "Do they think it was a heart attack?"

"We're waiting for word from the hospital," I told her. Then, turning to the bandleader, I asked, "Did Bix have any health problems?"

"He's only been with me a few months, but he seemed healthy enough. Let me ask Spider." He called to the black musician who'd helped me break in the door earlier. "This is Spider Downs, a damn fine saxophone man. He and Bix joined the band together. Spider, you knew him longer than I did. Were there any health problems?"

Spider was a short, bald man who was built like a barrel. He was probably no older than me and his chest and shoulders were those of a weight lifter or piano mover. "Nothing to kill him," Spider assured us. "His lip gave him some trouble once in a while, but that's not unusual for horn men. We live with it."

I spotted Bob Yale hurrying into the hall, bound for Sheriff Lens, and I wanted to hear his report. I joined them just as he was saying, "The preliminary result is that death was due to respiratory failure caused by an intravenous injection of methylmorphine."

Sheriff Lens looked blank. "Methylmorphine?"

"Better known as codeine," I explained.

"I take that stuff in cough medicine," the sheriff said.

Dr. Yalen nodded. "This would have been a purer version, quite fatal even in small doses."

"The hypodermic needle?" I asked.

Yale nodded. "Full of it. There was a puncture mark in his thigh."

"Then he was murdered," the sheriff said.

I liked to caution against jumping to conclusions. "Suicide is always a possibility."

"Come on, Doc. Let's go talk to Lincoln Jones."

Linc had been sitting with his wife back at the table, and when the sheriff asked him to accompany us she started to come too. "What's this all about, Sheriff? What are you trying to say Linc did?"

"Nothing, yet. I just want to ask him some questions about what happened."

"He didn't do a thing! Bix Blake was always a troublemaker. Alive or dead, he's a troublemaker."

"Hush now!" Linc told her, rising to follow us.

The sheriff led us back to the death scene, as I knew he would. We pulled out three of the chairs facing the mirrors and Linc asked, right away, "What killed him?"

"The needle was full of codeine," I said quietly. "It was injected into his thigh."

Linc didn't seem too surprised. "He acted like he couldn't breathe."

"Tell us exactly what happened," the sheriff suggested.

"Well, I knew Bix from our high school days. Before the dance began I even took Sam up to meet him. We decided to catch up on things during the break between sets. We came in here together to talk."

"Who bolted the door?" I asked.

"Bix did. He said if anyone wanted a smoke he could go outside."

"Did you argue?" Sheriff Lens asked.

Linc averted his eyes. "We had nothing to argue about."

"Did you argue?" he repeated.

"Not really. He mentioned Charlene."

"Your wife?"

"He was engaged to her once, but that was long ago, in the old neighborhood."

"What did he say about Charlene?" I prodded.

"He said I'd stolen her away because I went to college. She wanted to marry a doctor and be wealthy. It was nothing new. He told Charlene the same thing twelve years ago."

"Did you fight?"

"Physically? Of course not! By that time I could see he was having trouble breathing."

"What about the needle?" the sheriff wanted to know.

"There was no needle. Not then."

"You'd better explain yourself."

Linc shifted on his chair. For the first time he appeared nervous. "Well, his breathing kept getting worse and I asked what was wrong. I just thought he was overwrought, but then I saw it was more than that. Suddenly he just collapsed—right about there, in the center of the room. Right where you found him. I dropped to my knees to examine him, then started giving artificial respiration. That was when I noticed the needle, lying near his foot. I picked it up to examine it just as you broke down the door."

"Is it possible that he injected the poison himself, that he meant to commit sucide?"

"No, no. That would have been impossible. His hands were in full view at all times. I was watching them because I feared he might take a punch at me."

"Refresh my memory," I said. "What happened to that needle after we burst into the room?"

"The sheriff asked me for it and I handed it to him."

Sheriff Lens nodded. "Wrapped it real careful in a clean handkerchief and turned it over to the ambulance people when they came for the body. Should have gotten some pictures of the scene, but we weren't sure it was murder then."

"You're not sure now," I reminded him.

"I'm sure. Dr. Jones, I'm goin' to have to hold you for further questioning, on suspicion of murder."

Linc sighed and stood up. "Let me speak with my wife. Then I'll come with you."

We went back to the hall and he crossed the floor to the table where Charlene sat with Mary Best. "You're making a big mistake, Sheriff."

"Tell me how else it could have been, Doc."

"I'm not ready to do that yet."

Charlene listened to Linc's quiet words and then started to cry. "They can't do this to you! That damned Bix Blake! You never killed him."

"I know that, darlin'. Just see what you can do about getting me a good lawyer. And take care of the kids till I get back."

The dance had been on a Friday night, and the next morning everyone in town was talking about it. Bob Yale was talking about squeezing in a few more tables for that evening because so many people wanted to come. "It's going to make more money for us, Sam."

I'd walked down the hall to his office in the hospital wing, wanting to clarify a few things. "Some would consider it blood money," I pointed out. "You know Linc is innocent."

"I'd like to think he is. There's pretty nasty talk around town, though. They know Lincoln would never harm a hair on their heads, but this Bix was someone from his past—another Negro —and they were arguing about a black woman."

"She happens to be Linc's wife, and I hardly think he killed someone over her after all these years. Bix Blake was certainly no threat to their marriage."

"How do you know?"

I walked out in disgust, deciding I'd rather talk to Linc down at the jail. When I arrived, Charlene was with him. I decided to talk with Sheriff Lens instead.

"He'll be taken before the judge on Monday, Doc, and proba-bly held for the grand jury. He's got motive: the fight about his wife. He's got opportunity, the only one with opportunity. And he's got method. I figure the codeine is available at the hospi-tal."

"Yes," I admitted.

"How long does it take to kill someone with it?"

"If you swallow it in that strength you'd get sleepy and have trouble breathing within twenty minutes. Injected into the bloodstream, the effects are immediate."

"It kills instantly?"

"Theoretically, yes. In practice, the victim's size, health, and drug tolerance would be factors that could slow the action for several minutes."

"Did you get a look at the needle, Doc?"

"Briefly, yes."

"I understand from Dr. Yale it's the sort used at Pilgrim Memorial."

"It's the sort used just about everywhere, the most popular brand. Anyone who's diabetic probably has one at home."

Sheriff Lens chewed on his lower lip. He was holding Linc Jones for a judge, but I could see he wasn't happy about it. "Let's look at the possibilities, Doc. Did Blake kill himself? No, because Lincoln Jones never saw the needle in his hand. Did someone else hide in the room and jab him with the needle? No, because there was no hiding place."

"I haven't quite agreed to that yet. I'll want another look at the room."

"Was he jabbed after you burst into the room? No, because Jones was already holding the needle and Blake was dead."

"Agreed."

"If he didn't kill himself, and Lincoln Jones was the only person with him, then Lincoln Jones must have killed him. It's as simple as that, Doc."

"It's not that simple, because he didn't do it. You don't go to a dance with a hypodermic needle full of poison because you might encounter someone you disagreed with twelve years earlier. Linc approached him as an old friend, not an enemy."

"Maybe Bix Blake brought the poison to kill Jones, they struggled, and he got jabbed in the leg."

"Same argument, Sheriff. Would he have brought poison to use on Linc, after all those years? Linc, at least, didn't even realize there was still animosity over his marriage to Charlene. Besides, if it happened that way, in self-defense, Linc would have no reason to lie about what occurred."

Sheriff Lens sighed. "Then it's another one of your locked-room puzzles, Doc."

"Maybe," I glanced at my watch. It was after noon and I wanted to speak with Sweeney Lamb. "I'm going to shove off now. Tell Linc I didn't want to interrupt his visit with Charlene. I'll be back to see him later."

Most of the band was at Northmont's only hotel, but Helen McDonald told me Sweeney was out at the bus. "I'll take you there if you'd like," she offered.

"That would be helpful."

It was parked about a block from the hotel in an undeveloped field. "I feel terrible about Bix," she said as we walked. "I'd gotten to be real friendly with him in the months since he joined the band."

"Was he at the hotel with the rest of you?"

"Oh, sure. Spider's there too. We don't have much trouble in New England."

"What happens when there is trouble?"

"Bix and Spider have been known to sleep on the bus."

I could see it was a vehicle with many miles on it, in need of a paint job. Sweeney Lamb was seated inside, going over some sheet music arrangements for the evening performance. "Gotta make it a bit different from last night's selection," he explained. "And someone else has to play Bix's part."

"Who'll that be?"

"Probably Spider. He doubles on the trumpet."

I thought about that. "Is it a job to kill for?"

Lamb and Helen both laughed. "Not hardly," the bandleader replied. "They pay the same, and the trumpet and sax both get solos in different numbers."

I picked up a scrapbook that was lying on the seat next to him. There were newspaper ads for the band and pictures of their performances. One from last summer showed them playing in short-sleeved shirts at a Coney Island jazz festival. "You play all sorts of music," I said.

"Well, jazz and pop."

I flipped over a few more pages and found a two-year-old photo of Helen McDonald in a sexy strapless gown. I smiled at her. "I thought you were just out of high school."

"Don't I wish!"

"Did either of you ever see Bix with a hypodermic needle?" I asked.

Sweeney Lamb frowned. "I don't allow no drugs in my band. Any needles, they're out! I had a drummer die of a heroin overdose just last summer."

"Have the police been on you about it?"

"They don't bother us," Helen replied. "Sweeney runs a clean crew."

I decided there was nothing more to be learned there. "We'll be looking forward to tonight."

He nodded. "A fresh start. I'll open with a little tribute to Bix and then we take off with a new beginning."

I left Helen on the bus and headed back to my office at Pilgrim Memorial. I had no patients scheduled that Saturday, but Mary was in the office and there was always the possibility of an emergency.

"Not a thing," she told me, "except Charlene Jones. She stopped by after visiting Linc at the jail."

"Where is she now?"

She nodded toward my inner office, where the door was standing open. I could see Charlene in the patients' chair by my desk. I walked in and asked, "How's Linc doing?"

"Not bad. He knows he's innocent. It's just some terrible mistake."

"Tell me about you and Bix. Did you break your engagement to him?"

"That was right out of high school. We were all awfully young. He admitted it was the right thing."

"Might he have killed himself and tried to frame Linc?"

"I hadn't seen him in maybe twelve years. Neither grudges nor romances last that long without a little fuel. Whatever happened to Bix had nothing to do with either Linc or me."

I pressed my lips together, thinking. "Could you come down to the Grange Hall with me, Charlene? Right now?"

"What for?"

"I want to try something."

"All right."

The place was already open for the evening's dance and I led the way at once to the makeshift dressing room. "This is where it happened," I told her. "The men changed their clothes here."

"What about the girl singer?"

"She used it later, during their first few instrumentals."

Charlene was a small woman, but I could see at once that my first theory was a loser. She was far too large to have hidden in one of the boxes of tablecloths. "Would you stand behind that rack of coats, please?"

She didn't move. She just stood there staring at me. "My God, Sam, you think I killed him somehow!"

"No, no—"

"Yes, you do! What motive could I have had? Even if I'd done it, do you think I'd let Linc go to jail in my place?"

"Please, Charlene, just stand behind the coats."

This time she did as I asked, but I could clearly see her feet beneath the coats. "Could you grab the pipe and pull yourself up?" She gamely tried it and the pipe almost pulled free from

the wall. Surely there'd been no one hiding in the room either
before or after Bix's death.

"Satisfied?" she asked.

"I just had to check all the possibilities. You were away from
the table during the crucial period."

She left the room without another word, and I feared that I
had lost a friend.

I went back to the hospital next, and found Sheriff Lens with
Bob Yale outside the latter's office. "Hi, Doc. Just stopped by to
pick up the dead man's clothes." He held up a paper bag.

"Stop in my office before you leave, Sheriff."

A couple of minutes later he appeared in my door. "What's
up, Doc?"

"I just had an idea. I'd like to see the clothes Bix was
wearing."

The sheriff opened the bag and dumped them on my examining table. "I went over them quick and didn't find anything."

I started checking the pockets and the sheriff chuckled.
"Nothin' in that one but a hole."

There was indeed a small hole in the side pants pocket. I
stuck my finger through it and wondered about the workings of
fate. "Where's Bix's body, Sheriff?"

"Still here at the hospital, waitin' for instructions from the
next of kin."

"Let's go take a look at it."

I'd never gotten used to examining day-old corpses, but it
took me only a moment to find what I was looking for. "See
this, Sheriff? And *this?*"

"What does it mean?"

"Tonight we're going to catch ourselves a murderer."

The dance that evening might have been a replica of the
previous night's affair. Most everyone was dressed in the same
clothes, and before the music started I asked Sweeney Lamb to
duplicate everything he'd done on Friday night. "You mean play
the same tunes?"

"Exactly," I said. "They'll get new music in the second set."

People looked around at one another as Sweeney Lamb and

Dr. Yale made their opening remarks again, then really began to feel spooked when the band opened with their theme and then switched into *Pennies from Heaven.*

"Is this your idea?" Mary Best asked.

"It is," I admitted. "We'll see if it's a good one."

Spider Downs was playing Bix's part on the trumpet, and his own chair was empty. Otherwise everything was the same. Helen McDonald appeared on cue wearing the same pink gown and launched into *It's a Sin to Tell a Lie.*

A number of couples were on the dance floor, but others remained at their tables as if waiting to see what would happen. As the set drew near its concluding number I caught the eye of Sheriff Lens. Sweeney Lamb was on the bandstand, passing out the sheet music for the final arrangement, just as he had the night before. Helen McDonald hesitated, then took one and passed it on to Spider, seated in Bix's place.

"Come on!" I told the sheriff.

She turned pale as she saw us coming and tried to leave the bandstand. But I had one arm and Sheriff Lens had the other. "You'd better come with us, Miss McDonald," he told her. "We want to ask you about the murder of Bix Blake."

"I didn't—"

"Yes, you did," I told her. "You killed him and we're going to prove it."

News of the killing had reached New York, and by the time the second night's dance ended there were big-city reporters waiting with their questions. I was glad we had a few answers.

With Bob Yale from the hospital and Sweeney Lamb both standing nearby, Sheriff Lens began. "We expect a full statement from Miss McDonald shortly, and Dr. Lincoln Jones will be released from jail within the hour. For the rest of it, I'm going to turn you over to Dr. Sam Hawthorne, who played an important part in assisting with my investigations."

I stood to address the gathering.

"It appeared at first that Bix Blake had been murdered by an injection of codeine while in a locked room with only Lincoln Jones present," I began, capturing their attention from the start. "However, further investigation suggested another possibility.

Bix may have been injected with the poison before he entered the room and locked the door."

Bob Yale interrupted. "Codeine injected in that strong of a dosage usually takes effect immediately."

I nodded. "But its symptoms can be delayed a few minutes or longer by a drug tolerance, which is exactly what Bix Blake had. It's not unheard-of among musicians these days. I believe he was a heroin addict. He injected the hypodermic needle into his own thigh at the end of the first set, through a hole in his pants pocket. A close examination of the body this afternoon revealed previous needle marks in the thighs. They'd been missed on the initial examination because of his dark skin."

"You're saying he committed suicide?"

"Hardly. A hypo full of an almost clear codeine solution could easily be mistaken for white heroin. Bix wouldn't have chosen to kill himself in front of his old friend Linc, at least not without telling him the reason. I think Bix was murdered by his drug supplier, who gave him a needle full of codeine instead of heroin. That's why I wanted a repeat performance tonight that followed last evening's events exactly.

"I thought I remembered something from last night, but I had to see it again to be sure. When Sweeney here passed out the sheet music arrangements for the final song of the set, Helen McDonald took one, even though it was an instrumental in which she had no part. She then folded the sheet music and passed it to Bix. Tonight I saw her take the sheet music, but she didn't fold it when she passed it to Spider in Bix's chair. Last night she passed Bix the deadly hypo in the fold of that sheet music. I noticed the pain on his face as he left the bandstand to meet Linc, immediately after injecting himself. And he told Linc he'd be better next set, meaning when the drug took effect. But there was no next set for Bix. As he grew weaker and died in that dressing room, the needle slipped through the hole in his pocket and fell to the floor next to his feet, where Lincoln Jones found it."

Lamb could only shake his head. "Why was he injecting it into his thigh rather than his arm?"

"Because your band wears short-sleeved shirts in the summer, I saw the picture in your scrapbook."

"But even if she was supplying Bix with drugs, why would Helen kill him?"

Sheriff Lens answered that one. "Her initial statement indicates he's been blackmailing her for free drugs, threatening to tell you that she was responsible for the heroin death of your drummer last year. They both knew how you felt about drugs in the band."

Lamb seemed crushed by what had happened. Perhaps the tragedy of it, for Bix and Helen and his drummer, was only now sinking in. I left him and went down to the jail, so I'd be there when Linc was released. Charlene saw me coming and even managed a smile.

"Thank you," she said. "Thank you for getting him out."

WENDY HORNSBY

NINE SONS

Wendy Hornsby, a California writer with two novels to her credit, has not been well known in the short-story field until now. This tale of the ordinary-turned-dreadful is the sort that Shirley Jackson would have appreciated. It won the MWA Edgar Award as the best short mystery of the year.

I saw Janos Bonachek's name in the paper this morning. There was a nice article about his twenty-five years on the federal bench, his plans for retirement. The Boy Wonder, they called him, but the accompanying photograph showed him to be nearly bald, a wispy white fringe over his ears the only remains of his once remarkable head of yellow hair.

For just a moment, I was tempted to write him, or call him, to put to rest forever questions I had about the death that was both a link and a wedge between us. In the end I didn't. What was the point after all these years? Perhaps Janos's long and fine career in the law was sufficient atonement, for us all, for events that happened so long ago.

It occurred on an otherwise ordinary day. It was April, but spring was still only a tease. If anything stood out among the endless acres of black mud and gray slush, it was two bright dabs of color: first the blue crocus pushing through a patch of dirty snow, then the bright yellow head of Janos Bonachek as he ran along the line of horizon toward his parents' farm after school. Small marvels maybe, the spring crocus and young Janos, but in that frozen place, and during those hard times, surely they were miracles.

The year was 1934, the depths of the Great Depression. Times were bad, but in the small farm town where I had been posted by the school board, hardship was an old acquaintance.

I had arrived the previous September, fresh from teachers'

college, with a new red scarf in my bag and the last piece of my
birthday cake. At twenty, I wasn't much older than my high
school-age pupils.

Janos was ten when the term began and exactly the height of
ripe wheat. His hair was so nearly the same gold as the bearded
grain that he could run through the uncut fields and be no
more noticeable than the ripples made by a prairie breeze. The
wheat had to be mown before Janos could be seen at all.

On the northern plains, the season for growing is short, a
quick breath of summer between the spring thaw and the first
frost of fall. Below the surface of the soil, and within the people
who forced a living from it, there seemed to be a layer that
never had time to warm all the way through. I believe to this
day that if the winter hadn't been so long, the chilling of the
soul so complete, we would not have been forced to bury Janos
Bonachek's baby sister.

Janos came from a large family, nine sons. Only one of them,
Janos, was released from chores to attend school. Even then, he
brought work with him in the form of his younger brother,
Boya. Little Boya was then four or five. He wasn't as brilliant as
Janos, but he tried hard. Tutored and cajoled by Janos, Boya
managed to skip to the second-grade reader that year.

Around Halloween, that first year, Janos was passed up to me
by the elementary teacher. She said she had nothing more to
teach him. I don't know that I was any better prepared than she
was, except that the high school textbooks were on the shelves
in my room. I did my best.

Janos was a challenge. He absorbed everything I had to offer
and demanded more, pushing me in his quiet yet insistent way
to explain or to find out. He was eager for everything. Except
geography. There he was a doubter. Having lived his entire life
on a flat expanse of prairie, Janos would not believe the earth
was a sphere, or that there were bodies of water vaster than the
wheatfields that stretched past his horizon. The existence of
mountains, deserts, and oceans he had to take on faith, like the
heavenly world the nuns taught me about in catechism.

Janos was an oddball to his classmates, certainly. I can still
see that shiny head bent close to his books, the brow of his
pinched little face furrowed as he took in a new set of universal

truths from the world beyond the Central Grain Exchange. The other students deferred to him, respected him, though they never played with him. He spent recesses and lunch periods sitting on the school's front stoop, waiting for me to ring the big brass bell and let him back inside. I wonder how that affected him as a judge, this boy who never learned how to play.

Janos shivered when he was cold, but he seemed otherwise oblivious to external discomfort or appearances. Both he and Boya came to school barefoot until there was snow on the ground. Then they showed up in mismatched boots sizes too big, yet no one called attention to them, which I found singular. Janos's coat, even in blizzards, was an old gray blanket that I'm sure he slept under at night. His straight yellow hair stuck out in chunks as if it had been scythed like the wheat. He never acknowledged that he was in any way different from his well-scrubbed classmates.

While this oblivion to discomfort gave Janos an air of stoic dignity, it did impose some hardship on me. When the blizzards came and I knew school should be closed, I went out anyway because I knew Janos would be there, with Boya. If I didn't come to unlock the classroom, I was sure they would freeze waiting.

Getting there was itself a challenge. I boarded in town with the doctor and his wife, my dear friend Martha. When the snow blew in blinding swirls and the road was impassable to any automobile, I would persuade the doctor to harness his team of plow horses to his cutter and drive me out. The doctor made only token protest after the first trip: the boys had been at the school for some time before we arrived, huddled together on the stoop like drifted snow.

Those were the best days, alone, the two boys and I. I would bring books from Martha's shelves, books not always on the school board's approved list. We would read together and talk about the world on the far side of the prairie and how one day we would see it for ourselves. As the snow drifts piled up to the sills outside, we would try to imagine the sultry heat of the tropics, the pitch and roll of the oceans, men in pale suits in electric-lit parlors discussing being and nothingness while they sipped hundred-year-old sherry.

We had many days together. That year the first snow came on All Saints Day and continued regularly until Good Friday. I would have despaired during the ceaseless cold if it weren't for Janos and the lessons I received at home on the evenings of those blizzardy days.

Invariably, on winter nights when the road was impassable and sensible people were at home before the fire, someone would call for the doctor's services. He would harness the cutter and go. Martha, of course, couldn't sleep until she heard the cutter return. We would keep each other entertained, sometimes until after the sun came up.

Martha had gone to Smith or Vassar. I'm not sure which because Eastern girls' schools were so far from my experience that the names meant nothing to me then. She was my guide to the world I had seen only in magazines and slick-paged catalogues, where people were polished to a smooth and shiny perfection, where long underwear, if indeed any was worn, never showed below their hems. These people were oddly whole, no scars, no body parts lost to farm machinery. In their faces I saw a peace of mind I was sure left them open to the world of ideas. I longed for them, and was sure Martha did as well.

Martha took life in our small community with grace, though I knew she missed the company of other educated women. I had to suffice.

Just as I spent my days preparing Janos, Martha spent her evenings teaching me the social graces I would need if I were ever to make my escape. Perhaps I was not as quick a pupil as Janos, but I was as eager.

Lessons began in the attic where Martha kept her trunks. Packed in white tissue was the elegant trousseau she had brought with her from the East, gowns of wine-colored taffeta moire and green velvet and a pink silk so fine I feared touching it with my calloused hands.

I had never actually seen a live woman in an evening gown, though I knew Martha's gowns surpassed the mail-order gowns that a woman might order for an Eastern Star ritual, if she had money for ready-made.

Martha and I would put on the gowns and drink coffee with brandy and read to each other from Proust, or take turns at the piano. I might struggle through a Strauss waltz or the "Fat Lady Polka." She played flawless Dvorak and Debussy. This was my finishing school, long nights in Martha's front parlor, waiting for the cutter to bring the doctor home, praying the cutter hadn't overturned, hoping the neighbor he had gone to tend was all right.

When he did return, his hands so cold he needed help out of his layers of clothes, Martha's standard greeting was, "Delivering Mrs. Bonachek?" This was a big joke to us, because, of course, Mrs. Bonachek delivered herself. No one knew how many pregnancies she had had beyond her nine living sons. Poor people, they were rich in sons.

That's what I kept coming back to that early spring afternoon as I walked away from the Bonachek farm. I had seen Janos running across the fields after school. If he hadn't been hurrying home to help his mother, then where had he gone? And where were his brothers?

It lay on my mind.

As I said, the day in question had been perfectly ordinary. I had stayed after my students to sweep the classroom, so it was nearly four before I started for home. As always, I walked the single-lane road toward town, passing the Bonachek farm about halfway. Though underfoot the black earth was frozen hard as tarmac, I was looking for signs of spring, counting the weeks until the end of the school term.

My feet were cold inside my new Sears and Roebuck boots and I was mentally drafting a blistering letter to the company. The catalogue copy had promised me boots that would withstand the coldest weather, so, as an act of faith in Sears, I had invested a good chunk of my slim savings for the luxury of warm feet. Perhaps the copywriter in a Chicago office could not imagine ground as cold as this road.

I watched for Janos's mother as I approached her farm. For three days running, I had seen Mrs. Bonachek working in the fields as I walked to school in the morning, and as I walked back to town in the dusky afternoon. There was no way to avoid her. The distance between the school and the Bonachek farm was uninterrupted by hill or wall or stand of trees.

Mrs. Bonachek would rarely glance up as I passed. Unlike the other parents, she never greeted me, never asked how her boys were doing in school, never suggested I let them out earlier for farm chores. She knew little English, but neither did many of the other parents, or my own.

She was an enigma. Formless, colorless, Mrs. Bonachek seemed no more than a piece of the landscape as she spread seed grain onto the plowed ground from a big pouch in her apron. Wearing felt boots, she walked slowly along the straight furrows, her thin arm moving in a sweep as regular as any motor-powered machine.

Hers was an odd display of initiative, I thought. No one else was out in the fields yet. It seemed to me she risked losing her seed to mildew or to a last spring freeze by planting so early. Something else bothered me more. While I was a dairyman's daughter and knew little about growing wheat, I knew what was expected of farm children. There were six in my family, my five brothers and myself. My mother never went to the barns alone when there was a child at hand. Mrs. Bonachek had nine sons. Why, I wondered, was she working in the fields all alone?

On the afternoon of the fourth day, as had become my habit, I began looking for Mrs. Bonachek as soon as I locked the schoolhouse door. When I couldn't find her, I felt a pang of guilty relief that I wouldn't have to see her that afternoon, call out a greeting that I knew she wouldn't return.

So I walked more boldly, dressing down Sears in language I could never put on paper, enjoying the anarchy of my phrases even as I counted the blue crocus along the road.

Just as I came abreast of the row of stones that served to define the beginning of the Bonachek driveway, I saw her. She sat on the ground between the road and the small house, head bowed, arms folded across her chest. Her faded calico apron, its big seed pocket looking flat and empty, was spread on the ground beside her. She could have been sleeping, she was so still. I thought she might be sick, and would have gone to her, but she turned her head toward me, saw me, and shifted around until her back was toward me.

I didn't stop. The road curved and after a while I couldn't see her without turning right around. I did look back once and saw Mrs. Bonachek upright again. She had left her apron on the ground, a faded red bundle at the end of a furrow. She gathered up the skirt of her dress, filled it with seed grain, and continued her work. So primitive, I thought. How was it possible she had spawned the bright light that was Janos?

I found Martha in an extravagant mood when I reached home. The weather was frigid, but she, took, had seen the crocus. She announced that we would hold a tea to welcome spring. We would put on the tea frocks from her trunk and invite in some ladies from town. It would be a lark, she said, a coming out. I could invite anyone I wanted.

I still had Mrs. Bonachek on my mind. I couldn't help picturing her rising from her squat in the muddy fields to come sit on Martha's brocade sofa, so I said I would invite her first. The idea made us laugh until I had hiccups. I said the woman had no daughters and probably needed some lively female company.

Martha went to the piano and banged out something suitable for a melodrama. I got a pan of hot water and soaked my cold feet while we talked about spring and the prospect of being warm again, truly warm, in all parts at once. I wondered what magazine ladies did at teas.

We were still planning little sandwiches and petit fours and onions cut into daisies when the doctor came in for supper. There were snowflakes on his beard and I saw snow falling outside, a lacy white curtain over the evening sky. When Martha looked away from the door, I saw tears in her eyes.

"You're late," Martha said to the doctor, managing a smile. "Out delivering Mrs. Bonachek?"

"No such luck." The doctor seemed grim. "I wish that just once the woman would call me in time. She delivered herself again. The baby died, low body temperature I suspect. A little girl. A pretty, perfect little girl."

I was stunned but I managed to blurt, "But she was working in the fields just this afternoon."

Martha and the doctor exchanged a glance that reminded me how much I still had to learn. Then the doctor launched into a speech about some people not having sense enough to take to their beds and what sort of life could a baby born into such circumstances expect, anyway?

"The poor dear," Martha said when he had run down. "She finally has a little girl to keep her company and it dies." She grabbed me by the arm. "We must go offer our consolation."

We put on our boots and coats and waited for the doctor to get his ancient Ford back out of the shed. It made a terrible racket, about which Martha complained gently, but there wasn't enough snow for the cutter. We were both disappointed—the cutter gave an occasion a certain weight.

"Say your piece, then leave," the doctor warned as we rattled over the rutted road. "These are private people. They may not understand your intentions."

He didn't understand that Martha and I were suffering a bit of guilt from the fun we had had at poor Mrs. Bonachek's expense. And we were bored. Barn sour, my mother would say. Tired of being cooped up all winter and in desperate need of some diversion.

We stormed the Bonachek's tiny clapboard house, our offers of consolation translated by a grim-faced Janos. Martha was effusive. A baby girl should have a proper send-off, she said. There needed to be both a coffin and a dress. When was the funeral?

Mrs. Bonachek looked from me to Martha, a glaze over her mud-colored eyes. Janos shrugged his skinny shoulders. There was no money for funerals, he said. When a baby died, you called in the doctor for a death certificate, then the county came for the remains. That was all.

Martha patted Mrs. Bonachek's scaly hands. Not to worry. We would take care of everything. And we did. Put off from our spring tea by the sudden change in the weather, we diverted our considerable social energy to the memorial services.

I found a nice wooden box of adequate size in the doctor's storeroom and painted it white. Martha went up to the attic and brought down her beautiful pink silk gown and an old feather pillow. She didn't even wince as she ran her sewing shears up the delicate hand-turned seams. I wept. She hugged me and talked about God's will being done and Mrs. Bonachek's peasant strength. I was thinking about the spoiled dress.

We worked half the night. We padded the inside of the box with feathers and lined it with pink silk. We made a tiny dress and bonnet to match. The doctor had talked the county into letting us have a plot in the cemetery. It was such a little bit of ground, they couldn't refuse.

We contacted the parish priest, but he didn't want to perform the services. The county cemetery wasn't consecrated and he didn't know the Bonacheks. We only hoped it wasn't a rabbi that was needed because there wasn't one for miles. Martha reasoned that heaven was heaven and the Methodist preacher would have to do, since he was willing.

By the following afternoon everything was ready. The snow had turned to slush but our spirits weren't dampened. We set off, wearing prim navy blue because Martha said it was more appropriate for a child's funeral than somber black.

When the doctor drove us up to the small house, the entire Bonachek family, scrubbed and brushed, turned out to greet us.

Janos smiled for the first time I could remember. He fingered a frayed necktie that hung below his twine belt. He looked very awkward, but I knew he felt elegant. Everyone, even Boya, wore some sort of shoes. It was a gala, if solemn event.

Mr. Bonachek, a scrawny, pale-faced man, relieved us of the makeshift coffin and led us into the single bedroom. The baby, wrapped in a scrap of calico, lay on the dresser. I unfolded the little silk dress on the bed while Martha shooed Mr. Bonachek out of the room.

"We should wash her," Martha said. A catch in her voice showed that her courage was failing. She began to unwrap the tiny creature. It was then I recognized the calico—Mrs. Bonachek's faded apron.

I thought of the nine sons lined up in the next room and Mrs. Bonachek sitting in the field with her apron spread on the cold ground beside her. Mrs. Bonachek who was rich in sons.

I needed to know how many babies, how many girls, had died before this little one wrapped in the apron. Janos would tell me, Janos who had been so matter-of-fact about the routine business of death. I hadn't the courage at that moment to ask him.

Martha was working hard to maintain her composure. She had the baby dressed and gently laid her in the coffin. The baby was beautiful, her porcelain face framed in soft pink silk. I couldn't bear to see her in the box, like a shop-window doll.

I wanted to talk with Martha about the nagging suspicion that was taking shape in my mind. I hesitated too long.

Janos appeared at the door and I didn't want him to hear what I had to say. Actually, his face was so thin and expectant that it suddenly occurred to me that we hadn't brought any food for a proper wake.

"Janos," Martha whispered. "Tell your mother she may come in now."

Janos led his mother only as far as the threshold when she stopped stubbornly. I went to her, put my arm around her and impelled her to come closer to the coffin. When she resisted, I pushed. I was desperate to see some normal emotion from her. If she had none, what hope was there for Janos?

Finally, she shuddered and reached out a hand to touch the baby's cheek. She said something in her native language. I could understand neither the words nor the tone. It could have been a prayer, it could have been a curse.

When I let her go, she turned and looked at me. For the barest instant there was a flicker in her eyes that showed neither fear nor guilt about what I might have seen the afternoon before. I was disquieted because, for the length of that small glimmer, she was beautiful. I saw who she might have become at another time, in a different place. When the tears at last came to my eyes, they were for her and not for the baby.

Janos and Boya carried the coffin out to the bare front room and set it on the table. The preacher arrived and he gave his best two-dollar service even though there would be no payment. He spoke to the little group, the Bonacheks, Martha, the doctor and I, as if we were a full congregation. I don't remember what he said. I wasn't listening. I traced the pattern of the cheap, worn linoleum floor with my eyes and silently damned the poverty of the place and the cold that seeped in under the door.

We were a small, depressed-looking procession, walking down the muddy road to the county cemetery at the edge of town, singing along to hymns only the preacher seemed to know. At the gravesite, the preacher prayed for the sinless soul and consigned her to the earth. It didn't seem to bother him that his principal mourners didn't understand a word he said.

Somehow, the doctor dissuaded Martha from inviting all of the Bonacheks home for supper—she, too, had belatedly thought about food.

As we walked back from the cemetery, I managed to separate the doctor from the group. I told him what was on my mind, what I had seen in the fields the day before. She had left her bundled apron at the end of a furrow and gone back to her work. I could not keep that guilty knowledge to myself.

The doctor wasn't as shocked as I expected him to be. But he was a man of worldly experience and I was merely a dairyman's daughter—the oldest child, the only girl in a family of five boys.

As the afternoon progressed, the air grew colder, threatening more snow. To this day, whenever I am very cold, I think of that afternoon. Janos, of course, fills that memory.

I think the little ceremony by strangers was a sort of coming out for him. He was suddenly not only a man of the community but of the world beyond the road that ran between his farm and the schoolhouse, out where mountains and oceans were a possibility. It had been a revelation.

Janos called out to me and I stopped to wait for him, watching him run. He seemed incredibly small, outlined against the flat horizon. He was golden, and oddly ebullient.

Pale sunlight glinted off his bright head as he struggled through the slush on the road. Mud flew off his big boots in thick gobs and I thought his skinny legs would break with the weight of it. He seemed not to notice—mud was simply a part of the season's change, a harbinger of warmer days.

When he caught up, Janos was panting and red in the face. He looked like a wise little old man for whom life held no secrets. As always, he held himself with a stiff dignity that I imagine suited him quite well when he was draped in his judge's robes.

Too breathless to speak, he placed in my hand a fresh blue crocus he had plucked from the slush.

"Very pretty," I said, moved by his gesture. I looked into his smiling face and found courage. "What was the prayer your mother said for the baby?"

He shrugged and struggled for breath. Then he reached out and touched the delicate flower that was already turning brown from the warmth of my hand.

"No prayer," he said. "It's what she says. 'Know peace. Your sisters in heaven wait to embrace you.' "

I put my hand on his shoulder and looked up at the heavy, gathering clouds. "If it's snowing tomorrow," I said, "which books shall I bring?"

STUART M. KAMINSKY
PUNISHMENT

It's a pleasure to welcome Edgar-winning novelist Stuart M. Kaminsky to this series with one of his infrequent short stories. I say infrequent because virtually all of Kaminsky's short-story output since 1965 is available in one slender volume, Opening Shots, *published last year by Mystery Scene Press. With novels often set in the past, or in modern-day Russia, it's not surprising that Kaminsky should combine both themes into this unique detective story set in the Russia of long ago. His sleuth is none other than police inspector Porfiry Petrovich, from Dostoevsky's* Crime and Punishment. *Journey with Stuart Kaminsky back to St. Petersburg in the years following the American Civil War.*

Peasants and poverty-stricken students, peddlers and beggars moved around the tall man who stood in the Hay Market of St. Petersburg on that hot August afternoon in the year 1867. The tall man did not seem to notice the crowds, the dank choking smell of human sweat, the voices of housewives haggling with peddlers, whose carts carried everything from wilting vegetables to thimbles and thread.

There was something forbidding, something foreign about the man. He was, perhaps, forty-five years of age, thin, well dressed in a dark suit complete with the stylish tie of the period. He was certainly the best-dressed person among the several hundred who scurried and cried, sold and bought, coughed and fled. Beggars would normally have besieged him with pleas and sad stories, showed the place where arms and legs had once been attached, given the names of their consumptive wives and tubercular children. But the American's face was too forbidding to approach, hollow-cheeked, hair yellow—white and gray eyes focused beyond the cart in front of him owned by Yuri Kolodonov.

94

Business had not been particularly good for Kolodonov that day. He had brought his fifteen-year-old daughter, Natalya, with him in the hope that her clear skin and blue eyes would draw lustful husbands to his cart, where they would guiltily buy a set of four blue bowls and a quintet of brown cups made by the Kolodonovs in their own kiln and with their own hands right here in the city.

At first, the presence of the tall, well-dressed man had given Kolodonov some hope. He did not remember when the man had appeared, but he did remember the moment when he had looked up and saw him there. Kolodonov had smiled. He had nodded to Natalya to smile, but the tall man did not smile back and he did not approach.

After an hour as the sun dropped ever so little, Kolodonov decided that the man would not approach and buy but would only look from a distance. His presence became annoying. An hour later it became oppressive, and he feared that the tall man was driving customers away.

"Ask him what he wants," Kolodonov finally told his daughter as he pretended to rearrange his wares in the wooden cart.

Natalya did not look at the tall man. Instead she looked at the cart of Sofia Ivanova, who was doing a brisk sale in dirt-covered radishes that promised to send her home well before darkness came.

"I'm afraid," said Natalya stealing a glance at the man. "He may be mad or ill."

"Nonsense, nonsense," puffed her father. "He is a gentleman. He simply wants to . . . to be coaxed. I think he is shy, a foreigner."

"I'm afraid," Natalya repeated.

"And I am your father," said Kolodonov, touching his beard to remind himself that his age and station gave him the right to send his offspring off to face pale strangers. And Natalya obeyed. She wiped her hands on her smock, adjusted her blue blouse, assumed a smile she did not feel, and made her way past a pair of fat but dwarfishly small women with baskets under their arms who were arguing about whose turn it was to make dinner the next day.

"Sir," Natalya said, standing before him.

He looked down at her, a touch of irony in the corner of his mouth or, perhaps, only the illusion of a wasted smile. An argument exploded at a nearby cart. Two voices, both men, rose loud and animal-like. The tall man did not seem to hear though Natalya could not help glancing toward the squabble.

"Sir," she repeated, "could I help you?"

This time he did smile, a smile that indicated even to this most unworldly girl that he believed he was beyond help of any sort.

And then the man answered in a language which might have been gibberish but was, in fact, English:

By a route obscure and lonely,
Haunted by ill angels only,
Where an Eldolon, named Night,
On a black throne reigns upright,
I have reached these lands but newly
From an ultimate dim Thule—
From a wild weird clime that lieth, sublime,
Out of Space—out of Time.

"I don't understand," Natalya said as the man's right hand came up and touched her arm. She stepped back and into a woman with a child who mumbled a curse. The man's long fingers gripped her arm. Natalya turned to her father for help, but he was engaged with a customer. Natalya was considering a scream when a man's voice, a bit high-pitched, said,

"Edgar Allan Poe."

And then a hand came out, a white pudgy hand. It touched the hand of the tall man that gripped Natalya, and the tall man released her.

"That was in English, something by the American Poe," the man with the pudgy hand said. "Somber man. My English is poor, but I recognize the pattern, remember the words but can't place them."

The tall man's face did not change. Natalya looked at her rescuer, and though she was grateful as she fought to keep from touching the place where the tall man's fingers had bruised her arm, she was not impressed.

The man was well dressed, about forty, short, fat and clean-shaven. His hair was short, and he had a large round head that was unusually bulbous in the back. His soft, round, snub-nosed face was yellowish in color as if he had seldom ventured out into the daylight. He was definitely smiling, the smile of a man who has a secret and longs to share it with you. There was something decidedly feminine about the man except for his eyes below almost white lashes, moist eyes that were quite serious. Something in those eyes told Natalya to turn away now and return to her father.

When she made her way through the crowd to the cart and looked back, the two men were gone. Her father paused in his sweating effort to persuade an uncertain woman to buy the bowls. He looked up, saw the tall man was gone, and nodded approvingly to his daughter. She did not respond.

For the first time in her life, the possibility of death had looked down at her and touched her. Though it was hot enough to cause the old to seek shelter from the sun, Natalya shuddered and crossed herself.

"My name is Porfiry Petrovich," the small man said, guiding the tall man out of the Hay Market and toward the river. "You speak Russian, I hope. My English is poor."

"My Russian is also poor," the tall man said in Russian with a voice so dry that it seemed to have gone unused for years.

"But it is better than my English," said Porfiry Petrovich. "I go to the market often to see the faces, feel the life."

The tall man grunted as they walked.

"Actually," said Porfiry Petrovich, "that is not true. I seldom go to the market. I don't like the smell. Look there. See. They're putting in gas lights on the main streets. Civilization. St. Petersburg is becoming like Paris. You want to see the city? I can . . . Are you all right?"

The tall man had stopped and was breathing heavily.

"Wound," he said. "During the war."

"The war?" mulled the fat little man. "You are an American. You mean your Civil War. You were a soldier? Which side?"

"Confederacy," said the man in English.

"Confederacy," Porfiry Petrovich repeated as crowds moved past them. "That was the South?"

"Yes," said the man.

"You were an officer?"

"A colonel," said the man, finding his breath. "Bullet in the lung. Still there."

"Your war fascinates me," said Porfiry Petrovich. "I'm fond of reading all military histories. I've missed my proper calling. I should have been a soldier, not a general, a Napolean or your Grant—I'm sorry. Your Lee, but I might have been a major. Yes, a major."

The tall American was ready to move again.

"What is your career, if I may ask?" the American said.

"I'm a lawyer," said Porfiry Petrovich with a deep sigh, as if the confession would lose him his new and closest friend. "And you?"

"Ulysses," said the man, walking again at the little man's side. "I wander. I made a living as a soldier and a cotton farmer. That was when I was alive. I died in the war. My wife, my daughter, died in the war."

"I'm sorry," said Porfiry Petrovich. "I myself am and have always been a bachelor. Look, look there. The cathedral. The czar himself goes to the cathedral."

The tall man grunted and Porfiry Petrovich suddenly stopped and pulled him down so he could whisper into his ear.

"The truth is that the czar seldom goes to the cathedral. Tonight he will probably go. A member of his own guards was found dead not far from here yesterday. Murdered. Service will be today. Perhaps the czar will attend. Perhaps he won't. His wife, the czarina . . . but that's another story, Colonel Franklin, another story for a quiet . . . here, here, a cafe I know."

Though he was half the size of the tall American, Porfiry Petrovich dragged him through the wooden door and into a noisy, smoke-filled room in which a haggard woman with stringy hair was playing French-sounding songs on a concertina.

"Smells in here, but the food is good," said Porfiry Petrovich, leading him to a wooden table that was almost clean though it would never be rid of the smell of fish. They sat and Porfiry

Petrovich waved furiously at a bearded waiter and called for drinks and food.

"You've never been in here before," the American said, fixing his eyes on the smiling little man who was surveying the room.

Porfiry Petrovich raised his hands, palms open to show that he had been caught in a lie.

"And you knew my name," said the man. "I didn't tell you my name."

Porfiry Petrovich grinned sheepishly and said, "Valve is badly off in that concertina, a distraction. I think the woman is too drunk to notice."

"You're a policeman," said Franklin without emotion.

"An examining lawyer in the department of investigation of criminal causes," said Porfiry Petrovich, shaking his head. "A person of no consequence. Ah, the food."

The waiter with the beard plopped two plates on the table, the smell of onions and chopped fish rose before them. Cucumbers lay sliced around the fish. A large square of dark, rough bread rested heavily on the edge of each plate.

"Vodka, Colonel?" Porfiry Petrovich asked. "I seldom drink, but today, a new acquaintance. Wine?"

Franklin sat unsmiling and silent.

"Make it wine," Porfiry Petrovich told the waiter. "Good wine. Take no liberties with my palate."

The waiter did not bother to respond but walked away to the call of other patrons. Porfiry Petrovich began to eat, carefully pronging pieces of fish, onion, and cucumber, ushering it to his mouth with a piece of bread.

"What do you want?" asked Franklin in Russian.

"Want? From you? To practice my English. To learn about your war. To show a cultivated visitor around our historic city. I like to talk. It is my passion, my need. I live alone, have few acquaintances outside of my profession."

"How did you find me in the market?" Franklin went on, this time in English.

Porfiry Petrovich paused in mid-bite to understand and translate the words.

"Eat, you have nothing on your bones. I have too much, I confess.

"I was looking for you. I went to your hotel. Your name, obviously American or English, was in the registry. The names and home addresses of all visitors to St. Petersburg are brought by each hotel to central registry.

"And I happened to be looking through the registry on a case and saw your name. I was intrigued."

"A case?" said the American ignoring his food as the little policeman finished his own.

The waiter brought a bottle of red wine and plunked it with two glasses on the table. Porfiry Petrovich inserted a finger into his mouth and poured the red liquid into the two glasses.

"Fish bone," said the inspector. "There, I've got it. Yes, a case. The same case I mentioned a little while ago. Might interest you. Count Nicolai Bognerov, one of the czar's guards. Murdered. Strangled. Obviously by someone very strong, very determined. The count, though confidentially he did drink, some say to excess, was not a small man. He fought in your war. On the side of the South. Small group of Cossack volunteers led by the count, an adventure, a lark, who knows, maybe deep conviction. You never ran into him in your country?"

"No," said Franklin.

"No," repeated Porfiry Petrovich. "If you are not going to eat . . . ?"

Franklin pushed the plate toward the inspector, reached for the wine, and downed it in one gulp.

"No, no, no, my friend," sighed Porfiry Petrovich, "not on an empty stomach. You'll lose control. Say things you might regret. Believe me. I know the cheap wine of such places. Trust me."

And then the inspector laughed. He laughed so hard that bits of bread sprayed from his mouth. He reached for the wine and drank it to stifle his laughter. The room was so crowded and noisy that no one but Franklin heard or saw the display.

"Forgive me," he said, tapping his chest. "The drink, the food, the company. I'm already a bit giddy."

"How did you find me in the market?" asked Franklin.

"I told you," said the inspector, wiping a tear of laughter from the corner of his right eye. "I went to your hotel and . . ."

". . . and they knew I was in the Hay Market," Franklin said in slow, precise English. "How would they know where I had gone?"

Porfiry Petrovich pushed his plate away, poured more wine for both of them, and folded his pale fat hands on the table in front of him. Beads of sweat were evident on his forehead.

"I followed you," said the inspector.

Franklin nodded almost imperceptibly and took a drink.

"May I ask you a question? Tell me if I'm prying and we'll go. Would you like to see where we work, where criminal investigations are pursued? But that is not the question. Actually, I have two questions."

"Ask," said Franklin, after finishing his second glass of wine. The bottle was already almost empty.

"First, when and why did you learn to speak Russian?"

"I began to learn in the hospital where I was treated after I was wounded at the end of the war," said Franklin. "I had business in Russia."

"And you have taken care of your business?"

"I have," said the tall American.

"I'll not ask you what that business is," said Porfiry Petrovich. "It is not my concern."

"I'm not sure I see how you determine what is and is not your business," said Franklin.

"Second question," said Porfiry Petrovich, "Why were you standing in the market and looking at the peddler and his daughter?"

"She looks like Melinda," said Franklin, pouring himself another drink.

"Melinda? Your daughter? Wife?"

"Perhaps both. Both were named Melinda."

Porfiry Petrovich nodded.

"And they died in the war?" Porfiry Petrovich said, almost too softly to be heard over the noise.

Franklin answered with a nod.

"Come, you are a military man. I want to show you something."

Porfiry Petrovich whispered, a finger to his full, pale lips.

"Is this an order?" asked Franklin softly.

"An order? You mean in connection with my? . . . no, no. A request. A plea for help."

He stood and Franklin leaned over to drink one final glass of wine. Porfiry Petrovich pulled out a rouble note and dropped it on the table.

"My treat," he said. "My pleasure. Worth it for the company and to get away from that desk. This way."

The fat little man made his way around the tables and to the door with the tall man following him, still steady on his feet, still military of bearing in spite of consuming most of the bottle of wine without food.

Back in the street Porfiry Petrovich stamped first one foot and then another.

"Circulation," he said. "Returns the circulation. The sun is still well in the sky. Does it stay light in the summer till late at night in your country?"

"No," said Franklin following the little man.

"Blessing and a curse," said Porfiry Petrovich with an exaggerated sigh. "More hours to fill. Darkness is an excuse to be alone."

"I believe you said you are a lonely man," said Franklin as they crossed the street behind a large rambling cart and avoided the recent droppings of a horse.

"Yes, lonely," admitted Porfiry Petrovich, "but sometimes a lonely man enjoys his solitude. Though of course solitude, only oneself for company, can result in strange thoughts, delusions. Only last year, not far from this very spot, a young student murdered two old women with an ax. Solitude had created delusion. A sad sight. Are you a solitary man, Colonel Franklin?"

Colonel Franklin did not answer as they turned a corner side by side.

"There, right there, that entrance," said the inspector pointing at a large double wooden doorway with large hasps. The stone building looked ancient.

"You recognize it?" asked Porfiry Petrovich with a smile.

Franklin did not answer.

"I only ask because the style of the building is very English and I understand many of the city buildings in your Charlotte and Natchez are . . . Here."

Porfiry Petrovich opened the door with a key and ushered Franklin into the near darkness.

"Is your wound bothering you? Watch your step. See the light to the left? Walk carefully. It's a courtyard near the steps. I'm right ahead of you."

Their footsteps echoed across the stone hallway as Franklin followed the outline of the inspector and his eyes began to adjust to the near total darkness. As they approached the stairs, the light from the courtyard gave him a reasonably clear picture of the wooden stairway that arched upward.

"Can you move ahead of me?" said Porfiry Petrovich, panting as they reached the second landing. "I'm not a military man and my legs . . . I'll catch up. Fourth landing. Door on the right. What I have to show you is in there."

They moved upward, silently except for the sound of their footsteps on the creaking stairs, the tortured breathing of Colonel Franklin, and the panting of Porfiry Petrovich.

Ahead of the inspector, the American had stopped on a landing and turned to his left. The inspector caught up with him as Colonel Franklin stood in front of a door waiting. Porfiry Petrovich caught his breath and looked at both the man before him and the door.

"Strange," said the inspector.

"What is?" asked Franklin.

"I told you we were going to an apartment on the fourth floor. You stopped on the third."

"Sorry," said Franklin, moving back toward the stairs.

"No," said Porfiry Petrovich. "The error was mine. This is the right door. Perhaps you miscounted?"

"Perhaps," said the American softly.

The inspector moved to the door, inserted his key, and opened it.

The two men entered. The room was large and surprisingly light with a window facing east. The furniture was fashionable, solid tables, chairs, and desk, a wood-trimmed sofa and two comfortable chairs covered in satiny red material with little red buttons. The walls were lined with military paintings except for one small bookcase toward which Porfiry Petrovich moved. "Right here," he said. "It's right here. The murderer wasn't interested or simply overlooked it."

"Murderer?" said Franklin, remaining erect near the door, the only sign of his drinking a small band of moisture on his upper lip.

Porfiry Petrovich stopped suddenly, turned to Franklin, and hit himself in the forehead with the open palm of his right hand.

"The heat. The wine. Forgive me once again," he said, resuming his move toward the bookcase. "This is the apartment of Count Nicholai Bognerov. His family has an estate not far from the city. It was in this very room he was murdered yesterday, right there by the desk. The desk drawer was open. Something had been taken from it. You might look in the drawer while I find the book . . . here it is."

Franklin did not move. He stood on the corner of a once-elegant but now faded Oriental rug and watched without passion.

"You don't want to look in the drawer? Very well. I'll tell you. It is filled with photographs, some of them on those etched metals the French invented. Most if not all of them appear to be from your country. Soldiers in uniform, women, even children."

Porfiry Petrovich looked up and thought he saw the gaunt man shudder.

"You might know someone . . ."

"Thank you, no," said Franklin.

"Very well," said the Inspector with a wave of his hand to dismiss the offer. He moved to the sofa and gestured to Franklin to join him and still the American did not move. Porfiry Petrovich held the book up so the light from the now orange sun would hit the pages as he flipped through them in search of the passage he sought.

"Do you like the ballet, Colonel?" the inspector said, slowing down the pages just a bit.

Still no answer.

"I am fascinated by it, but, alas, I'm usually too busy. The passage. Right here. This is the count's diary. Listen. I'll read slowly. It's in Russian." He read: " 'This morning we followed

General Smith into Charleston. We were attached to the 17th
Cavalry. The goal was to drive the Union troops under Dun-
steader back and provide time to join the . . .'

"I'll skip a bit of this," said Porfiry Petrovich, "and pick it up,
let's see, here: 'The house had been part of a cotton plantation
but did not look as if it had been tilled since the early days of
the war. My cossacks and I were detached, alone. There were
only women in the house and one wounded man who spoke
with the accent of the North. I took him for a deserter and
determined that the women had harbored him and were,
therefore, traitors. I shot the deserter, and, as we had done
before, I left the women to the cossacks. We dined in the house
and the next morning set fire to it before moving north to join
General Smith.' "

Porfiry Petrovich looked up. Franklin was rigid, at attention.

"Is that passage familiar to you?" he asked.

Franklin did not speak.

"The last entry in the diary is January 6, 1864," said Porfiry
Petrovich. "Two weeks before the count returned to Europe. I
understand that he left rather hurriedly and had to leave many
of his belongings behind. I have spoken to the woman who has
cleaned this room every day for six years. She tells me that this
diary was not here yesterday morning before the count died."

"And?" asked Colonel Franklin.

"Who knows? Perhaps she simply never noticed it or the
count moved it from someplace else yesterday just before he
was murdered. Or, and this is the theory I wanted to ask you
about, perhaps the murderer put the book on the shelf."

The sun was definitely dropping now and shadows had fallen
over Franklin's face, masking it.

"Why?"

Porfiry Petrovich stood now and placed the book in his
pocket.

He began to pace the room with one hand behind his back as
if he were about to dictate a letter.

"Perhaps the diary was left in your country," he said. "Perhaps
it got into the hands of someone who, by the count's own
words, had wronged that person. When he had finished murder-
ing the count, the killer no longer needed the diary. He re-

turned it to the shelf, a final gesture. The act of completion. You see where I am taking this?"

And Franklin said nothing.

"Do you have just a little more time? One more stop?"

"I have nowhere I have to be now," Franklin said.

"Good," said Porfiry Petrovich and led him out the door.

The sun was almost gone when they entered Porfiry Petrovich's office in the department of investigation twenty minutes later. A few clerks were in the outer offices, but the inspector's room was empty. Porfiry Petrovich moved ahead to light the two lamps on the desk. The lamps were helped by the uncovered windows, which caught the last of the sun.

Franklin stood just inside the door. The room was neither large nor small. Porfiry Petrovich moved behind his writing table, which stood before a sofa upholstered in checkered material, a bureau, a bookcase in the corner, and several chairs, all government issued, of polished yellow wood. In one corner was a closed door. Next to it was a heavy wooden clock with a gold pendulum that ticked loudly.

"My den," said Porfiry Petrovich. "Please sit. Tea? Coffee? It will take a few minutes only."

Franklin moved slowly into the room and sat on the sofa, his eyes never leaving the inspector, who took the count's diary from his pocket and placed it on the writing table. He smiled and then opened the drawer of the writing table to pull out a small wooden box. He placed the box on the table, folded his hands, and looked at his guest dreamily. The clock ticked.

"My favorite time of the day," said Porfiry Petrovich softly. "Neither night nor day. The lost time. The time for contemplation and silence between the smile and the tear. I wish I could say it like your Poe. I'm pleased that we both admire your Poe."

They sat for perhaps ten minutes till the sun was completely gone and there was nothing but the clock and their own breathing.

Finally, Porfiry Petrovich opened the small box. He removed four flat and heavy rectangular objects and laid them before him on the writing table.

The silence was broken by Franklin, who stood suddenly, stepped forward, and pounded his fist on the writing desk.

"Sir," he said evenly. "These photographs are mine."

"They are," Porfiry Petrovich conceded without moving. "I took them from your room."

Franklin scooped the photographs up and shoved them in his pocket.

"Your wife and daughter?" the inspector asked, looking up at Franklin. "They do look like the girl in the Hay Market. And one of you with them. And the older woman?"

"My wife's mother," said Franklin. "Sir, I plan to leave this room now."

"Well," said Porfiry Petrovich with an enormous sigh and a wave of both hands, "I was hoping you could be of help."

"You plan to arres—" Franklin began, but Porfiry Petrovich sprang to his feet and interrupted him with, "Indulge me, Colonel, for just a moment, please."

Franklin hesitated.

"It is my theory," said the inspector, "that the count, who has a reputation for gambling, womanizing, and bad debts, a rarity in the aristocracy, had a confrontation with someone, perhaps one of his former cossacks, after a night of revelry. A neighbor reports seeing a tall man of military bearing enter the count's apartment slightly before the murder.

"That same neighbor reported that he heard the count speak to someone in a foreign language the neighbor did not understand. The death of a member of the aristocracy is not to be taken lightly. The life of a count is, as my superior said yesterday, worth that of a hundred peasants. My responsibility in this investigation, because of my humble ability to speak English, was to join others in questioning the handful of Americans and Englishmen in the city. You were the fourth I found. I have determined that you are quite innocent of any involvement in or knowledge of this horrible deed. It is possible that the savage murderer will never be brought to justice by man. He will have to stand before God. With that I am content."

And with that, Colonel Franklin, late of the Army of the Confederacy, sat back on the sofa and wept. For the first time since he had begun to watch him that morning, Porfiry Petrovich thought he detected a flicker of life in the gaunt man.

"There is a train to Moscow at seven in the morning," said the inspector, turning his chair to the window so that he could see the flickering lights of the city.

"I shall be on it, sir," Franklin said, dignity returning to his voice.

"Can you find your way back to your hotel?" Porfiry Petrovich asked, still watching the lights of the city he loved.

"Of course."

"Have a good journey home," said the inspector.

Behind him, the office door opened and Colonel Franklin went into the hall, closing the door behind him. Porfiry Petrovich was alone with his ticking clock.

And before he could stop them and from where they came he knew not, lines of Poe came to him:

Thy soul shall find itself alone
'Mid dark thoughts of the gray tomb-stone—
Not one, of all the crowd, to pry
Into thine hour of secrecy.

PETER LOVESEY

THE CRIME OF MISS OYSTER BROWN

I suppose this tale of mystery in a quiet English town would be classified these days as a "cozy." Somehow, when Peter Lovesey's writing it, there's nothing very cozy about what happens. This story was the winner of the annual EQMM Readers Award, chosen by a vote of the magazine's readers. It's easy to understand why it stuck in their memory.

Miss Oyster Brown, a devout member of the Church of England, joined passionately each Sunday in every prayer of the Morning Service—except for the general Confession, when, in all honesty, she found it difficult to class herself as a lost sheep. She was willing to believe that everyone else in church had erred and strayed. In certain cases she knew exactly how, and with whom, and she would say a prayer for them. On her own account, however, she could seldom think of anything to confess. She tried strenuously, more strenuously—dare I say it?—than you or me to lead an untainted life. She managed conspicuously well. Very occasionally, as the rest of the congregation joined in the Confession, she would own up to some trifling sin.

You may imagine what a fall from grace it was when this virtuous woman committed not merely a sin but a crime. She lived more than half her life before it happened.

She resided in a Berkshire town with her twin sister, Pearl, who was a mere three minutes her senior. Oyster and Pearl—a flamboyance in forenames that owed something to the fact that their parents had been plain John and Mary Brown. Up to the moment of birth the Browns had been led to expect one child, who, if female, was to be named Pearl. In the turmoil created

109

by a second, unscheduled, daughter, John Brown jokingly suggested naming her Oyster. Mary, bosky from morphine, seized
on the name as an inspiration, a delight to the ear when said in
front of dreary old Brown.

Of course the charm was never so apparent to the twins, who
got to dread being introduced to people. Even in infancy, they
were aware that their parents' friends found the names amusing.
At school they were taunted as much by the teachers as the
children. The names never ceased to amuse. Fifty years on,
things were still said just out of earshot and laced with pretended sympathy. "Here come Pearl and Oyster, poor old ducks.
Fancy being stuck with names like that."

No wonder they faced the world defiantly. In middle age,
they were a formidable duo, stalwarts of the choir, the Bible-
reading Circle, the Townswomen's Guild, and the Magistrates'
Bench. Neither sister had married. They lived together in Lime
Tree Avenue, in the mock-Tudor house where they were born.
They were not short of money.

There are certain things people always want to know about
twins, the more so in mystery stories. I can reassure the wary
reader that Oyster and Pearl were not identical. Oyster was an
inch taller, more sturdy in build than her sister and slower of
speech. They dressed individually, Oyster as a rule in tweed
skirts and check blouses that she made herself, always from the
same Butterick pattern; Pearl in a variety of mail-order suits in
pastel blues and greens. No one confused them.

As for that other question so often asked about twins, neither
sister could be characterized as "dominant." Each possessed a
forceful personality by any standard. To avoid disputes they had
established a household routine, a division of the duties that
worked pretty harmoniously, all things considered. Oyster did
most of the cooking and the gardening, for example, and Pearl
attended to the housework and paid the bills when they became
due. They both enjoyed shopping, so they shared it. They did
the church flowers together when their turn came, and they
always ran the bottle stall at the church fete. Five vicars had
held the living at St. Saviour's in the twins' time as worshipers
there. Each new incumbent was advised by his predecessor that

Pearl and Oyster were the mainstays of the parish. Better to fall foul of the diocesan bishop himself than the Brown twins.

All of this was observed from a distance, for no one, not even a vicar making his social rounds, was allowed inside the house on Lime Tree Avenue. The twins didn't entertain, and that was final. They were polite to their neighbors without once inviting them in. When one twin was ill, the other would transport her to the surgery in a state of high fever rather than call the doctor on a visit.

It followed that people's knowledge of Pearl and Oyster was limited. No one could doubt that they lived an orderly existence; there were no complaints about undue noise or unwashed windows or neglected paintwork. The hedge was trimmed and the garden mown. But what really bubbled and boiled behind the regularly washed net curtains—the secret passion that was to have such a dire result—was unsuspected until Oyster committed her crime.

She acted out of desperation. On the last Saturday in July 1990, her well-ordered life suffered a seismic shock. She was parted from her twin sister. The parting was sudden, traumatic, and had to be shrouded in secrecy. The prospect of anyone finding out what had occurred was unthinkable.

So for the first time in her life Oyster had no Pearl to change the light bulbs, pay the bills, and check that all the doors were locked. Oyster—let it be understood—was not incapable or dim-witted. Bereft as she was, she managed tolerably well until the Friday afternoon, when she had a letter to post, a letter of surpassing importance, capable—God willing—of easing her desolation. She had agonized over it for hours. Now it was crucial that the letter caught the last post of the day. Saturday would be too late. She went to the drawer where Pearl always kept the postage stamps and—calamity—not one was left.

Stamps had always been Pearl's responsibility. To be fair, the error was Oyster's; she had written more letters than usual and gone through the supply. She should have called at the Post Office when she was doing the shopping.

It was too late. There wasn't time to get there before the last post at 5:15. She tried to remain calm and consider her options.

It was out of the question to ask a neighbor for a stamp; she and Pearl had made it a point of honor never to be beholden to anyone else. Neither could she countenance the disgrace of despatching the letter without a stamp in the hope that it would get by, or the recipient would pay the amount due.

This left one remedy, and it was criminal.

Behind one of the Staffordshire dogs on the mantelpiece was a bank statement. She had put it there for the time being because she had been too busy to check where Pearl normally stored such things. The significant point for Oyster at this minute was not the statement but the envelope containing it. More precisely, the top right-hand corner of the envelope, because the first-class stamp had somehow escaped being cancelled.

Temptation stirred and uncoiled itself.

Oyster had never in her life steamed an unfranked stamp from an envelope and used it again. Nor, to her knowledge, had Pearl. Stamp collectors sometimes removed used specimens for their collections, but what Oyster was contemplating could in no way be confused with philately. It was against the law. Defrauding the Post Office. A crime.

There was under twenty minutes before the last collection.

I couldn't, she told herself. *I'm on the Parochial Church Council. I'm on the Bench.*

Temptation reminded her that she was due for a cup of tea in any case. She filled the kettle and pressed the switch. While waiting, watching the first wisp of steam rise from the spout, she weighed the necessity of posting the letter against the wickedness of reusing a stamp. It wasn't the most heinous of crimes, Temptation whispered. And once Oyster began to think about the chances of getting away with it, she was lost. The kettle sang, the steam gushed, and she snatched up the envelope and jammed it against the spout. Merely, Temptation reassured her, to satisfy her curiosity as to whether stamps could be separated from envelopes by this method.

Those who believe in retribution will not be in the least surprised that the steam was deflected by the surface of the envelope and scalded three of Oyster's fingers quite severely. She cried out in pain and dropped the envelope. She ran the cold tap and plunged her hand under it. Then she wrapped the sore fingers in a piece of kitchen towel.

Her first action after that was to turn off the kettle. Her second was to pick up the envelope and test the corner of the stamp with the tip of her fingernail. It still adhered to some extent, but with extreme care she was able to ease it free, consoled that her discomfort had not been entirely without result. The minor accident failed to deter her from the crime. On the contrary, it acted like a prod from Old Nick.

There was a bottle of gum in the writing desk, and she applied some to the back of the stamp, taking care not to use too much, which might have oozed out at the edges and discolored the envelope. When she had positioned the stamp neatly on her letter, it would have passed the most rigorous inspection. She felt a wicked frisson of satisfaction at having committed an undetectable crime. Just in time, she remembered the post and had to hurry to catch it.

There we leave Miss Oyster Brown to come to terms with her conscience for a couple of days.

We meet her again on the Monday morning in the local chemist's shop. The owner and pharmacist was John Trigger, whom the Brown twins had known for getting on for thirty years, a decent, obliging man with a huge mustache who took a personal interest in his customers. In the face of strong competition from a national chain of pharmacists, John Trigger had persevered with his old-fashioned service from behind a counter, believing that some customers still preferred it to filling a wire basket themselves. But to stay in business, he had been forced to diversify by offering some electrical goods.

When Oyster Brown came in and showed him three badly scalded fingers out in blisters, Trigger was sympathetic as well as willing to suggest a remedy. Understandably, he inquired how Oyster had come by such a painful injury. She was expecting the question and had her answer ready, adhering to the truth as closely as a God-fearing woman should.

"An accident with the kettle."

Trigger looked genuinely alarmed. "An electric kettle? Not the one you bought here last year?"

"I didn't," said Oyster at once.

"Must have been your sister. A Steamquick. Is that what you've got?"

"Er, yes."

"If there's a fault—"

"I'm not here to complain, Mr. Trigger. So you think this ointment will do the trick?"

"I'm sure of it. Apply it evenly, and don't attempt to pierce the blisters, will you?" John Trigger's conscience was troubling him. "This is quite a nasty scalding, Miss Brown. Where exactly did the steam come from?"

"The kettle."

"I know that. I mean was it the spout?"

"It really doesn't matter," said Oyster sharply. "It's done."

"The lid, then? Sometimes if you're holding the handle you get a rush of steam from that little slot in the lid. I expect it was that."

"I couldn't say," Oyster fudged, in the hope that it would satisfy Mr. Trigger.

It did not. "The reason I asked is that there may be a design fault."

"The fault was mine, I'm quite sure."

"Perhaps I ought to mention it to the manufacturers."

"Absolutely not," Oyster said in alarm. "I was careless, that's all. And now, if you'll excuse me—" She started backing away and then Mr. Trigger ambushed her with another question.

"What does your sister say about it?"

"My sister?" From the way she spoke, she might never have had one.

"Miss Pearl."

"Oh, nothing. We haven't discussed it," Oyster truthfully stated.

"But she must have noticed your fingers."

"Er, no. How much is the ointment?"

Trigger told her and she dropped the money on the counter and almost rushed from the shop. He stared after her, bewildered.

*   *   *

The next time Oyster Brown was passing, Trigger took the trouble to go to the door of his shop and inquire whether the hand was any better. Clearly she wasn't overjoyed to see him. She assured him without much gratitude that the ointment was working. "It was nothing. It's going to clear up in a couple of days."

"May I see?"

She held out her hand.

Trigger agreed that it was definitely on the mend. "Keep it dry, if you possibly can. Who does the washing up?"

"What do you mean?"

"You or your sister? It's well known that you divide the chores between you. If it's your job, I'm sure Miss Pearl won't mind taking over for a few days. If I see her, I'll suggest it myself."

Oyster reddened and said nothing.

"I was going to remark that I haven't seen her for a week or so," Trigger went on. "She isn't unwell, I hope."

"No," said Oyster. "Not unwell."

Sensing correctly that this was not an avenue of conversation to venture along at this time, he said instead, "The Steamquick rep was in yesterday afternoon, so I mentioned what happened with your kettle."

She was outraged. "You had no business!"

"Pardon me, Miss Brown, but it *is* my business. You were badly scalded. I can't have my customers being injured by the products I sell. The rep was very concerned, as I am. He asked if you would be so good as to bring the kettle in next time you come so that he can check if there's a fault."

"Absolutely not," said Oyster. "I told you I haven't the slightest intention of complaining."

Trigger tried to be reasonable. "It isn't just your kettle. I've sold the same model to other customers."

"Then they'll complain if they get hurt."

"What if their children get hurt?"

She had no answer.

"If it's inconvenient to bring it in, perhaps I could call at your house."

"No," she said at once.

"I can bring a replacement. In fact, Miss Brown, I'm more than a little concerned about this whole episode. I'd like you to have another kettle with my compliments. A different model. Frankly, the modern trend is for jug kettles that couldn't possibly scald you as yours did. If you'll kindly step into the shop, I'll give you one now to take home."

The offer didn't appeal to Oyster Brown in the least. "For the last time, Mr. Trigger," she said in a tight, clipped voice, "I don't require another kettle." With that, she walked away up the high street.

Trigger, from the motives he had mentioned, was not content to leave the matter there. He wasn't a churchgoer, but he believed in conducting his life on humanitarian principles. On this issue, he was resolved to be just as stubborn as she. He went back into the shop and straight to the phone. While Oyster Brown was out of the house, he would speak to Pearl Brown, the sister, and see if he could get better cooperation from her.

Nobody answered the phone.

At lunchtime, he called in to see Ted Collins, who ran the garden shop next door, and asked if he had seen anything of Pearl Brown lately.

"I had Oyster in this morning," Collins told him.

"But you haven't seen Pearl?"

"Not in my shop. Oyster does all the gardening, you know. They divide the work."

"I know."

"I can't think what came over her today. Do you know what she bought? Six bottles of Rapidrot."

"What's that?"

"It's a new product. An activator for composting. You dilute it and water your compost heap and it speeds up the process. They're doing a special promotion to launch it. Six bottles are far too much, and I tried to tell her, but she wouldn't be told."

"Those two often buy in bulk," said Trigger. "I've sold Pearl a dozen tubes of toothpaste at a go, and they must be awash with Dettol."

"They won't use six bottles of Rapidrot in twenty years,"

Collins pointed out. "It's concentrated stuff, and it won't keep all that well. It's sure to solidify after a time. I told her one's plenty to be going on with. She's wasted her money, obstinate old bird. I don't know what Pearl would say. Is she ill, do you think?"

"I've no idea," said Trigger, although in reality an idea was beginning to form in his brain. A disturbing idea. "Do they get on all right with each other? Daft question," he said before Collins could answer it. "They're twins. They've spent all their lives in each other's company."

For the present he dismissed the thought and gave his attention to the matter of the electric kettles. He'd already withdrawn the Steamquick kettles from sale. He got on the phone to Steamquick and had an acrimonious conversation with some little Hitler from their public-relations department who insisted that thousands of the kettles had been sold and the design was faultless.

"The lady's injury isn't imagined, I can tell you," Trigger insisted.

"She must have been careless. Anyone can hurt themselves if they're not careful. People are far too ready to put the blame on the manufacturer."

"People, as you put it, are your livelihood."

There was a heavy sigh. "Send us the offending kettle, and we'll test it."

"That isn't so simple."

"Have you offered to replace it?"

The man's whole tone was so condescending that Trigger had an impulse to frighten him rigid. "She won't let the kettle out of her possession. I think she may be keeping it as evidence."

"Evidence?" There was a pause while the implication dawned. "Blimey."

On his end of the phone, Trigger permitted himself to grin.

"You mean she might take us to court over this?"

"I didn't say that."

"Ah."

"But she does know the law. She's a magistrate."

An audible gasp followed, then: "Listen, Mr., er—"

"Trigger."

"Mr. Trigger. I think we'd better send someone to meet this lady and deal with the matter personally. Yes, that's what we'll do."

Trigger worked late that evening, stocktaking. He left the shop about 10:30. Out of curiosity he took a route home via Lime Tree Avenue and stopped the car opposite the Brown sisters' house and wound down the car window. There were lights upstairs and presently someone drew a curtain. It looked like Oyster Brown.

"Keeping an eye on your customers, Mr. Trigger?" a voice close to him said.

He turned guiltily. A woman's face was six inches from his. He recognized one of his customers, Mrs. Wingate. She said, "She's done that every night this week."

"Oh?"

"Something fishy's going on in there," she said. "I walk my little dog along the verge about this time every night. I live just opposite them, on this side, with the wrought-iron gates. That's Pearl's bedroom at the front. I haven't seen Pearl for a week, but every night Oyster draws the curtains and leaves the light on for half an hour. What's going on, I'd like to know. If Pearl is ill, they ought to call a doctor. They won't, you know."

"That's Pearl's bedroom, you say, with the light on?"

"Yes, I often see her looking out. Not lately."

"And now Oyster switches on the light and draws the curtains?"

"And pulls them back at seven in the morning. I don't know what *you* think, Mr. Trigger, but it looks to me as if she wants everyone to think Pearl's in there, when it's obvious she isn't."

"Why is it obvious?"

"All the windows are closed. Pearl always opens the top window wide, winter and summer."

"That is odd, now you mention it."

"I'll tell you one thing," said Mrs. Wingate, regardless that she had told him several things already, "whatever game she's up to, we won't find out. Nobody ever sets foot inside that house except the twins themselves."

* * *

At home and in bed that night, Trigger was troubled by a gruesome idea, one that he'd tried repeatedly to suppress. Suppose the worst had happened a week ago in the house on Lime Tree Avenue, his thinking ran. Suppose Pearl Brown had suffered a heart attack and died. After so many years of living in that house as if it were a fortress, was Oyster capable of dealing with the aftermath of death, calling in the doctor and the undertaker? In her shocked state, mightn't she decide that anything was preferable to having the house invaded, even if the alternative was disposing of the body herself?

How would a middle-aged woman dispose of a body? Oyster didn't drive a car. It wouldn't be easy to bury it in the garden, or hygienic to keep it in a cupboard in the house. But if there was one thing every well-bred English lady knew about, it was gardening.

Oyster was the gardener.

In time, everything rots in a compost heap. If you want to accelerate the process, you buy a preparation like Rapidrot.

Oyster Brown had purchased six bottles of the stuff. And every night she drew the curtains in her sister's bedroom to give the impression that she was there.

He shuddered.

In the fresh light of morning, John Trigger told himself that his morbid imaginings couldn't be true. They were the delusions of a tired brain. He decided to do nothing about them.

Just after 11:30, a short fat man in a dark suit arrived in the shop and announced himself as the Area Manager of Steamquick. His voice was suspiciously like the one Trigger had found so irritating when he had phoned their head office. "I'm here about this allegedly faulty kettle," he announced.

"Miss Brown's?"

"I'm sure there's nothing wrong at all, but we're a responsible firm. We take every complaint seriously."

"You want to see the kettle? You'll be lucky."

The Steamquick man sounded smug. "That's all right. I telephoned Miss Brown this morning and offered to go to the house. She wasn't at all keen on that idea, but I was very firm with the lady and she compromised. We're meeting here at noon. She's agreed to bring the kettle for me to inspect. I don't know why you found her so intractable."

"High noon, eh? Do you want to use my office?"

Trigger had come to a rapid decision. If Oyster was on her way to the shop, he was going out. He had two capable assistants.

This was a heaven-sent opportunity to lay his macabre theory to rest. While Oyster was away from the house on Lime Tree Avenue, he would drive there and let himself into the back garden. Mrs. Wingate or any other curious neighbor watching from behind the lace curtains would have to assume he was trying to deliver something. He kept his white coat on, to reinforce the idea that he was on official business.

Quite probably, he told himself, the compost heap will turn out to be no bigger than a cowpat. The day was sunny and he felt positively cheerful as he turned up the avenue. He checked his watch. Oyster would be making mincemeat of the Steam-quick man about now. It would take her twenty minutes, at least, to walk back.

He stopped the car and got out. Nobody was about, but just in case he was being observed he walked boldly up the path to the front door and rang the bell. No one came.

Without appearing in the least furtive, he stepped around the side of the house. The back garden was in a beautiful state. Wide, well stocked, and immaculately weeded borders enclosed a finely trimmed lawn, yellow roses on a trellis, and a kitchen garden beyond. Trigger took it in admiringly, and then remembered why he was there. His throat went dry. At the far end, beyond the kitchen garden, slightly obscured by some runner beans on poles, was the compost heap—as long as a coffin and more than twice as high.

The flesh on his arms prickled.

The compost heap was covered with black-plastic bin liners weighted with stones. They lay across the top, but the sides were exposed. A layer of fresh green garden refuse, perhaps half a meter in depth, was on the top. The lower part graduated in color from a dull yellow to earth brown. Obvious care had been taken to conserve the shape, to keep the pressure even and assist the composting process.

Trigger wasn't much of a gardener. He didn't have the time for it. He did the minimum and got rid of his garden rubbish with bonfires. Compost heaps were outside his experience, except that as a scientist he understood the principle by which they generated heat in a confined space. Once, years ago, an uncle of his had demonstrated this by pushing a bamboo cane into his heap from the top. A wisp of steam had issued from the hole as he withdrew the cane. Recalling it now, Trigger felt a wave of nausea.

He hadn't the stomach for this.

He knew now that he wasn't going to be able to walk up the garden and probe the compost heap. Disgusted with himself for being so squeamish, he turned to leave, and happened to notice that the kitchen window was ajar, which was odd considering that Oyster wasn't at home. Out of interest, he tried the door handle. The door was unlocked.

He said, "Anyone there?" and got no answer.

From the doorway he could see a number of unopened letters on the kitchen table. After the humiliation of turning his back on the compost heap, this was like a challenge, a chance to regain some self-respect. This, at least, he was capable of doing. He stepped inside and picked up the letters. There were five, all addressed to Miss P. Brown. The postmarks dated from the beginning of the previous week.

Quite clearly, Pearl had not been around to open her letters.

Then his attention was taken by an extraordinary lineup along a shelf. He counted fifteen packets of cornflakes, all open, and recalled his conversation with Ted Collins about the sisters buying in bulk. If Collins had wanted convincing, there was ample evidence here: seven bottles of decaffeinated coffee, nine jars of the same brand of marmalade, and a tall stack of boxes of paper tissues. Eccentric housekeeping, to say the least. Perhaps, he reflected, it meant that the buying of six bottles of Rapidrot had not, after all, been so sinister.

But now that he was in the house, he wasn't going to leave without seeking an answer to the main mystery, the disappearance of Pearl. His mouth was no longer dry and the gooseflesh had gone from his arms. He made up his mind to go upstairs and look into the front bedroom.

On the other side of the kitchen door, more extravagance was revealed. The passage from the kitchen to the stairway was lined on either side with sets of goods that must have overflowed from the kitchen. Numerous tins of cocoa, packets of sugar, pots of jam, gravy powder, and other grocery items were stored as if for a siege, stacked along the skirting boards in groups of at least half a dozen. Trigger began seriously to fear for the mental health of the twins. Nobody had suspected anything like this behind the closed doors. The stacks extended halfway upstairs.

As he stepped upward, obliged to tread close to the banister, he was gripped by the sense of alienation that must have led to hoarding on such a scale. The staid faces that the sisters presented to the world gave no intimation of this strange compulsion. What was the mentality of people who behaved as weirdly as this?

An appalling possibility crept into Trigger's mind. Maybe the strain of so many years of appearing outwardly normal had finally caused Oyster to snap. What if the eccentricity so apparent all around him now were not so harmful as it first appeared? No one could know what resentments, what jealousies lurked in this house, what mean-minded cruelties the sisters may have inflicted on each other. What if Oyster had fallen out with her sister and attacked her? She was a sturdy woman, physically capable of killing.

If she'd murdered Pearl, the compost-heap method of disposal would certainly commend itself.

Come now, he told himself, this is all speculation.

He reached the top stair and discovered that the stockpiling had extended to the landing. Toothpaste, talcum powder, shampoos, and soap were stacked up in profusion. All the doors were closed. It wouldn't have surprised him if when he opened one he was knee-deep in toilet rolls.

First he had to orientate himself. He decided that the front bedroom was to his right. He opened it cautiously and stepped in.

What happened next was swift and devastating. John Trigger heard a piercing scream. He had a sense of movement to his left and a glimpse of a figure in white. Something crashed against his head with a mighty thump, causing him to pitch forward.

About four, when the Brown twins generally stopped for tea, Oyster filled the new kettle that the Steamquick Area Manager had exchanged for the other one. She plugged it in. It was the newfangled jug type and she wasn't really certain if she was going to like it, but she certainly needed the cup of tea.

"I know it was wrong," she said, "and I'm going to pray for forgiveness, but I didn't expect that steaming a stamp off a letter would lead to this. I suppose it's a judgment."

"Whatever made you do such a wicked thing?" her sister Pearl asked, as she put out the cups and saucers.

"The letter had to catch the post. It was the last possible day for the Kellogg's Cornflakes competition, and I'd thought of such a wonderful slogan. The prize was a fortnight in Venice."

Pearl clicked her tongue in disapproval. "Just because I won the Birds Eye trip to the Bahamas, it didn't mean *you* were going to be lucky. We tried for twenty years and only ever won consolation prizes."

"It isn't really gambling, is it?" said Oyster. "It isn't like betting."

"It's all right in the Lord's eyes," Pearl told her. "It's a harmless pastime. Unfortunately, we both know that people in the church won't take a charitable view. They wouldn't expect us to devote so much of our time and money to competitions. That's why we have to be careful. You didn't tell anyone I was away?"

"Of course not. Nobody knows. For all they know, you were ill, if anyone noticed at all. I drew the curtains in your bedroom every night to make it look as if you were here."

"Thank you. You know I'd do the same for you."

"I *might* win," said Oyster. "Someone always does. I put in fifteen entries altogether, and the last one was a late inspiration."

"And as a result we have fifteen packets of cornflakes with the tops cut off," said Pearl. "They take up a lot of room."

"So do your frozen peas. I had to throw two packets away to make some room in the freezer. Anyway, I felt entitled to try. It wasn't much fun being here alone, thinking of you sunning yourself in the West Indies. To tell you the truth, I didn't really think you'd go and leave me here. It was a shock."

Oyster carefully poured some hot water into the teapot to warm it. "If you want to know, I've also entered the Rapidrot Trip of a Lifetime competition. A week in San Francisco followed by a week in Sydney. I bought six bottles to have a fighting chance."

"What's Rapidrot?"

"Something for the garden." She spooned in some tea and poured on the hot water. "You must be exhausted. Did you get any sleep on the plane?"

"Hardly any," said Pearl. "That's why I went straight to bed when I got in this morning." She poured milk into the teacups. "The next thing I knew the doorbell was going. I ignored it, naturally. It was one of the nastiest shocks I ever had, hearing the footsteps coming up the stairs. I could tell it wasn't you. I'm just thankful that I had the candlestick to defend myself with."

"Is there any sign of life yet?"

"Well, he's breathing, but he hasn't opened his eyes, if that's what you mean. Funny, I would never have thought Mr. Trigger was dangerous to women."

Oyster poured the tea. "What are we going to do if he doesn't recover? We can't have people coming into the house." Even as she was speaking, she put down the teapot and glanced out the kitchen window toward the end of the garden. She had the answer herself.

BARRY N. MALZBERG
FOLLY FOR THREE

A mystery story is not always a detective story. Occasionally the mystery can arise from the manner in which the story is told, as in this striking tale by Barry Malzberg. His contributions to the science fiction field have tended to overshadow Malzberg's ventures into the mystery, but no one since Woolrich has delivered such a dark vision of the way we live. Malzberg's 1976 novel The Running of Beasts, *written in collaboration with Bill Pronzini, remains a classic study of a psychopathic killer.*

Good, he said again, this is very good. Just turn a little, let the light catch you. I want to see you in profile, against the light. There, he said, that's good. That's what I want. His voice had thickened, whether with passion or contempt she had no idea. They were still at that tentative state of connection where all moves were suspect, all signals indeterminate.

Ah, he said, you're a piece all right. That's what you are.

I've never done this before, she said. I've never done anything like this before. I want you to know that. She looked out the window, the gray clouds on the high floor hammering at the panes. Way, way up now. For everything there's a first time, she said.

Right, he said, humoring her. Whatever you say. I'm your first. Best in the world. Anything for a hump. He backed against a chair, crouched, fell into the cushions, stared at her from that angle, looking upward intently, checking out her crotch, then the high angle of her breasts, pulled upward within the brassiere, arching. He muttered something she could not hear and raised a hand.

What is it? she said. What do you want?

Come here. I want you to come here right now.

Tell me why.

I don't want games, he said. We'll have time for that later. You want to fool around, play with yourself. Come over here. Move it.

Can't you be a little kinder? I told you, I've never done anything like this before.

You want a commendation? he said. A Congressional Medal of Honor? He cleared his throat, looked at her with an odd and exacting impatience. Everybody has to have a first time, he said. Even I did once. I got through it. You'll get through it too. But you have to close your eyes and jump. Move it over here now.

This isn't the way I thought it would be, she said.

How did you think it would be? Flowers and wine? Tchaikovsky on the turntable? White Russians with straws? This is the setup, he said, this is what a nooner feels like. You don't hang out in bars midday if you're not looking for a nooner.

She looked at him, almost as if for the first time, noting the age spots on his arms, the fine, dense wrinkling around the eyes, which she had not noticed in the bar. Could she back out now? No, she thought, she couldn't. This was not the way it was done. That was all behind her now. I'm on the forty-eighth floor and that's all there is to it and no one in the world except this man knows I'm here. Not the kids, not Harry, not the cops. Okay, she said, I'm coming. She went toward him, trying to make her stockings glide, trying to move the way they moved in this kind of scene on "Dallas." Maybe she could break him on the anvil of desire. Maybe she could quit him. Maybe—

There was a pounding on the door. Open up, someone in the hall said, open it! Open it now! The voice was huge, insistent.

For God's sake, she said, who is that?

He was trembling. I don't know, he said, what have you put us into? Detectives? Photographers? You got me into this, bitch. He backed away from her. His lips moved but there was no sound.

The noises in the hall were enormous, like nothing she had ever heard. The hammering was regular, once every three or four seconds now, an avid panting just beyond earshot. Like fucking, that's how it sounded. Last chance, the voice said, you open that goddamned door or we break it down.

What have you done? she said to the man. Stunned, absolutely without response, he ran his hands over his clothing, looked stupidly at the belt. This wasn't supposed to happen, she said. This wasn't part of it. *Who is out there?*

Nothing. He had nothing to say. He brought his clothing against him helplessly in the thin off-light in which she had so recently posed. She heard the sound of keys in the hallway. They were going to open the door.

An hour earlier in the bar she had said, Let's go now. I have a room in the Lenox around the corner.

Fast mover, he had said. His briefcase was on his lap, concealing an erection she supposed, one elbow draped over it awkwardly, clutching the briefcase there, the other hand running up and down her bare arm. She could feel the tremor in his fingers. He wanted her. Well, that was *his* problem.

I can be fast when I want, she said. Other times I can be slow. Whatever you say, big boy, I'm on your side. Who can believe these lines? she thought. This is what it's come to now.

Okay, he said. Just let me finish this drink. He raised the cocktail glass. I paid for it, he said, it's mine, I ought to have it.

She pressed his arm. You only think you're paying, she said. *I'm* paying. All the way, up and down the line. In his face she could see the pallor of acknowledgment, a blush of realization. *I've got a hot one here,* that face was saying. Well, that's the idea all right.

Let's go, friend, she said. She pushed away her own glass, clung to him for an instant, then pulled him upright. Let's see how fast you are where it counts. Out in the clean fresh air and then forty-eight stories *up,* that's the right place to put it.

He released her, yanked upright from the stool, took out a twenty, and put it on the bar. We'll see how fast I am, he said. He took the briefcase against his side, gripped the handle. Now, he said. The lust on his face seemed to struggle for just a moment with doubt, then faded to a kind of bleakness as she reached out again and stroked him. Now and now. He rose gravely to her touch. For God's sake, he said. For God's sake—

Now, she said.

They struggled toward the door. The man on the stool

nearest the entrance looked up at them, his glasses dazzling in the strobe and said, You too? Every one of you?

She stared. She had never seen this man in her life. Of course, she reminded herself, the salesman with the briefcase was new also. Two strangers, one maybe as good as the other when she had walked in, but the salesman was the one she had picked and in whom the time had been invested. No looking back. She said nothing, started toward the door.

Fornicators, the seated man said, infidels. Desolate lost angels of the Lord. Have you no shame? No hope?

Out on the street, the salesman said, Another bar, another crazy. They're all over the place. This city—

I don't want to hear about the city, she said. Please. Just take me to the hotel. Right now. She was appalled by the thought that the man at the bar would come after them. The thought was crazy but there it was. To the hotel, she said. I'm burning up, can't you tell. She yanked at his wrist. Now, she said, let's go.

She began to tug at him, he broke into a small trot. Hey, he said, hey look, it's all right. We've got all afternoon. I'm not going anywhere, we have hours. We have—

I'm afraid he's following us, she said. There, it was out, be done with it. I'm afraid he's going to come after us.

Who? The guy from the bar?

His footsteps, she said, I know them. He's coming up behind us. She turned and pointed, ready for a confrontation right there, but of course there was nothing. A couple of secretaries giggling, a man with a dog, a beggar with a sign saying I AM BLIND, that was all. Quickly, she said, before he finds us. I know he's on the way.

She moved rapidly then, dropping her grip, striding out, making the salesman race. Let him struggle, she thought. Let him chase her a little. She was afraid of the man in the bar whether or not he was coming. Desolate lost angels of the Lord. Fornicators, she thought. We're all fornicators, but some of us know more than others. There was something to come to terms with in this, but she simply could not. All she wanted to do was get to the forty-eighth floor of the Hotel Lenox, take him into that room, get it over with, take him as deep as her brains. Make it happen, make it done. Get it into her. She was burning. Burning.

That morning in the kitchen he had said, I don't know how late I'll be. There's a conference midday and then I have to go out with the accounts exec again. I could be tied up till midnight with this guy, he's a professional drunk. If that's it I'll just get a room in the city and sleep in.

That's nice, she said. That's the third time I've heard that this month. Why bother coming home at all?

Hey, he said, his head tilting to attention, you think I'm lying? You think this is some kind of crap here, that I'm making up a story? Then just say it.

I didn't say a thing.

You think I'm running around? he said. I'm knocking my brains out to keep us in this $250,000 house we can't afford and can't sell and you're running tabs on me? Maybe we ought to have a discussion about that.

We're not going to have a discussion about anything, she said. He looks forty, she thought, and his gut is starting to swell. The sideburns are ragged and at night, the nights that he's next to me, he breathes like an old man, a sob in his throat. He's not going to last but who lasts? What stays? Ten years ago we made plans and every one of them worked out. I'm having trouble getting wet. AIDS is crossing the Huguenot line. The kids are no longer an excuse. We moved here expecting the usual, who was to know the joke was on us? I'm entitled to something too, she said, just think of that.

What does that mean? he said indifferently. He stood, gathered papers, stacked them, and leaned to open his briefcase. You trying to tell me something?

Nothing, she said, nothing at all. Make of it what you will.

Because if that's the deal, two can play you know. I don't have to get a heart attack at forty-two to keep you in a place like this. I can just let it go.

Forget it, she said. I didn't mean anything. It was just an expression. Pushing it, she thought. We're starting to push it now. It used to be easier; now we've got to get closer and closer to the bull.

Everything's an expression, he said. He opened the briefcase, inserted the papers, closed it with a snap. There's no time to discuss this now, he said, maybe later we ought to settle a few goddamned things. Maybe we'll sit down this weekend and talk.

I'll make an appointment, she said.

Enough, he said, enough of this. I'm out the door. You got something to say, maybe you write it down in words of one syllable, we fix it so a simple guy like me can see this. We're practical in the sales department, we only know what's in front of us. You got to spell it out.

Me and my imaginary friend, she said.

Imaginary friend? Is that what you call him now?

You'll be late for the bus, she said. You'll miss your connections and what will happen midday? He stared at her. You've got a schedule to meet, I mean, she said. In four years he won't be able to come, she thought. He'll be a heavy, barking lump next to me and I'll be counting the heartbeats, waiting for the hammer. That's what's going to happen. You bet it would have to be imaginary, she said.

He laughed, a strangulated groan. Too much, he said, you're too much for me. Always were. Always ahead of me. He leaned forward, kissed her cheek, his eyes flicking down indifferently, taking in her body, then moving away, all of him moving away, arching toward the wall and then the door. Keep it going, he said, just take a tip from me and keep it going. He reached toward the door.

Just like I do, he said, and with a wink was gone.

She followed him, closed the heavy service door, sat on the stool, ran her feet in and around her slippers, looking at the clock. In her mind she ran the day forward, spun the hours, turned it until it was one in the afternoon and she would be in the Lenox waiting to be taken. She had worked it all out. But that still left hours, even figuring in the time at the bar and the arrangements to be made there. Too much time altogether. She thought of that.

She thought of it for a long time and of other things, the kids off at school, the difficult arc of the morning already getting passed. What do you think? she said to herself, what do you really think of this? Does it make any sense at all? Is this what we wanted?

Desolation, a voice said. That isn't what you wanted, that's what you've got. So you do the best you can. You make it up as you go along. That's the suburban way of life.

Well, there was nothing to say to that. There almost never was. What she could say would destroy the game. She kicked off her slippers and moved toward the stairs, ready to get dressed, ready to pull herself together. Again. Playing it out.

Two years before that, a Thursday in summer she had said, I can't go on this way anymore, Harry. Can you understand that? It's too much for me, it's not enough for me, it's a grayness, a vastness, I can't take it. I need something else. I can't die this way. She had run her hand on his thigh, felt the cooling, deadly torment of his inanition.

It's not just you, she said. It's everything. It's everybody.

We can work it out, he said. There are things we can do.

We can't do anything. I've thought it through. It's just the situation and it's too much. It's not enough, it's—

It's not just the two of us, he said. There are things to be done.

No shrinks, she said. No counselors. We've had enough of them. We're not getting anywhere.

I don't mean that, he said. There are other things. Things we can do on our own, things that will change.

Oh, Harry, she said, Harry, you have answers, but there *are* no answers, there are only plagues out there, and darkness.

So we'll do something, he said, practically. He was a practical man. Because of the plagues, the risks. No one goes out there now if they can help it. I don't want to go out there and neither do you. So we have to work something out.

What? she said. What do you want? What's the answer?

He clutched her hand. We know all about it in the sales game, he said, and I can teach you.

Teach me what?

Masks, he said.

Masks? Halloween?

Repertory theater, he said. That's what we're going to have

here. A little repertory theater. So get ready for the roles of your life.

Once she had loved him, she supposed. She must have loved him a lot. In deference to that, then, she laid back in the bed wide-eyed, listened to the tempo of his breathing as it picked up, touched him.

Okay, she said. Tell me more. I'm listening.

Yes, he said. Yes.

In the darkness, as he spoke, it was as if there were now another presence heaped under the bedclothes, an imaginary friend maybe, *her* imaginary friend, listening.

He told her what he had in mind.

He sold her on it.

On the forty-eighth floor, she backed against the high window in the hotel room, her eyes fixed on the door, listening to the sound of the key turning. No, she said, no.

The man hobbling toward the door, half-dressed, turned, stared. No what? he said.

No more of this, she said. There's someone out there, she said. There's someone really out there with the key in the lock. We're in over our heads.

She could hear the key turning, turning. It encountered an obstruction, then suddenly it didn't and it was through. The door was moving.

The terror was clambering within her like an animal. He looks forty, she thought, and his gut is starting to swell. He's breathing like an old man *Over our heads,* she said. I don't know what to do.

He looked at her, speechless. Wait a minute, he said. Now just wait—

The door was open. The man from the bar was there smiling, holding a gun now, pointing it. Fornicators, he said, I knew what you were up to. I have the key and I followed you here. Now you're going to pay. You disgust me.

She moved toward the window. Harry was rooted in place.

She looked at the priestly little man with the gun and sadly she looked at her husband, waiting now for whatever would happen.

Curtain, Harry, she said.

BILL PRONZINI

LA BELLEZZA DELLE BELLEZZE

Bill Pronzini's stories about his Nameless Detective are often compassionate studies of human frailty. In this novelette he examines life and death in the North Beach Italian community of San Francisco, where the old men still play bocce and the young still try to escape to their own lives.

That Sunday, the day before she died, I went down to Aquatic Park to watch the old men play bocce. I do that sometimes on weekends when I'm not working, when Kerry and I have nothing planned. More often than I used to, out of nostalgia and compassion and maybe just a touch of guilt, because in San Francisco bocce is a dying sport.

Only one of the courts was in use. Time was, all six were packed throughout the day and there were spectators and waiting players lined two and three deep at courtside and up along the fence on Van Ness. No more. Most of the city's older Italians, to whom bocce was more a religion than a sport, have died off. The once large and close-knit North Beach Italian community has been steadily losing its identity since the fifties—families moving to the suburbs, the expansion of Chinatown, and the gobbling up of North Beach real estate by wealthy Chinese—and even though there has been a small new wave of immigrants from Italy in recent years, they're mostly young and upscale. Young, upscale Italians don't play bocce much, if at all; their interests lie in soccer, in the American sports where money and fame and power have replaced a love of the game itself. The Di Massimo bocce courts at the North Beach Playground are mostly closed now; the only place you can find a game every Saturday and Sunday is on the one Aquatic Park court. And the players get older, and sadder, and fewer each year.

There were maybe fifteen players and watchers on this Sunday, almost all of them older than my fifty-eight. The two courts nearest the street are covered by a high, pillar-supported roof, so that contests can be held even in wet weather; and there are wooden benches set between the pillars. I parked myself on one of the benches midway along. The only other seated spectator was Pietro Lombardi, in a patch of warm May sunlight at the far end, and this surprised me. Even though Pietro was in his seventies, he was one of the best and spryest of the regulars, and also one of the most social. To see him sitting alone, shoulders slumped and head bowed, was puzzling.

Pining away for the old days, maybe, I thought—as I had just been doing. And a phrase popped into my head, a line from Dante that one of my uncles was fond of quoting when I was growing up in the Outer Mission: *Nessun maggior dolore che ricordarsi del tempo felice nella miseria.* The bitterest of woes is to remember old happy days.

Pietro and his woes didn't occupy my attention for long. The game in progress was spirited and voluble, as only a game of bocce played by elderly *'paesanos* can be, and I was soon caught up in it.

Bocce is simple—deceptively simple. You play it on a long narrow packed-earth pit with low wooden sides. A wooden marker ball the size of a walnut is rolled to one end; the players stand at the opposite end and in turn roll eight larger, heavier balls, grapefruit-sized, in the direction of the marker, the object being to see who can put his bocce ball closest to it. One of the required skills is slow-rolling the ball, usually in a curving trajectory, so that it kisses the marker and then lies up against it—the perfect shot—or else stops an inch or two away. The other required skill is knocking an opponent's ball away from any such close lie without disturbing the marker. The best players, like Pietro Lombardi, can do this two out of three times on the fly—no mean feat from a distance of fifty feet. They can also do it by caroming the ball off the pit walls, with topspin or reverse spin after the fashion of pool-shooters.

Nobody paid much attention to me until after the game in

progress had been decided. Then I was acknowledged with hand gestures and a few words—the tolerant acceptance accorded to known spectators and occasional players. Unknowns got no greeting at all; these men still clung to the old ways, and one of the old ways was clannishness.

Only one of the group, Dominick Marra, came over to where I was sitting. And that was because he had something on his mind. He was in his mid-seventies, white-haired, white-mustached; a bantamweight in baggy trousers held up by galluses. He and Pietro Lombardi had been close friends for most of their lives. Born in the same town—Agropoli, a village on the Gulf of Salerno not far from Naples; moved to San Francisco with their families a year apart, in the late twenties; married cousins, raised large families, were widowed at almost the same time a few years ago. The kind of friendship that is almost a blood tie. Dominick had been a baker; Pietro had owned a North Beach trattoria that now belonged to one of his daughters.

What Dominick had on his mind was Pietro. "You see how he sits over there, hah? He's got trouble—*la miseria.*"

"What kind of trouble?"

"His granddaughter. Gianna Fornessi."

"Something happen to her?"

"She's maybe go to jail," Dominick said.

"What for?"

"Stealing money."

"I'm sorry to hear it. How much money?"

"Two thousand dollars."

"Who did she steal it from?"

"*Che?*"

"Who did she steal the money from?"

Dominick gave me a disgusted look. "She don't steal it. Why you think Pietro he's got *la miseria,* hah?"

I knew what was coming now; I should have known it the instant Dominick started confiding to me about Pietro's problem. I said, "You want me to help him and his granddaughter."

"Sure. You a detective."

"A busy detective."

"You got no time for old man and young girl? *Compaesani?*"

I sighed, but not so he could hear me do it. "All right, I'll talk to Pietro. See if he wants my help, if there's anything I can do."

"Sure he wants your help. He just don't know it yet."

We went to where Pietro was sitting alone in the sun. He was taller than Dominick, heavier, balder. And he had a fondness for Toscanas, those little twisted black Italian cigars; one protruded now from a corner of his mouth. He didn't want to talk at first, but Dominick launched into a monologue in Italian that changed his mind and put a glimmer of hope in his sad eyes. Even though I've lost a lot of the language over the years, I can understand enough to follow most conversations. The gist of Dominick's monologue was that I was not just a detective but a miracle worker, a cross between Sherlock Holmes and the messiah. Italians are given to hyperbole in times of excitement or stress, and there isn't much you can do to counteract it—especially when you're one of the *compaesani* yourself.

"My Gianna, she's good girl," Pietro said. "Never give trouble, even when she's little one. *La bellezza delle bellezze,* you understand?"

The beauty of beauties. His favorite grandchild, probably. I said, "I understand. Tell me about the money, Pietro."

"She don't steal it," he said. *"Una ladra,* my Gianna? No, no, it's all big lie."

"Did the police arrest her?"

"They got no evidence to arrest her."

"But somebody filed charges, is that it?"

"Charges," Pietro said. "Bah," he said and spat.

"Who made the complaint?"

Dominick said, "Ferry," as if the name were an obscenity.

"Who's Ferry?"

He tapped his skull. *"Caga di testa,* this man."

"That doesn't answer my question."

"He live where she live. Same apartment building."

"And he says Gianna stole two thousand dollars from him."

"Liar," Pietro said. "He lies."

"Stole it how? Broke in or what?"

"She don't break in nowhere, not my Gianna. This Ferry, this *bastardo,* he says she take the money when she's come to pay rent and he's talk on telephone. But how she knows where he keep his money? Hah? How she knows he have two thousand dollars in his desk?"

"Maybe he told her."

"Sure, that's what he says to police," Dominick said. "Maybe he told her, he says. He don't tell her nothing."

"Is that what Gianna claims?"

Pietro nodded. Threw down what was left of his Toscana and ground it into the dirt with his shoe—a gesture of anger and frustration. "She don't steal that money," he said. "What she need to steal money for? She got good job, she live good, she don't have to steal."

"What kind of job does she have?"

"She sell drapes, curtains. In . . . what you call that business, Dominick?"

"Interior decorating business," Dominick said.

"*Si.* In interior decorating business."

"Where does she live?" I asked.

"Chestnut Street."

"Where on Chestnut Street? What number?"

"Seventy-two fifty."

"You make that Ferry tell the truth, hah?" Dominick said to me. "You fix it up for Gianna and her goombah?"

"I'll do what I can."

"*Va bene.* Then you come tell Pietro right away."

"If Pietro will tell me where he lives—"

There was a sharp whacking sound as one of the bocce balls caromed off the side wall near us, then a softer clicking of ball meeting ball, and a shout went up from the players at the far end: another game won and lost. When I looked back at Dominick and Pietro they were both on their feet. Dominick said, "You find Pietro okay, good detective like you," and Pietro said, *"Grazie, mi amico,"* and before I could say anything else the two of them were off arm in arm to join the others.

Now *I* was the one sitting alone in the sun, holding up a burden. Primed and ready to do a job I didn't want to do, probably couldn't do, and would not be paid well for if at all. Maybe this man Ferry wasn't the only one involved who had *caga di testa*—shit for brains. Maybe I did too.

2

The building at 7250 Chestnut Street was an old three-storied, brown-shingled job, set high in the shadow of Coit Tower and across from the retaining wall where Telegraph Hill falls off steeply toward the Embarcadero. From each of the apartments, especially the ones on the third floor, you'd have quite a view of the bay, the East Bay, and both bridges. Prime North Beach address, this. The rent would be well in excess of two thousand a month.

A man in a tan trenchcoat was coming out of the building as I started up the steps to the vestibule. I called out to him to hold the door for me—it's easier to get apartment dwellers to talk to you once you're inside the building—but either he didn't hear me or he chose to ignore me. He came hurrying down without a glance my way as he passed. City-bred paranoia, I thought. It was everywhere these days, rich and poor neighborhoods both, like a nasty strain of social disease. Bumpersticker for the nineties: *Fear Lives.*

There were six mailboxes in the foyer, each with Dymo-Label stickers identifying the tenants. Gianna Fornessi's name was under box #4, along with a second name: Ashley Hansen. It figured that she'd have a roommate; salespersons working in the interior design trade are well but not extravagantly paid. Box #1 bore the name George Ferry and that was the bell I pushed. He was the one I wanted to talk to first.

A minute died away, while I listened to the wind that was savaging the trees on the hillside below. Out on the bay hundreds of sailboats formed a mosaic of white on blue. Somewhere among them a ship's horn sounded—to me, a sad false note. Shipping was all but dead on this side of the bay, thanks to wholesale mismanagement of the port over the past few decades.

The intercom crackled finally and a male voice said, "Who is it?" in wary tones.

I asked if he was George Ferry, and he admitted it, even more guardedly. I gave him my name, said that I was there to ask him a few questions about his complaint against Gianna Fornessi. He said, "Oh Christ." There was a pause, and then, "I called you people yesterday, I told Inspector Cullen I was dropping the charges. Isn't that enough?"

He thought I was a cop. I could have told him I wasn't; I could have let the whole thing drop right there, since what he'd just said was a perfect escape clause from my commitment to Pietro Lombardi. But I have too much curiosity to let go of something, once I've got a piece of it, without knowing the particulars. So I said, "I won't keep you long, Mr. Ferry. Just a few questions."

Another pause. "Is it really necessary?"

"I think it is, yes."

An even longer pause. But then he didn't argue, didn't say anything else—just buzzed me in.

His apartment was on the left, beyond a carpeted, dark-wood staircase. He opened the door as I approached it. Mid-forties, short, rotund, with a nose like a blob of putty and a Friar Tuck fringe of reddish hair. And a bruise on his left cheekbone, a cut along the right corner of his mouth. The marks weren't fresh, but then they weren't very old either. Twenty-four hours, maybe less.

He didn't ask to see a police ID; if he had I would have told him immediately that I was a private detective, because nothing can lose you a California investigator's license faster than impersonating a police officer. On the other hand, you can't be held accountable for somebody's false assumption. Ferry gave me a nervous once-over, holding his head tilted downward as if that would keep me from seeing his bruise and cut, then stood aside to let me come in.

The front room was neat, furnished in a self-consciously masculine fashion: dark woods, leather, expensive sporting prints. It reeked of leather, dust, and his lime-scented cologne.

As soon as he shut the door Ferry went straight to a liquor cabinet and poured himself three fingers of Jack Daniels, no water or mix, no ice. Just holding the drink seemed to give him courage. He said, "So. What is it you want to know?"

"Why you dropped your complaint against Gianna Fornessi."

"I explained to Inspector Cullen . . ."

"Explain to me, if you don't mind."

He had some of the sour mash. "Well, it was all a mistake . . . just a silly mistake. She didn't take the money after all."

"You know who did take it, then?"

"Nobody took it. I . . . misplaced it."

"Misplaced it. Uh-huh."

"I thought it was in my desk," Ferry said. "That's where I usually keep the cash I bring home. But I'd put it in my safe-deposit box along with some other papers, without realizing it. It was in an envelope, you see, and the envelope got mixed up with the other papers."

"Two thousand dollars is a lot of cash to keep at home. You make a habit of that sort of thing?"

"In my business . . ." The rest of the sentence seemed to hang up in his throat; he oiled the route with the rest of his drink. "In my business I need to keep a certain amount of cash on hand, both here and at the office. The amount I keep here isn't usually as large as two thousand dollars, but I—"

"What business are you in, Mr. Ferry?"

"I run a temp employment agency for domestics."

"Temp?"

"Short for temporary," he said. "I supply domestics for part-time work in offices and private homes. A lot of them are poor, don't have checking accounts, so they prefer to be paid in cash. Most come to the office, but a few—"

"Why did you think Gianna Fornessi had stolen the two thousand dollars?"

". . . What?"

"Why Gianna Fornessi? Why not somebody else?"

"She's the only one who was here. Before I thought the money was missing, I mean. I had no other visitors for two days and there wasn't any evidence of a break-in."

"You and she are good friends, then?"

"Well . . . no, not really. She's a lot younger . . ."

"Then why was she here?"

"The rent," Ferry said. "She was paying her rent for the month. I'm the building manager, I collect for the owner. Before I could write out a receipt I had a call, I was on the phone for quite a while and she . . . I didn't pay any attention to her and I thought she must have . . . you see why I thought she'd taken the money?"

I was silent.

He looked at me, looked at his empty glass, licked his lips, and went to commune with Jack Daniels again.

While he was pouring I asked him, "What happened to your face, Mr. Ferry?"

His hand twitched enough to clink bottle against glass. He had himself another taste before he turned back to me. "Clumsy," he said, "I'm clumsy as hell. I fell down the stairs, the front stairs, yesterday morning." He tried a laugh that didn't come off. "Fog makes the steps slippery. I just wasn't watching where I was going."

"Looks to me like somebody hit you."

"Hit me? No, I told you . . . I fell down the stairs."

"You're sure about that?"

"Of course I'm sure. Why would I lie about it?"

That was a good question. Why would he lie about that, and about all the rest of it too? There was about as much truth in what he'd told me as there is value in a chunk of fool's gold.

3

The young woman who opened the door of apartment #4 was not Gianna Fornessi. She was blond, with the kind of fresh-faced Nordic features you see on models for Norwegian ski wear. Tall and slender in a pair of green silk lounging pajamas; arms decorated with hammered gold bracelets, ears with dangly gold triangles. Judging from the expression in her pale eyes, there wasn't much going on behind them. But then, with her physical attributes, not many men would care if her entire brain had been surgically removed.

"Well," she said, "hello."

"Ashley Hansen?"

"That's me. Who're you?"

When I told her my name her smile brightened, as if I'd said something amusing or clever. Or maybe she just liked the sound of it.

"I knew right away you were Italian," she said. "Are you a friend of Jack's?"

"Jack?"

"Jack Bisconte." The smile dulled a little. "You are, aren't you?"

"No," I said, "I'm a friend of Pietro Lombardi."

"Who?"

"Your roommate's grandfather. I'd like to talk to Gianna, if she's home."

Ashley Hansen's smile was gone now; her whole demeanor had changed, become less self-assured. She nibbled at a corner of her lower lip, ran a hand through her hair, fiddled with one of her bracelets. Finally she said, "Gianna isn't here."

"When will she be back?"

"She didn't say."

"You know where I can find her?"

"No. What do you want to talk to her about?"

"The complaint George Ferry filed against her."

"Oh, that," she said. "That's all been taken care of."

"I know. I just talked to Ferry."

"He's a creepy little prick, isn't he."

"That's one way of putting it."

"Gianna didn't take his money. He was just trying to hassle her, that's all."

"Why would he do that?"

"Well, why do you think?"

I shrugged. "Suppose you tell me."

"He wanted her to do things."

"You mean go to bed with him?"

"Things," she said. "Kinky crap, *real* kinky."

"And she wouldn't have anything to do with him."

"No way, José. What a creep."

"So he made up the story about the stolen money to get back at her, is that it?"

"That's it."

"What made him change his mind, drop the charges?"

"He didn't tell you?"

"No."

"Who knows?" She laughed. "Maybe he got religion."

"Or a couple of smacks in the face."

"Huh?"

"Somebody worked him over yesterday," I said. "Bruised his cheek and cut his mouth. You have any idea who?"

"Not me, mister. How come you're so interested, anyway?"

"I told you, I'm a friend of Gianna's grandfather."

"Yeah, well."

"Gianna have a boyfriend, does she?"

". . . Why do you want to know that?"

"Jack Bisconte, maybe? Or is he yours?"

"He's just somebody I know." She nibbled at her lip again, did some more fiddling with her bracelets. "Look, I've got to go. You want me to tell Gianna you were here?"

"Yes." I handed her one of my business cards. "Give her this and ask her to call me."

She looked at the card; blinked at it and then blinked at me. "You . . . you're a detective?"

"That's right."

"My God," she said, and backed off, and shut the door in my face.

I stood there for a few seconds, remembering her eyes—the sudden fear in her eyes when she'd realized she had been talking to a detective.

What the hell?

4

North Beach used to be the place you went when you wanted *pasta fino*, expresso and biscotti, conversation about *la dolce vita* and *il patria d'Italia*. Not anymore. There are still plenty of Italians in North Beach, and you can still get the good food and some of the good conversation; but their turf continues to shrink a little more each year, and despite the best efforts of the entrepreneurial new immigrants, the vitality and most of the Old World atmosphere are just memories.

The Chinese are partly responsible, not that you can blame them for buying available North Beach real estate when Chinatown, to the west, began to burst its boundaries. Another culprit is the Bohemian element that took over upper Grant Avenue in the fifties, paving the way for the hippies and the introduction of hard drugs in the sixties, which in turn paved the way for the jolly current mix of motorcycle toughs, aging hippies, coke and crack dealers, and the pimps and small-time crooks who work the flesh palaces along lower Broadway. Those "Silicone Alley" nightclubs, made famous by Carol Doda in the late sixties, also share responsibility: they added a smutty leer to the gaiety of North Beach, turned the heart of it into a ghetto.

Parts of the neighborhood, particularly those up around Coit Tower where Gianna Fornessi lived, are still prime city real estate; and the area around Washington Square Park, *il giardino* to the original immigrants, is where the city's literati now congregates. Here and there, too, you can still get a sense of what it was like in the old days. But most of the landmarks are gone—Enrico's, Vanessi's, The Bocce Ball where you could hear mustachioed waiters in gondolier costumes singing arias from operas by Verdi and Puccini—and so is most of the flavor. North Beach is oddly tasteless now, like a week-old mostaccioli made without good spices or garlic. And that is another thing that is all but gone: twenty-five years ago you could not get within a thousand yards of North Beach without picking up the fine, rich fragrance of garlic. Nowadays you're much more likely to smell fried egg roll and the sour stench of somebody's garbage.

Parking in the Beach is the worst in the city; on weekends you can drive around its hilly streets for hours without finding a legal parking space. So today, in the perverse way of things, I found a spot waiting for me when I came down Stockton.

In a public telephone booth near Washington Square Park I discovered a second minor miracle: a directory that had yet to be either stolen or mutilated. The only Bisconte listed was Bisconte Florist Shop, with an address on upper Grant a few blocks away. I took myself off in that direction, through the usual good-weather Sunday crowds of locals and gawking sightseers and drifting homeless.

Upper Grant, like the rest of the area, has changed drastically over the past few decades. Once a rock-ribbed Little Italy, it has become an ethnic mixed bag: Italian markets, trattorias, pizza parlors, bakeries cheek by jowl with Chinese sewing-machine sweat shops, food and herb vendors, and fortune-cookie companies. But most of the faces on the streets are Asian and most of the apartments in the vicinity are occupied by Chinese.

The Bisconte Florist Shop was a hole-in-the-wall near Filbert, sandwiched between an Italian saloon and the Sip Hing Herb Company. It was open for business, not surprisingly on a Sunday in this neighborhood: tourists buy flowers too, given the opportunity.

The front part of the shop was cramped and jungly with cut flowers, ferns, plants in pots, and hanging baskets. A small glass-fronted cooler contained a variety of roses and orchids. There was nobody in sight, but a bell had gone off when I entered and a male voice from beyond a rear doorway called, "Be right with you." I shut the door, went up near the counter. Some people like florist shops; I don't. All of them have the same damp, cloyingly sweet smell that reminds me of funeral parlors; of my mother in her casket at the Figlia Brothers Mortuary in Daly City nearly forty years ago. That day, with all its smells, all its painful images, is as clear to me now as if it were yesterday.

I had been waiting about a minute when the voice's owner came out of the back room. Late thirties, dark, on the beefy side; wearing a professional smile and a floral-patterned apron that should have been ludicrous on a man of his size and coloring but wasn't. We had a good look at each other before he said, "Sorry to keep you waiting—I was putting up an arrangement. What can I do for you?"

"Mr. Bisconte? Jack Bisconte?"

"That's me. Something for the wife, maybe?"

"I'm not here for flowers. I'd like to ask you a few questions, if you don't mind."

The smile didn't waver. "Oh? What about?"

"Gianna Fornessi."

"Who?"

"You don't know her?"

"Name's not familiar, no."

"She lives up on Chestnut with Ashley Hansen."

"Ashley Hansen . . . I don't know that name either."

"She knows you. Young, blond, looks Norwegian."

"Well, I know a lot of young blondes," Bisconte said. He

winked at me. "I'm a bachelor and I get around pretty good, you know?"

"Uh-huh."

"Lot of bars and clubs in North beach, lot of women to pick and choose from." He shrugged. "So how come you're asking about these two?"

"Not both of them. Just Gianna Fornessi."

"That so? You a friend of hers?"

"Of her grandfather's. She's had a little trouble."

"What kind of trouble?"

"Manager of her building accused her of stealing some money. But somebody convinced him to drop the charges."

"That so?" Bisconte said again, but not as if he cared.

"Leaned on him to do it. Scared the hell out of him."

"You don't think it was me, do you? I told you, I don't know anybody named Gianna Fornessi."

"So you did."

"What's the big deal anyway?" he said. "I mean, if the guy dropped the charges, then this Gianna is off the hook, right?"

"Right."

"Then why all the questions?"

"Curiosity," I said. "Mine and her grandfather's."

Another shrug. "I'd like to help you, pal, but like I said, I don't know the lady. Sorry."

"Sure."

"Come back any time you need flowers," Bisconte said. He gave me a little salute, waited for me to turn and then did the same himself. He was hidden away again in the back room when I let myself out.

Today was my day for liars. Liars and puzzles.

He hadn't asked me who I was or what I did for a living; that was because he already knew. And the way he knew, I thought, was that Ashley Hansen had gotten on the horn after I left and told him about me. He knew Gianna Fornessi pretty well too, and exactly where the two women lived.

He was the man in the tan trenchcoat I'd seen earlier, the one who wouldn't hold the door for me at 7250 Chestnut.

5

I treated myself to a plate of linguine and fresh clams at a ristorante off Washington Square and then drove back over to Aquatic Park. Now, in mid-afternoon, with fog seeping in through the Gate and the temperature dropping sharply, the number of bocce players and kibitzers had thinned by half. Pietro Lombardi was one of those remaining; Dominick Marra was another. Bocce may be dying easy in the city but not in men like them. They cling to it and to the other old ways as tenaciously as they cling to life itself.

I told Pietro—and Dominick, who wasn't about to let us talk in private—what I'd learned so far. He was relieved that Ferry had dropped his complaint but just as curious as I was about the Jack Bisconte connection.

"Do you know Bisconte?" I asked him.

"No. I see his shop but I never go inside."

"Know anything about him?"

"*Niente.*"

"How about you, Dominick?"

He shook his head. "He's too old for Gianna, hah? Almost forty, you say—that's too old for girl twenty-three."

"If that's their relationship," I said.

"Men almost forty they go after young woman, they only got one reason. *Fatto 'na bella chiavata.* You remember, eh, Pietro?"

"*Pazzo!* You think I forget *'na bella chiavata?*"

I asked Pietro, "You know anything about Gianna's roommate?"

"Only once I meet her," he said. "Pretty, but not so pretty like my Gianna, *la bellezza delle bellezze.* I don't like her too much."

"Why not?"

"She don't have respect like she should."

"What does she do for a living, do you know?"

"No. She don't say and Gianna don't tell me."

"How long have they been sharing the apartment?"

"Eight, nine months."

"Did they know each other long before they moved in together?"

He shrugged. "Gianna and me, we don't talk much like when she's little girl," he said sadly. "Young people now, they got no time for *la familia.*" Another shrug, a sigh. *"Ognuno pensa per sè."* he said. Everybody thinks only of himself.

Dominick gripped his shoulder. Then he said to me, "You find out what's happen with Bisconte and Ferry and those girls. Then you see they don't bother them no more. Hah?"

"If I can, Dominick. If I can."

The fog was coming in thickly now and the other players were making noises about ending the day's tournament. Dominick got into an argument with one of them; he wanted to play another game or two. He was outvoted, but he was still pleading his case when I left. Their Sunday was almost over. So was mine.

I went home to my flat in Pacific Heights. And Kerry came over later on and we had dinner and listened to some jazz. I thought maybe Gianna Fornessi might call, but she didn't. No one called. Good thing, too. I would not have been pleased to hear the phone ring after eight o'clock; I was busy then.

Men in their late fifties are just as interested in *'na bella chiavata.* Women in their early forties, too.

6

At the office in the morning I called TRW for credit checks on Jack Bisconte, George Ferry, Gianna Fornessi, and Ashley Hansen. I also asked my partner, Eberhardt, who has been off the cops just a few years and who still has plenty of cronies sprinkled throughout the SFPD, to find out what Inspector Cullen and the Robbery Detail had on Ferry's theft complaint, and to have the four names run through R&I for any local arrest record.

The report out of Robbery told me nothing much. Ferry's complaint had been filed on Friday morning; Cullen had gone to investigate, talked to the two principals, and determined that there wasn't enough evidence to take Gianna Fornessi into custody. Thirty hours later Ferry had called in and withdrawn the complaint, giving the same flimsy reason he'd handed me. As far as Cullen and the department were concerned, it was all very minor and routine.

The TRW and R&I checks took a little longer to come through, but I had the information by noon. It went like this:

Jack Bisconte. Good credit rating. Owner and sole operator, Bisconte Florist Shop, since 1978; lived on upper Greenwich Street, in a rented apartment, same length of time. No listing of previous jobs held or previous local addresses. No felony or misdemeanor arrests.

George Ferry. Excellent credit rating. Owner and principal operator, Ferry Temporary Employment Agency, since 1972. Resident of 7250 Chestnut since 1980. No felony arrests; one DWI arrest and conviction following a minor traffic accident in May 1981, sentenced to ninety days in jail (suspended), driver's license revoked for six months.

Gianna Fornessi. Fair to good credit rating. Employed by Home Draperies, Showplace Square, as a sales representative since 1988. Resident of 7250 Chestnut for eight months; address prior to that, her parents' home in Daly City. No felony or misdemeanor arrests.

Ashley Hansen. No credit rating. No felony or misdemeanor arrests.

There wasn't much in any of that, either, except for the fact that TRW had no listing on Ashley Hansen. Almost everybody uses credit cards these days, establishes some kind of credit— especially a young woman whose income is substantial enough to afford an apartment in one of the city's best neighborhoods. Why not Ashley Hansen?

She was one person who could tell me; another was Gianna Fornessi. I had yet to talk to Pietro's granddaughter and I thought it was high time. I left the office in Eberhardt's care, picked up my car, and drove south of Market to Showplace Square.

The Square is a newish complex of manufacturer's show-rooms for the interior decorating trade—carpets, draperies, lighting fixtures, and other types of home furnishings. It's not open to the public, but I showed the photostat of my license to one of the security men at the door and talked him into calling

the Home Draperies showroom and asking them to send Gianna
Fornessi out to talk to me.

They sent somebody out, but it wasn't Gianna Fornessi.
It was a fluffy looking little man in his forties named Lundquist, who said, "I'm sorry, Ms. Fornessi is no longer employed
by us."

"Oh? When did she leave?"

"Eight months ago."

"Eight *months?*"

"At the end of September."

"Quit or terminated?"

"Quit. Rather abruptly, too."

"To take another job?"

"I don't know. She gave no adequate reason."

"No one called afterward for a reference?"

"No one," Lundquist said.

"She worked for you two years, is that right?"

"About two years, yes."

"As a sales representative?"

"That's correct."

"May I ask her salary?"

"I really couldn't tell you that . . ."

"Just this, then: Was hers a high-salaried position? In excess
of thirty thousand a year, say?"

Lundquist smiled a faint, fluffy smile. "Hardly," he said.

"Were her skills such that she could have taken another,
better-paying job in the industry?"

Another fluffy smile. And another "Hardly."

So why had she quit Home Draperies so suddenly eight
months ago, at just about the same time she moved into the
Chestnut Street apartment with Ashley Hansen? And what was
she doing to pay her share of the rent?

7

There was an appliance store delivery truck double-parked in
front of 7250 Chestnut, and when I went up the stairs I found
the entrance door wedged wide open. Nobody was in the
vestibule or lobby, but the murmur of voices filtered down

from the third floor. If I'd been a burglar I would have rubbed my hands together in glee. As it was, I walked in as if I belonged there and climbed the inside staircase to the second floor.

When I swung off the stairs I came face to face with Jack Bisconte.

He was hurrying toward me from the direction of apartment #4, something small and red and rectangular clutched in the fingers of his left hand. He broke stride when he saw me; and then recognition made him do a jerky double take and he came to a halt. I stopped, too, with maybe fifteen feet separating us. That was close enough, and the hallway was well-lighted enough, for me to get a good look at his face. It was pinched, sweat-slicked, the eyes wide and shiny—the face of a man on the cutting edge of panic.

Frozen time, maybe five seconds of it, while we stood staring at each other. There was nobody else in the hall; no audible sounds on this floor except for the quick rasp of Bisconte's breathing. Then we both moved at the same time—Bisconte in the same jerky fashion of his double take, shoving the red object into his coat pocket as he came forward. And then, when we had closed the gap between us by half, we both stopped again as if on cue. It might have been a mildly amusing little pantomime if you'd been a disinterested observer. It wasn't amusing to me. Or to Bisconte, from the look of him.

I said, "Fancy meeting you here. I thought you didn't know Gianna Fornessi or Ashley Hansen."

"Get out of my way."

"What's your hurry?"

"Get out of my way. I mean it." The edge of panic had cut into his voice; it was thick, liquidy, as if it were bleeding.

"What did you put in your pocket, the red thing?"

He said, "Christ!" and tried to lunge past me.

I blocked his way, getting my hands up between us to push him back. He made a noise in his throat and swung at me. It was a clumsy shot; I ducked away from it without much effort, so that his knuckles just grazed my neck. But then the son of a bitch kicked me, hard, on the left shinbone. I yelled and went down. He kicked out again, this time at my head; didn't connect because I was already rolling away. I fetched up tight against the wall and by the time I got myself twisted back around he was pelting toward the stairs.

I shoved up the wall to my feet, almost fell again when I put weight on the leg he'd kicked. Hobbling, wiping pain-wet out of my eyes, I went after him. People were piling down from the third floor; the one in the lead was George Ferry. He called something that I didn't listen to as I started to descend. Bisconte, damn him, had already crossed the lobby and was running out through the open front door.

Hop, hop, hop down the stairs like a contestant in a one-legged race, using the railing for support. By the time I reached the lobby, some of the sting had gone out of my shinbone and I could put more weight on the leg. Out into the vestibule, half running and half hobbling now, looking for him. He was across the street and down a ways, fumbling with a set of keys at the driver's door of a new silver Mercedes.

But he didn't stay there long. He was too wrought up to get the right key into the lock, and when he saw me pounding across the street in his direction, the panic goosed him and he ran again. Around behind the Mercedes, onto the sidewalk, up and over the concrete retaining wall. And gone.

I heard him go sliding or tumbling through the undergrowth below. I staggered up to the wall, leaned over it. The slope down there was steep, covered with trees and brush, strewn with the leavings of semi-humans who had used it for a dumping ground. Bisconte was on his buttocks, digging hands and heels into the ground to slow his momentum. For a few seconds I thought he was going to turn into a one-man avalanche and plummet over the edge where the slope ended in a sheer bluff face. But then he managed to catch hold of one of the tree trunks and swing himself away from the bluff, in among a tangle of bushes where I couldn't see him anymore. I could hear him —and then I couldn't. He'd found purchase, I thought, and was easing himself down to where the backside of another apartment building leaned in against the cliff.

There was no way I was going down there after him. I turned and went to the Mercedes.

It had a vanity plate, the kind that makes you wonder why somebody would pay twenty-five dollars extra to the DMV to put it on his car: BISFLWR. If the Mercedes had had an external hood release I would have popped it and disabled the engine; but it didn't, and all four doors were locked. All right. Chances were, he wouldn't risk coming back soon—and even if he ran the risk, it would take him a good long while to get here.

I limped back to 7250. Four people were clustered in the vestibule, staring at me—Ferry and a couple of uniformed deliverymen and a fat woman in her forties. Ferry said as I came up the steps, "What happened, what's going on?" I didn't answer him. There was a bad feeling in me now; or maybe it had been there since I'd first seen the look on Bisconte's face. I pushed through the cluster—none of them tried to stop me—and crossed the lobby and went up to the second floor.

Nobody answered the bell at apartment #4. I tried the door, and it was unlocked, and I opened it and walked in and shut it again and locked it behind me.

She was lying on the floor in the living room, sprawled and bent on her back near a heavy teak coffee table, peach-colored dressing gown hiked up over her knees; head twisted at an off-angle, blood and a deep triangular puncture wound on her left temple. The blood was still wet and clotting. She hadn't been dead much more than an hour.

In the sunlight that spilled in through the undraped windows, the blood had a kind of shimmery radiance. So did her hair— her long gold blond hair.

Goodbye Ashley Hansen.

8

I called the Hall of Justice and talked to a Homicide inspector I knew slightly named Craddock. I told him what I'd found, and about my little skirmish with Jack Bisconte, and said that yes, I would wait right here and no, I wouldn't touch anything. He didn't tell me not to look around and I didn't say that I wouldn't.

Somebody had started banging on the door. Ferry, probably. I went the other way, into one of the bedrooms. Ashley Hansen's: there was a photograph of her prominently displayed on the dresser, and lots of mirrors to give her a live image of herself. A narcissist, among other things. On one nightstand was a telephone and an answering machine. On the unmade bed, tipped on its side with some of the contents spilled out, was a fancy leather purse. I used the backs of my two index fingers to stir around among the spilled items and the stuff inside. Everything you'd expect to find in a woman's purse—and one thing that should have been there and wasn't.

Gianna Fornessi's bedroom was across the hall. She also had a telephone and an answering machine; the number on the telephone dial was different from her roommate's. I hesitated for maybe five seconds, then I went to the answering machine and pushed the button marked "playback calls" and listened to two old messages before I stopped the tape and rewound it. One message would have been enough.

Back into the living room. The knocking was still going on. I started over there; stopped after a few feet and stood sniffing the air. I thought I smelled something—a faint lingering acrid odor. Or maybe I was just imagining it . . .

Bang, bang, bang. And Ferry's voice: "What's going on in there?"

I moved ahead to the door, threw the bolt lock, yanked the door open. "Quit making so damned much noise."

Ferry blinked and backed off a step; he didn't know whether to be afraid of me or not. Behind and to one side of him, the two deliverymen and the fat woman looked on with hungry eyes. They would have liked seeing what lay inside; blood attracts some people, the gawkers, the insensitive ones, the same way it attracts flies.

"What's happened?" Ferry asked nervously.

"Come in and see for yourself. Just you."

I opened up a little wider and he came in past me, showing reluctance. I shut and locked the door again behind him. And when I turned he said, "Oh my God," in a sickened voice. He was staring at the body on the floor, one hand pressed up under his breastbone. "Is she. . . ?"

"Very."

"Gianna . . . is she here?"

"No."

"Somebody did that to Ashley? It wasn't an accident?"

"What do you think?"

"Who? Who did it?"

"You know who, Ferry. You saw me chase him out of here."

"I . . . don't know who he is. I never saw him before."

"The hell you never saw him. He's the one put those cuts and bruises on your face."

"No," Ferry said, "that's not true." He looked and sounded even sicker now. "I told you how that happened . . ."

"You told me lies. Bisconte roughed you up so you'd drop your complaint against Gianna. He did it because Gianna and Ashley Hansen have been working as call girls and he's their pimp and he didn't want the cops digging into her background and finding out the truth."

Ferry leaned unsteadily against the wall, facing away from what was left of the Hansen woman. He didn't speak.

"Nice quiet little operation they had," I said, "until you got wind of it. That's how it was, wasn't it? You found out and you wanted some of what Gianna's been selling."

Nothing for ten seconds. Then, softly, "It wasn't like that, not at first. I . . . loved her."

"Sure you did."

"I *did.* But she wouldn't have anything to do with me."

"So then you offered to pay her."

". . . Yes. Whatever she charged."

"Only you wanted kinky sex and she wouldn't play."

"No! I never asked for anything except a night with her . . . one night. She pretended to be insulted; she denied that she's been selling herself to men. She . . . she said she'd never go to bed with a man as . . . ugly . . ." He moved against the wall—a writhing movement, as if he were in pain.

"That was when you decided to get even with her."

"I wanted to hurt her, the way she'd hurt me. It was stupid, I know that, but I wasn't thinking clearly. I just wanted to hurt her . . ."

"Well, you succeeded," I said. "But the one you really hurt is Ashley Hansen. If it hadn't been for you, she'd still be alive."

He started to say something but the words were lost in the sudden summons of the doorbell.

"That'll be the police," I said.

"The police? But . . . I thought you were . . ."

"I know you did. I never told you I was, did I?"
I left him holding up the wall and went to buzz them in.

9

I spent more than two hours in the company of the law,
alternately answering questions and waiting around. I told
Inspector Craddock how I happened to be there. I told him
how I'd come to realize that Gianna Fornessi and Ashley Hansen
were call girls, and how George Ferry and Jack Bisconte figured
into it. I told him about the small red rectangular object I'd
seen Bisconte shove into his pocket—an address book, no
doubt, with the names of some of Hansen's johns. That was the
common item that was missing from her purse.

Craddock seemed satisfied. I wished I was.

When he finally let me go I drove back to the office. But I
didn't stay long; it was late afternoon, Eberhardt had already
gone for the day, and I felt too restless to tackle the stack of
routine paperwork on my desk. I went out to Ocean Beach and
walked on the sand, as I sometimes do when an edginess is on
me. It helped a little—not much.

I ate an early dinner out, and when I got home I put in a call
to the Hall of Justice to ask if Jack Bisconte had been picked up
yet. But Craddock was off duty and the inspector I spoke to
wouldn't tell me anything.

The edginess stayed with me all evening, and kept me awake
past midnight. I knew what was causing it, all right; and I knew
what to do to get rid of it. Only I wasn't ready to do it yet.

In the morning, after eight, I called the Hall again. Craddock
came on duty at eight, I'd been told. He was there and willing
to talk, but what he had to tell me was not what I wanted to
hear. Bisconte was in custody but not because he'd been
apprehended. At eight-thirty Monday night he'd walked into the
North Beach precinct station with his lawyer in tow and given
himself up. He'd confessed to being a pimp for the two women;
he'd confessed to working over George Ferry; he'd confessed
to being in the women's apartment just prior to his tussle with
me. But he swore up and down that he hadn't killed Ashley
Hansen. He'd never had any trouble with her, he said; in fact

he'd been half in love with her. The cops had Gianna Fornessi in custody too by this time, and she'd confirmed that there had never been any rough stuff or bad feelings between her room-mate and Bisconte.

Hansen had been dead when he got to the apartment, Bisconte said. Fear that he'd be blamed had pushed him into a panic. He'd taken the address book out of her purse—he hadn't thought about the answering machine tapes or he'd have erased the messages left by eager johns—and when he'd encountered me in the hallway he'd lost his head completely. Later, after he'd had time to calm down, he'd gone to the lawyer, who had advised him to turn himself in.

Craddock wasn't so sure Bisconte was telling the truth, but I was. I knew who had been responsible for Ashley Hansen's death; I'd known it a few minutes after I found her body. I just hadn't wanted it to be that way.

I didn't tell Craddock any of this. When he heard the truth it would not be over the phone. And it would not be from me.

10

It did not take me long to track him down. He wasn't home but a woman in his building said that in nice weather he liked to sit in Washington Square Park with his cronies. That was where I found him, in the park. Not in the company of anyone; just sitting alone on a bench across from the Saints Peter and Paul Catholic church, in the same slump-shouldered, bowed-head posture as when I'd first seen him on Sunday—the posture of *la miseria.*

I sat down beside him. He didn't look at me, not even when I said, *"Buon giorno,* Pietro."

He took out one of his twisted black cigars and lit it carefully with a kitchen match. Its odor was acrid on the warm morning air—the same odor that had been in his granddaughter's apartment, that I'd pretended to myself I was imagining. Nothing smells like a Toscana; nothing. And only old men like Pietro smoke Toscanas these days. They don't even have to smoke one in a closed room for the smell to linger after them; it gets into and comes off the heavy user's clothing.

"It's time for us to talk," I said.

"Che sopra?"

"Ashley Hansen. How she died."

A little silence. Then he sighed and said, "You already know, hah, good detective like you? How you find out?"

"Does it matter?"

"It don't matter. You tell police yet?"

"It'll be better if you tell them."

More silence, while he smoked his little cigar.

I said, "But first tell me. Exactly what happened."

He shut his eyes; he didn't want to relive what had happened.

"It was me telling you about Bisconte that started it," I said to prod him. "After you got home Sunday night you called Gianna and asked her about him. Or she called you."

"I call her," he said. "She's angry, she tell me mind my own business. Never before she talks to her goombah this way."

"Because of me. Because she was afraid of what I'd find out about her and Ashley Hansen and Bisconte."

"Bisconte." He spat the name, as if ridding his mouth of something foul.

"So this morning you asked around the neighborhood about him. And somebody told you he wasn't just a florist, about his little sideline. Then you got on a bus and went to see your granddaughter."

"I don't believe it, not about Gianna. I want her tell me it's not true. But she's not there. Only the other one, the *bionda.*"

"And then?"

"She don't want to let me in, that one. I go in anyway. I ask if she and Gianna are . . . if they sell themselves for money. She laugh. In my face she laugh, this girl what have no respect. She says what difference it make? She says I am old man—dinosaur, she says. But she pat my cheek like I am little boy or big joke. Then she . . . ah, *Cristo,* she come up close to me and she say you want some, old man, I give you some. To me she says this. Me." Pietro shook his head; there were tears in his eyes now. "I push her away. I feel . . . *feroce,* like when I am young man and somebody he make trouble with me. I push her too hard and she fall, her head hit the table and I see blood and she don't move . . . ah, *mio Dio!* She was wicked, that one, but I don't mean to hurt her . . ."

"I know you didn't, Pietro."

"I think, call doctor quick. But she is dead. And I hurt here, inside"—he tapped his chest—"and I think, what if Gianna she come home? I don't want to see Gianna. You understand? Never again I want to see her."

"I understand," I said. And I thought: Funny—I've never laid eyes on her, not even a photograph of her. I don't know what she looks like; now I don't want to know. I never want to see her either.

Pietro finished his cigar. Then he straightened on the bench, seemed to compose himself. His eyes had dried; they were clear and sad. He looked past me, across at the looming Romanesque pile of the church. "I make confession to priest," he said, "little while before you come. Now we go to police and I make confession to them."

"Yes."

"You think they put me in gas chamber?"

"I doubt they'll put you in prison at all. It was an accident. Just a bad accident."

Another silence. On Pietro's face was an expression of the deepest pain. "This thing, this accident, she shouldn't have happen. Once . . . ah, once . . ." Pause. *"Morto,"* he said.

He didn't mean the death of Ashley Hansen. He meant the death of the old days, the days when families were tightly knit and there was respect for elders, the days when bocce was king of his world and that world was a far simpler and better place. The bitterest of woes is to remember old happy days . . .

We sat there in the pale sun. And pretty soon he said, in a voice so low I barely heard the words, *"La bellezza delle bellezze."* Twice before he had used that phrase in my presence and both times he had been referring to his granddaughter. This time I knew he was not.

"Si, 'paesano," I said. *"La bellezza delle bellezze."*

RUTH RENDELL

MOTHER'S HELP

Ruth Rendell is probably the most honored mystery writer of our time, both in America and in her native England. She recently won the Crime Writers Association Gold Dagger for her Barbara Vine novel, King Solomon's Carpet, *bringing her total in England to a Diamond Dagger, four Gold Daggers, one Silver Dagger, an Arts Council National Book Award, the Angel Award, the Current Crime Silver Cup, and the Sunday Times Award for Literary Excellence. In America she has won three Edgars from MWA, one for best novel and two for best short story. This novelette, which had its first American appearance in her collection* The Copper Peacock and Other Stories, *is one of her best.*

1

The little boy would be three at the end of the year. He was big for his age. Nell, who was his nanny but modestly called herself a mother's help, was perturbed by his inability, or unwillingness, to speak. It was very likely no more than unwillingness, for Daniel was not deaf, that was apparent, and the doctor who carried out tests on him said he was intelligent. His parents and Nell knew that without being told.

He was inordinately fond of motor vehicles. No one knew why, since neither Ivan nor Charlotte took any particular interest in cars. They had one of course and both drove it, but Charlotte confessed that she had never understood the workings of the internal combustion engine. Their son's passion amused them. When he woke up in the morning he got into bed with them and ran toy trucks and miniature tractors over the pillows, shouting, "Brrm, brrm, brrm . . ."

"Say 'car,' Daniel," said Charlotte. "Say 'lorry.' "

"Brrm, brrm, brrm," said Daniel.

One of the things he liked to do was sit in the driver's seat on Ivan's knee or Charlotte's and, strictly supervised, pull the levers and buttons that worked the windscreen wipers, the lights, put the automatic transmission into "drive," make the light come on that flashed when the passenger failed to wear a seat belt, lift off the handbrake, and, naturally, sound the horn. All the time he was doing these things he was saying, "Brrm, brrm, brrm." The summer before he was three he said "car" and "tractor" and "engine" as well as "brrm, brrm, brrm." He had been able to say "Mummy" and "Daddy" and "Nell" for quite a long time. Soon his vocabulary grew large and Nell stopped worrying, though Daniel made no attempt to form sentences.

"It may be because he's an only child," she said to Ivan one evening when she came down from putting Daniel to bed.

"And likely to remain one," said Ivan, "under the circumstances."

He kept his voice low. Charlotte had stayed late at work, but she was home now, taking off her raincoat in the hall. Because Charlotte was there Nell made no reply to this cryptic remark of Ivan's. She tried to smile in a reproachful way but failed. Charlotte went upstairs to say goodnight to Daniel and in a little while Ivan went up too. Alone, Nell thought how handsome Ivan was and how there was something very masterful, not to say ruthless, about him. The idea of Ivan's ruthlessness made her feel quite excited. Charlotte was the sort of woman people call "attractive," without meaning that they, or any others in particular, were attracted by her. Nell guessed that she was quite a lot older than Ivan or perhaps she just looked older.

"I wish I'd met you four years ago," Ivan said one afternoon when Charlotte was at work and he had taken the day off. He had been married nearly four years. Nell had seen the cards he and Charlotte got for their third wedding anniversary.

"I was only seventeen then," she said. "I was still at school."

"What difference does that make?"

Daniel was pushing a miniature Land Rover along the windowsill and along the skirting board and up the side of the doorframe, saying, "Brrm, brrm." He got up onto a chair, fell off, and started screaming. Nell picked him up and held him in her arms.

"You look so lovely," said Ivan. "You look like a Murillo madonna."

Ivan was the owner of the picture gallery in Mayfair and knowledgeable about things like that. He asked Nell if it wasn't time for Daniel's sleep, but Nell said he was getting too old to sleep in the daytime and she usually took him out for a walk. "I shall come with you," said Ivan.

It was August and business was slack—though not Charlotte's business—and Ivan began taking days off more often. He told Charlotte he liked to be with Daniel as much as possible. Unless they weren't put to bed till some ridiculously late hour of the night, children grew up hardly knowing their fathers.

"Or their mothers," said Charlotte.

"No one obliges you to work."

"That's true. I'm thinking of giving up and then we wouldn't need to keep Nell on."

Nell couldn't drive. When she went shopping Ivan drove her. He came home specially early to do this. The house was a detached Victorian villa and the garage a converted coach house with a door that pulled down rather like a roller blind. When the car had been backed out it was tiresome to have to get out and pull down the door, but leaving the garage open was, as Charlotte said, an invitation to burglars. Nell sat in the front, in the passenger seat, and Daniel in the back. In those days safety belts in the rear of cars had scarcely been thought of and child seats were unusual.

It happened very suddenly. Ivan left the car in "park" and the handbrake on and went to close the garage door. Fortunately for him, he noticed a pool of what seemed to be oil at the back of the garage on the concrete floor and took a step or two inside to investigate. Daniel, with a shout of "Brrm, brrm!" but without any other warning, lunged forward across the top of the driver's seat and made a grab for the controls. He flipped on the lights, made the full beam blaze, whipped the transmission into "drive," sent sprays of water across the windscreen, and tugged off the handbrake.

The car shot forward with blazing lights. Nell screamed. She didn't know how to stop it, she didn't know what the handbrake was, where the footbrake was, she could only seize hold of laughing, triumphant Daniel. The car, descending the few feet of slope, charged into the garage, slowing as it met level ground, sliding almost to a stop while Ivan stood on tiptoe, flattening himself against the wall.

Nell began to cry. She was very frightened. Seeing Ivan in danger made her understand all kinds of things about herself and him she hadn't realized before. He came out and switched off the engine and carried Daniel back into the house. Nell followed, still crying. Ivan took her in his arms and kissed her. Her knees felt weak and she thought she might faint, from shock perhaps or perhaps not. Ivan forced her lips apart with his tongue and put his tongue in her mouth and said after a moment or two that they should go upstairs. Not with Daniel in the house, Nell moaned.

"Daniel is always in the bloody house," said Ivan.

When Charlotte came home they told her what Daniel had done. They didn't feel like talking, especially to Charlotte, but it would have looked unnatural to say nothing. Charlotte said Ivan should speak to Daniel, he should speak to him very gently but very firmly too and explain to him that what he had done was extremely naughty. It was dangerous and might have hurt Daddy. So Ivan took Daniel on his knee and gave him a lecture in a kind but serious way, impressing on him that he must never again do what he had done that afternoon.

"Daniel drive car," said Daniel.

It was the first sentence any of them had heard him speak, and Charlotte, in spite of the seriousness of the occasion, was enraptured. They thought it wiser to tell no one else about what had happened, but this resolve was quickly broken. Charlotte told her mother and her mother-in-law, and Nell confessed to Charlotte that she had told her boyfriend. Nell didn't in fact have a boyfriend, but she wanted Charlotte to think she had. Their doctor and his wife came to dinner and they told him. Ivan knew he had repeated the story to the doctor (and the four other guests at the table) because it was an example of the intelligence of a child some people might otherwise be starting to think of as backward. When an opportunity arose, he told the two women who worked for him at the gallery and Charlotte told her boss and the girl who did her typing.

In September Charlotte took two weeks' holiday. Business hadn't yet picked up at the gallery and they could have gone away somewhere but that would have meant taking Nell with them and Charlotte didn't want to pay some extortionate hotel bill for her as well. She was going to stay at home with her son and Nell could have the afternoons off. Charlotte's mother had said that in her opinion Nell was stealing Daniel's affections in an indefensible way. Ivan took Nell to a motel on the A12 where he pretended they were a married couple on their way to Harwich en route for a weekend in Amsterdam.

Nell had been nervous about this aspect of things at first but now she was so much in love with Ivan that she wanted him to be making love to her all the time. Every time she saw him, which was for hours of every day, she wanted him to be making love to her.

"I shall have to think what's to be done," said Ivan in the motel room. "We can't just go off together."

"Oh, no, I see that. You'd lose your little boy."

"I'd lose my house and half my income," said Ivan.

They got home very late, Ivan coming in first, Nell half an hour later by prearrangement. Ivan told Charlotte he had been working until eleven getting ready for a private view. She wasn't sure that she believed him, but she believed Nell when Nell said she had been to the cinema with her boyfriend. Nell was always out with this boyfriend, it was evidently serious, and Charlotte wasn't sorry. Nell would get married, and married women don't remain as live-in mother's helps. If Nell left she wouldn't have to sack her. She was having strange feelings about Nell, though she couldn't exactly define what they were, perhaps no more than fear of Daniel's preferring the mother's help to herself.

"He'll go to her before he goes to you," said Charlotte's mother. "You want to watch that."

He was always on Nell's lap, hugging her. He liked her to bathe him. It was Nell who was favored when a bedtime story was to be read, sweet-faced Nell with the soft blue eyes and the long fair hair. He seemed particularly to like the touch of her slim fingers and to press himself close against her. One Saturday morning when Nell was cutting up vegetables for his lunch, Daniel ran up behind her and threw his arms round her legs. Nell hadn't heard him coming, the knife slipped and she cut her left hand in a long gash across the forefinger and palm.

2

The cut extended from the first joint of the forefinger, diagonally across to the wrist, following the course of what palmists call the lifeline. The sight of blood, especially her own, upset Nell. She had given one loud cry, and now she was making frightened whimpering sounds. Blood was pouring out of her hand, spouting out in little leaps like an oil well she had seen on television. It dripped off the edge of the counter, and Daniel, who wasn't at all upset by the sight of it, caught the drips on his forefinger and drew squiggles on the cupboard door.

Charlotte, coming into the kitchen, guessed what had happened and was cross. If Nell hadn't encouraged Daniel in these displays of affection he wouldn't have hugged her like that and she wouldn't have cut herself. He should have been out in the fresh air hugging his mother who had a trowel, not a knife, in her hand. Charlotte had been looking forward to an early lunch so that she could spend the afternoon planting twelve Little Pet roses in the circular bed in the front garden.

"You'll have to have that stitched," she said. "You'll have to have an antitetanus injection." What Daniel was doing registered with her and she pulled him away. "That's very naughty and disgusting, Daniel!" Daniel began to scream and punch at Charlotte with his fists.

"Shall I have to go to hospital?" said Nell.

"Of course you will. We'll get that tied up; we'll have to try and stop the bleeding." Ivan was in the house, upstairs in the room he called his study. It would be more convenient for Charlotte if she could get Ivan to drive Nell to the hospital, but unaccountably she felt a sudden strong dislike of this idea. It hadn't occurred to her before, but she didn't want to leave Ivan alone with Nell again. "I'll drive you. We'll take Daniel with us."

"Couldn't we leave him with Ivan?" said Nell, who had wrapped a tea cloth tightly round her hand and was watching the blood work its way through the pattern, which was a map of Scotland. "We could tell Ivan and ask him to look after Daniel. Perhaps," she added hopefully, "we won't be very long."

"I'd appreciate it if you didn't interfere with my arrangements," said Charlotte very sharply.

Nell started crying. Daniel, who was still crying into Charlotte's shoulder, reached out his arms to her. With an exclamation of impatience, Charlotte handed him over. She washed the earth off her hands at the kitchen sink while Nell sniffled and crooned over Daniel. They took coats from the rack in the hall, Charlotte happening to grab an olive green padded jacket her mother-in-law had left behind, and went out through the front door. The twelve roses lay in a circle along the edge of the flowerbed, their roots wrapped in green plastic. Nell stood in the garage drive cuddling Daniel, the tea cloth not providing a very effective bandage. Blood had now entirely obscured Caithness and Sutherland. Looking down at it, Nell began to feel faint, and it was quite a different sort of faintness from the way she felt when Ivan started kissing her.

Charlotte raised the garage door, got into the car, and backed it out. She took Daniel from Nell and put him in the backseat, where he kept a fleet of small motor vehicles, trucks and tanks and saloon cars. Already regretting that she had spoken so harshly to Nell, she opened the passenger door for her. Pale, pretty Nell in a very becoming thin black raincoat, had grown fragile from shock and pain.

"You'd better sit down. Put your head back and close your eyes. You're as white as a sheet."

"Brrm, brrm," said Daniel, running a Triumph Dolomite up the back of the driver's seat.

Since Ivan was in the house there was no need to close the garage door. It occurred to Charlotte that, antagonistic toward him though she felt, she had better tell him they were going out and where they were going. But before she reached the front door it opened and Ivan came out.

"What's happened? Why was everyone yelling?"

She told him. He said, "I shall drive Nell to hospital. Naturally,

I want to drive her, I should have thought you'd know that. I can't understand why you didn't come and tell me as soon as this happened."

Charlotte said nothing. She was thinking. She seemed to hear in Ivan's voice a note of unusual concern, the kind of care a man might show for someone close and dear to him. And, incongruously, that look of his that had originally attracted her to him, had returned. More than ever he resembled some brigand or pirate who required for perfect conviction only a pair of gold earrings or a knife between his teeth.

"There's absolutely no need for you to go," he said in the rough way he had lately got into the habit of using to her. "It's pointless a great crowd of us going."

Putting two and two together, seeing all kinds of things fall delicately into place, recalling lonely evenings and bizarre excuses, Charlotte said, "I am certainly going. I am going to that hospital if it's the last thing I do."

"Suit yourself."

Ivan got into the driver's seat. He said to Nell. "Bear up, sweetheart, what a bloody awful thing to happen."

Nell opened her eyes and gave him a wan smile, pushing back with her good hand the curtain of daffodil colored hair that had fallen across her pale tearful face. In the back, Daniel put his arms round his father's neck from behind and ran the Triumph Dolomite up the lapels of his jacket.

"The least you could do is close the garage door," Charlotte shouted. "That's all we need, to come back and find someone's been in and nicked the stereo."

Ivan didn't move. He was looking at Nell. Charlotte walked down the drive to the garage door. With her back to the bonnet of the car, she reached up for the recessed handle in the door to pull it down. The green padded jacket went badly with the blue cord trousers and it made her look fat.

His hands on the steering wheel, Ivan turned slowly to look at her. Daniel was hanging on to his neck now, pushing the toy car up under Ivan's chin. "Brrm, brrm, brrm!"

"Stop that, Daniel, please. Don't do that."

"Drive car," said Daniel.

"All right," said Ivan. "Why not?"

He put the transmission into "drive," all the lights on, set the windscreen jets spouting, the wipers going, took off the hand-brake and stamped his foot hard on the accelerator. As the car plunged forward, Charlotte, who had pulled the door down to its fullest extent and was still bending over, sprang up, alerted by the blaze of light. She gave a loud scream, flinging out her hands as if to hold back the car. In that moment Nell, her eyes jerked open, her body propelled forward almost against the windscreen, saw Charlotte's face as if both their faces had swung to meet each other. Charlotte's face seemed to loom and grimace like a bogey in a ghost tunnel. It was a sight Nell was never to forget, Charlotte's expression of horror, and the knowl-edge that was also there, the awareness of why.

The weak hands, the desperate arms, were ineffectual against the juggernaut propulsion of the big car. Charlotte fell back-ward, crying out, screaming. The bonnet obscured her fall, the wheels went over her, as the car burst through the garage door, which against this onslaught was as flimsy as a roller blind.

Fragments of shattered door fell all over the bonnet and roof of the car. A triangular-shaped slice of it split the windscreen and turned it into a sheet of frosted glass. Nell was jumping up and down in her seat, making hysterical shrieks, but on the back seat, Daniel, who had retreated into the corner behind his father, was silent, holding a piece of the hem of his coat in his fingers and pushing it into his mouth.

Blinded by the whitening and cobwebbing of the glass, Ivan recoiled from it, put his foot on the brake, and pulled on the handbrake. The car emitted a deep musical note, like a rich chord drawn from a church organ, as it sometimes did when brought to a sudden stop. Ivan lifted his hands from the wheel, tossed his head as if to shake back a fallen lock of hair, and rested against the seat, closing his eyes. He breathed deeply and steadily, like someone about to fall asleep.

"Ivan," screamed Nell, "Ivan, Ivan, Ivan!"

He turned his head with infinite slowness, and when it was fully turned to face her, opened his eyes. Meeting his eyes had the immediate effect of silencing her. She whimpered. He put out his hand and touched the side of her cheek, not with his fingertips but very gently with his knuckles. He ran his knuckles along the line of her jaw and the curve of her neck.

"Your hand has stopped bleeding," he said in a whisper.

She looked down at the bundle in her lap, a red sodden mass. She didn't know why he said that or what he meant. "Oh, Ivan, Ivan, is she dead? She must be dead—is she?"

"I'm going to get you back into the house."

"I don't want to go into the house, I want to die, I just want to give up and die!"

"Yes, well, on second thought it might be best for you to stay where you are. Just for a while. And Daniel too. I shall go and phone the police."

She got hold of him as he tried to get out. She got hold of his jacket and held on, weeping. "Oh, Ivan, Ivan, what have you done?"

"Don't you mean," he said, "what has Daniel done?"

3

When he came back from his investigations underneath the car, Ivan knelt on the driver's seat. He brought his face very close to hers. "I'm going back into the house. I was in the house when it happened. I came running out when I heard the crash, and as soon as I saw what had happened I went back in to call the police and an ambulance."

"I don't understand what you mean," said Nell.

"Yes, you do. Think about it. I was upstairs in my study. You were alone in the car with Daniel, resting your head back with your eyes closed."

"Oh, no, Ivan, no. I couldn't say that, I couldn't tell people that."

"You needn't tell them anything. You can be in a state of shock, you are in a state of shock. Telling people things will come later. You'll be fine by then."

Nell put her hands up to her face, her right hand and the bandaged one. She peered out between her fingers like a child that has had a fright. "Is she—is she dead?"

"Oh, yes, she's dead," said Ivan.

"Oh my God, my God, and she said she was coming to the hospital if it was the last thing she did!"

"Closing the garage door was the last thing she did."

He went into the house. Nell started crying again. She sobbed, she hung her head and threw it back against the seat and howled. She had completely forgotten Daniel. He sat in the backseat munching on the hem of his coat, his fleet of motor vehicles ignored. The people next door, who had been eating their lunch when they heard the noise of the car going through the garage door, came down the drive to see what was the matter. They were joined by the man from a Gas Board van and a girl who had been distributing leaflets advertising double glazing. It was a dull gray day and the front gardens here were planted with tall trees and thick evergreen shrubs. Trees grew in the pavements. No one had seen the car go over Charlotte and through the garage door, no one had seen who was driving.

The people next door were helping Nell out of the car when Ivan emerged from the front door. Nell saw one of Charlotte's feet sticking out from under the car and Charlotte's blood on the concrete of the drive and the scattered bits of door and began screaming again. The woman from next door smacked her face. Her husband, conveniently doing the best part of Ivan's work for him, said, "What an appalling thing, what a ghastly tragedy. Who would have thought the poor little chap would get up to his tricks again with such tragic results?"

"Don't look at it, dear," said the double-glazing girl, making a screen out of her leaflets between Nell and the body, which lay half outside and half under the car. "Let's get you indoors."

Nell gave another wail when she saw the Little Pet roses all lying there waiting to be planted. The woman next door went into Charlotte's kitchen to make a cup of tea and her husband came in carrying Daniel, who, when he saw Nell, spoke another sentence of sorts.

"Daniel hungry."

"I'll see to him, I'll find something for him," said the woman next door, dispensing tea. "Bring him out here, poor little mite. He's not to blame, the little innocent, how was he to know?"

"You see," said Ivan when they were alone.

"You can't mean to tell people Daniel did it. You can't, Ivan."

"I can't, agreed, but you can. I wasn't there. I was up in my study."

"Ivan, the police will come and ask me."

"That's right and there'll be an inquest, certain to be. The coroner will ask you and police will probably ask you again and maybe solicitors will ask you, I don't know, a lot of different people, but they'll be kind to you, they'll be understanding."

"I can't tell lies to people like that, Ivan."

"Yes, you can, you're a very good liar. Remember all those lies you told to Charlotte. She believed you. Remember that boyfriend you invented and all the times you said you'd been to the cinema with him when you'd been with me? Besides, you don't have to lie. You only have to tell them what happened last time, only this time poor old Charlotte got in the way."

Nell burst into sobs. "Oh, I can't stop crying, I can't. What shall I do?"

"You don't have to stop crying. It's probably a very good thing for you to cry quite a lot. Now don't stop crying, but listen to me if you can. Daniel can't tell them because Daniel can't speak so's you'd notice. And it doesn't matter anyway because no one's going to blame him. You heard what Mrs. Whatever-her-name-is said about no one blaming him, the little innocent, how was he to know? Children aren't supposed to know what they're doing before they're seven, before the age of reason. Everyone is well aware of what Daniel gets up to in cars, everyone knows he did it before."

"But he didn't do it this time."

"Never say that again. Don't even think it. Everyone will assume it was Daniel and you will only have to confirm it."

"I don't think I can, Ivan. I don't think I can face it."

"You know what will happen to me if you can't face it, don't you?"

The police came before Nell had time to answer.

It was something of a dilemma for them because Daniel was so young, but he helped them by coming into the room where they were interviewing his father and confirming, so to speak, what Ivan had told them.

"Daniel drive."

They exchanged glances with Ivan and Nell, and one of them

wrote Daniel's words down. It was as if, Nell thought, they were taking down what he said to use it in evidence at his trial, only Daniel, naturally, wouldn't have a trial. He sat on her lap, holding one of his cars in his hand, but in silence. Nell said afterward to Ivan that from that day forward he never said "Brrm, brrm" again, but neither of them could be sure of this. When it was time for the police to go they took Nell with them to the hospital where at last she had her hand cleaned and the wound stitched. The sister in the Outpatients, who didn't know the circumstances, said it was a pity she hadn't come as soon as it had happened, for now she would probably be scarred for life.

"I expect I shall," said Nell.

"There's always plastic surgery," the sister said in a cheerful way.

By the time the inquest took place, the car had been fitted with a new windscreen and was scheduled for a respray, the garage had been measured for a new door, and Daniel had learned to utter several more sentences. But those who had power in these matters, a doctor or two and the coroner and the coroner's office, all agreed that it would be unwise from a psychological point of view to mention again in his hearing the events of that Saturday morning. Not, at least, until he was quite a lot older. It would be better not to attempt any questioning of him and admonition at this stage seemed useless. The wisest course, the coroner said when the inquest was almost over, was for his father to ensure that Daniel never again sat in the back of a car on his own unless he were strapped in or closely supervised.

Nell gave her evidence in a low, subdued voice. Several times she had to be asked to speak more loudly. She described how she had sat in the car, feeling faint, her eyes closed. There was no one in the driver's seat, Charlotte had gone to close the garage door, when suddenly Daniel, shouting "Brrm, brrm," had precipitated himself forward and, seizing the controls, switched on the lights, flashed up the full beam, pushed the transmission into "drive," set the water jets spraying across the windscreen, taken off the handbrake. No, it wasn't the first time he had done it, he had done it once before, only that time his mother wasn't in the path of the car, bending down to close the garage door.

The coroner asked if she had attempted to stop the child, but Nell burst into tears at this and, in a gesture that seemed dramatic but was in fact involuntary, held out, palm-upward, her wounded hand, at that time still thickly bandaged. She often found herself staring at that hand in the weeks, the months, the years to come, at the white scar that bisected it from the first joint of the forefinger to the fleshy pad that cushioned out at the point where hand met wrist. She looked at it when she held her third finger up for Ivan to put the wedding ring on.

"Death by misadventure" the verdict had been, "misadventure," Ivan said, meaning "accident." She had cut her finger by misadventure, and she sometimes wondered if any of this would have happened if she hadn't cut it. If, in point of fact, Daniel hadn't run up behind her and thrown his arms round her legs. So perhaps, in a curious way, it really was his fault after all. She said something of this to Ivan, who agreed, but he never mentioned anything about any of it again. Nell never mentioned it either. The event, which he had certainly witnessed, had no apparent ill effects on Daniel. He was four when they got married and talking like any other normal four-year-old. He didn't appear to miss his mother, but then, as Ivan said, he had always preferred Nell.

When Nell's daughter was born after they had been married five years and she was giving up hope of ever having a child, Daniel, eyeing the baby Emma, surprised her by asking about his mother. He asked her how Charlotte had died. In a car crash, Nell said, which was the answer she and Ivan had agreed on.

"One day you're going to have to tell him more," said Nell. "What are you going to tell him?"

4

Ivan didn't say anything. His expression was guarded yet calculating. As he got older the ruthlessness that had helped to give him his dashing piratical appearance now made him look wolfish. Nell repeated her question.

"What are you going to tell Daniel when he asks you how Charlotte died?"

"I shall say in a car crash."

"Well, he's not going to be satisfied with that, is he? He'll want to know details. He'll want to know who was driving and was anyone else involved and all that."

"I shall tell him the truth," said Ivan.

"You can't tell him the truth! How can you possibly? What's he going to think of you if you tell him that? He'll hate your guts. I mean, he may even go and tell people that his father—well, you know. I can't, frankly, bring myself to put it into words."

"I am delighted to hear there is something you can't bring yourself to put into words. It makes a pleasant change." When something riled him, Ivan had got into the habit of curling back his upper lip to expose his teeth and his red gums.

"What precisely do you intend to tell Daniel, Ivan?"

"When the occasion arises, I shall tell him the truth about Charlotte's death. I shall tell him that though he was technically responsible for it, he couldn't at his age be blamed. I shall tell him as honestly as I can that he got hold of the controls of the car and drove it into Charlotte."

"And that's the truth?"

"You should know," said Ivan, wolf-faced, his upper lip curling. "That's what you told the inquest."

Daniel had only asked about his mother, Nell thought, because he was jealous. He was jealous of Emma. Until then he had had all Nell's attention, or all the attention she could spare from Ivan. Seeing Nell with this newcomer, understanding perhaps that she would no longer be exclusively his, recalled to him that he had once had a real mother of his own.

There were many things to recall her to Nell. Each time—which was every day—she saw those Little Pet roses, she thought of Charlotte. Ivan had planted them himself, the day after Charlotte's funeral. They never used the car again, that went in part-exchange for a new one. When Emma was a year old they moved out of the house and into a larger, older one. Nell was happy to be rid of those roses, but she couldn't get rid of her own hand with the white scar across it that followed in

that sinister way the path of the lifeline. And she couldn't avoid
occasionally seeing a map of Scotland.

At the new house they lost their babysitter. The woman next
door had sat for them but wasn't prepared to travel ten miles.
Ivan had several times suggested they engage a mother's help,
but Nell was against this. She remembered the way Daniel had
always seemed to prefer her to his own mother. Besides, since
they married she had never been in what Ivan called gainful
employment. She had worked, of course, but this had been at
the tiring and time-consuming task of looking after Daniel and
then Emma too. And she had kept the house very clean and
beautiful, and learned to drive.

A girl who was employed by Ivan at the gallery lived no more
than a couple of streets away. She said she loved children and
offered to babysit for them once a week. Ivan told Nell she was
called Denise and was twenty-three but nothing else, and it
came as something of a shock to discover that she was also very
pretty and with long wavy chestnut hair. In fact, they needed
her less frequently than once a week, for Ivan so often worked
late that on the evenings he did come home in time for dinner
he didn't feel like going out again.

"Emma will grow up hardly knowing her father," said Nell.

"Go and be a mother's help then," said Ivan. "If you can earn
what I do, I'll be happy to retire and look after the kids."

Denise sat for them on the evening of their sixth wedding
anniversary and on Nell's birthday. Emma, whom Nell suspected
of being hyperactive, stayed awake most of the time Denise was
there, sitting on Denise's lap, playing with the contents of
Denise's handbag, and screaming when attempts were made to
put her back to bed. Denise said she didn't mind, she loved
children. Emma clung to her and hit out at Nell with her fists
when Nell tried to take her out of the girl's arms.

"I'll drive you home," said Nell.

"You don't need to do that," said Ivan. "I'll do that. You stay
here with Emma."

Denise had a boyfriend she was always talking about. When
she couldn't babysit it was because she was going out somewhere with her boyfriend. Ivan said he had seen him come for
Denise at the gallery, but when Nell asked what he was like the

best Ivan could do in the way of a description was to say he
was just ordinary and nothing in particular. Nell didn't know
where they would find another babysitter but sometimes she
hoped Denise was serious about her boyfriend because if this
were so she might get married and move away.

It was preposterous of Ivan to suggest, even in a satirical way,
that she might get a job herself. She had her hands full with
Emma, who had an abnormal amount of energy for a child of
eighteen months. Emma had walked when she was ten months
old and never slept for more than six hours a night, though
sometimes during the day she would collapse and fall asleep
through sheer exhaustion. It wasn't surprising that she hadn't
yet uttered a word, she was younger than all that activity made
her seem, and as Nell remarked to Daniel, she hadn't got time
to talk.

"You didn't talk till you were nearly three," said Nell, and
mistakenly as she quickly realized, "There must be something
about your father's children . . ."

"Yes," said Daniel, "there must be. It can't be you or my
mother. I'd like to know what happened to my mother."

"It was a car crash."

"Yes, I know. I mean I'd like to know details, I'd like to know
exactly what happened."

"Your father will tell you when you're older."

Nell had made a mystery of it, and this she knew was an
error. She intended to warn Ivan, but for days on end she hardly
saw him. They had made an arrangement to go out on Friday
evening, but Ivan phoned to say he was working late and that
he would get in touch with Denise and put her off. He got
home at midnight and nearly as late on Saturday. Daniel managed to catch him on Sunday morning.

"In some ways the sooner Daniel goes away to school the
better," Ivan said to Nell.

"That won't be for a year."

"It might be a good idea for him to go as a boarder somewhere for that year."

"I don't want him to go away, I want him to stay here. And
it's no good you saying he's not my child, it's nothing to do

with me, because he's more mine than yours. You've never
liked him."

Ivan's hair, once the black of a raven's wing, had begun to go
gray early. It was the color of a wolf's pelt now and the
mustache he had grown was iron gray. Perhaps it was the
contrast this provided that made the inside of his mouth look
so red and his teeth so white when he indulged in that ugly
mannerism of curling back his upper lip. If he were an animal,
Nell's mother said, you would call it a snarl, but men don't
snarl.

"Are you saying I don't like my own child?"

"Yes, I am. I am saying that. We don't like the people we've
injured, it's a well-known fact."

"What utter nonsense. How am I supposed to have injured
Daniel?"

Nell looked down at her left hand. This had become an
almost involuntary gesture with her, like a tic. She turned it
palm-downward and put her thumb across the base of her
forefinger to hide the scar.

"I suppose he asked you about Charlotte?" she said.

"I told him you were the only person who could tell him.
You were there and I wasn't. Of course, if you weren't prepared
to tell him, I said, that was your decision. I wish you'd have
something done about your hand. It doesn't get less unsightly
as you get older. They can do marvels with scars these days and
it isn't as if I'd grudge the expense."

It was six months since Denise had babysat for them. They
didn't need her because they never went out. Or they never
went out together. Ivan always went out. Nell stayed at home
and looked after Daniel and Emma and kept the house very
clean. She had become obsessive about it, her mother said, it
wasn't healthy.

One afternoon she was putting the vacuum cleaner away
when Emma, who had been running in and out, shut her in the
broom cupboard. The cupboard door, which was heavy and
solid in that old house, had a handle on the outside but not the
inside. Nell, determined not to panic, began cajoling Emma to
open the door and release her, please Emma, there's a good
girl, open the door Emma, let Mummy out . . .

5

For a little while Emma stood outside the door. Nell could hear her giggling.

"Let Mummy out, Emma. Emma's such a clever girl she can open the door but Mummy can't. Mummy's not clever enough to open the door."

Nell thought this flattery and self-abasement might have some effect on Emma. The giggling stopped. Nell waited in the dark. It was pitch dark in the cupboard and there wasn't even a line of light round the edge of the door. It fitted into its frame too well for that. The cupboard was in the middle of the house, between an interior wall and the solid brick of the chimney bay. The air there was thick and black and it smelt of dust and soot. Emma gave another very light soft giggle. Nell knew why it sounded so soft. Emma was moving away from the door.

"Emma, come back. Come back and let Mummy out. Just turn the handle and the door will open and Mummy can get out."

The little footsteps sounded very light as they retreated. They sounded too as if the feet that made them moved not with their customary swiftness but sluggishly. With a sinking of the heart, Nell realized what had happened. This was what often happened to Emma after a long frenzied spell of hyperactivity. She had tired herself out. Seizing her opportunity, Nell would lay Emma down in her cot and cover her up, but what would Emma do in Nell's absence?

Injure herself? Go outside and shut herself out? This was an additional worry. Nell began to hammer on the door with her fists. She began to kick at the door. Not only was she shut up in this cupboard but her child, her less than two-year-old baby, was wandering alone about this big old house of many steps and corners and traps for little children. Emma was tired, Emma was exhausted. Suppose she got the cellar door open and fell down the cellar steps? Suppose she put her fingers into the electricity sockets? Or found matches or knives? Nell couldn't see her hand in the dark, but she could feel with the fingers of her other hand the ridge of scar tissue that scored her palm. She hammered on the door and shouted, "Emma, Emma, come back and let Mummy out!"

As well as being black-dark in the cupboard, it was airless. Or Nell imagined it would soon be airless. No air could get in, and once she had used up what oxygen there was—she would die, wouldn't she? She would suffocate. Daniel wouldn't be home for hours, Ivan, to judge by his recent performance, not before midnight. The more she shouted, the more energy she used in beating at the door, the more oxygen her lungs needed.

It was Daniel who rescued her. About an hour after Emma shut Nell in the cupboard Daniel came home from school. He let himself in and found the house empty, which was most unusual. By that time Nell had stopped shouting and beating on the door. She was sitting on the stone floor with her arms clasped round her knees, keeping very still so as not to exhaust the oxygen in the dusty sooty air. Daniel wasn't expected home for another hour at least. He should have gone straight to his violin lesson from school, but he had forgotten his music and come home to fetch it.

Although it was almost unknown for Nell to be out when he came home, he knew he wasn't expected home yet. Perhaps she always went out while he was at his violin lesson. With very little time to spare, he would have gone straight up to his bedroom, fetched his music, and gone out again, but as he passed the living-room door he caught a glimpse of pink where no pink should be. This was his sister's pink jumpsuit. Emma was asleep on the rug in the living room, her thumb in her mouth, the small brush attachment from the vacuum cleaner lying by her side. The brush provided him with a clue and as he approached the broom cupboard, Nell heard his footsteps and shouted to him: "Daniel, Daniel, I'm in here, I'm in the cupboard!"

He released her. Nell staggered out of the cupboard with cobwebs in her hair and blinking her eyes at the light. Daniel seemed rather pleased to see Emma get into trouble, for even after nearly two years he hadn't quite got over his jealousy. He scolded Emma himself and for once Nell didn't stop him.

It was the first evening for weeks that Ivan had come home at a reasonable hour. He brought Denise with him. They had some unfinished work to get through and Ivan thought they might as well do it at home. Nell told them of the events of the afternoon and Denise said how clever and enterprising Daniel had been. If he had been less observant he would have left the house again immediately and where would poor Nell be now?

"It's hard to see what else he could have done," said Ivan. "You might say with more justice that this is the reverse of virtue rewarded. If Daniel hadn't been so careless as to leave his music behind he would never have come home when he did. How can you praise someone for that?"

He scowled unpleasantly, but not at Denise. He and Denise would get to work on the new catalogue until eight, and then he would take her out to eat somewhere. They had to have dinner, but there was no need for Nell to cook for them, he said more graciously, especially after her ordeal. Denise said she was terribly pleased Nell was all right. She couldn't wait to see her boyfriend's reaction when she told him the story.

Ivan came in very late. His brown wolf's eyes had a glazed look, sleepy and entranced, a look that Nell had once known very well. Next day she said to him, apropos of nothing in particular, that she thought the day was coming when she would feel obliged to tell Daniel the truth about what had happened to his mother. It might also mean having to tell others and therefore acknowledging that she had committed perjury at the inquest, but she couldn't help that, she would have to face that. Ivan said, didn't she mean *he* would have to face that? And then he said no one would believe her.

"If we split up," Nell said, "I should get custody of these children. Daniel not being my own wouldn't make any difference, I should get custody. But you wouldn't mind that, would you? You don't like children."

"What nonsense. Of course I like children."

"And you'd lose your house and half your income."

"Two-thirds," said Ivan.

"I think you'd like to see the back of Daniel. You can't stand him. And the reason you can't stand him is because one day you know you're either going to have to tell him the truth, which will be the end of you, or tell him a lie that will blight the rest of his life."

"How melodramatic you are," said Ivan, "and how wrong. Anyway, we aren't going to split up, are we?"

"I don't know. I can't go on living like this."

He took Emma on his knee and explained to her how extremely naughty she had been to shut Nell up in the broom cupboard. It was a very dangerous thing to do because there was no air in the cupboard and people need air in order to stay alive. Emma squirmed and fidgeted and struggled to get down. When Ivan held her firmly so that she couldn't get away, she bounced up and down on his lap. Suppose Emma herself had come to some harm, asked Ivan, who, judging others by himself, hadn't much faith in an appeal to altruism. Suppose she had fallen down the steps and hurt herself?

When Emma had gone to bed, Ivan suggested he and Nell make a fresh start. He would make an effort, he promised, to be home at a reasonable time in the evenings. Dismissing Denise would be tricky, but he thought she would leave of her own accord. And he wouldn't embark on these projects that necessitated working long hours.

"How about Daniel?" asked Nell.

Ivan smiled slightly. It was a sad smile, Nell thought. "I'm working out something to tell Daniel." She thought he was looking at the scar on her hand and she turned it palm-downward. "I shall tell him how it was you sitting in the passenger seat and he was in the back, playing with his cars, and the engine was running. I shall make it plain that he was in no way to blame. Of course I'll explain to him that you were feeling too ill to know what you were doing."

"You needn't make it sound as if I cut myself on purpose. I'm not going to die, you know. I'll be around to answer for myself."

Ivan didn't reply. He said it would be a nice idea to have a party for their seventh wedding anniversary.

The people Ivan had known during his first marriage he knew no longer, they had been left behind when he and Nell came to this house. But they invited Nell's mother and Nell's sister and brother-in-law and their doctor and his wife and the neighbors and the woman at the gallery with her husband and the girl who had taken over from Denise. It was a fine moonlit evening for a barbecue, and Emma was up and still rushing about the garden at nine, at ten. She was naughty and uncontrollable, Ivan told the doctor, brimming with energy, it was impossible to cope with her.

"Hyperactive, I suppose," said the doctor.

"Exactly," said Ivan. "For example, only a few weeks ago she shut Nell up in a cupboard, closed the door, and just ran off and left her there. If my son hadn't happened to forget something and come back for it, I don't know what would have happened. There's no air in that cupboard." Everyone had stopped talking and was listening to Ivan. Nell, handing round little cheese biscuits, stopped and listened to Ivan. "I gave her a talking-to, you can imagine the kind of thing, but she's only two. Precocious of course but basically a baby." Ivan's smile was so wolfish, he looked as if he was about to lift his head and bay at the moon. "I don't know why it is," he said, "but neither of my children ever do what they're told, they don't listen to a word I say."

Nell dropped the plate and screamed. She stood there screaming until the woman from the gallery went up to her and slapped her face.

PETER ROBINSON
INNOCENCE

Peter Robinson, a native of England who has lived in Canada since 1974, is the author of several detective novels but only a few short stories. This one, from the Canadian anthology Cold Blood III, *won the Canadian Crime Writers Arthur Ellis Award for the best short story of 1990. Since the anthology was not available in this country until January 1991, we're happy to judge it one of the best of 1991 as well.*

Francis must be late, surely, Reed thought as he stood waiting on the bridge by the railway station. He was beginning to feel restless and uncomfortable; the handles of his grip bit into his palm, and he noticed that the rain promised in the forecast that morning was already starting to fall.

Wonderful! Here he was, over two hundred miles away from home, and Francis hadn't turned up. But Reed couldn't be sure about that. Perhaps *he* was early. They had made the same arrangement three or four times over the past five years, but for the life of him, Reed couldn't remember the exact time they'd met.

Reed turned and noticed a plump woman in a threadbare blue overcoat come struggling against the wind over the bridge toward him. She pushed a large pram, in which two infants fought and squealed.

"Excuse me," he called out as she neared him, "could you tell me what time school gets out?"

The woman gave him a funny look—either puzzlement or irritation, he couldn't decide which—answered in the clipped, nasal accent peculiar to the Midlands: "Half past three." Then she hurried by, giving Reed a wide berth.

He was wrong. For some reason, he had got it into his mind that Francis finished teaching at three o'clock. It was only twenty-five past now, so there would be at least another fifteen minutes to wait before the familiar red Escort came into sight.

The rain was getting heavier and the wind lashed it hard against Reed's face. A few yards up the road from the bridge was the bus station, which was attached to a large modern shopping center, all glass and escalators. Reed could stand in the entrance there, just beyond the doors where it was warm and dry, and still watch for Francis.

At about twenty-five to four, the first schoolchildren came dashing over the bridge and into the bus station, satchels swinging, voices shrill and loud with freedom. The rain didn't seem to bother them, Reed noticed: hair lay plastered to skulls; beads of rain hung on the tips of noses. Most of the boys' ties were askew, their socks hung loosely around their ankles, and their shoelaces snaked along the ground. It was a wonder they didn't trip over themselves. Reed smiled, remembering his own school days.

And how alluring the girls looked as they ran smiling and laughing out of the rain into the shelter of the mall. Not the really young ones, the unformed ones, but the older, long-limbed girls, newly aware of their breasts and the swelling of their hips. They wore their clothes carelessly: blouses hanging out, black woolly tights twisted or torn at the knees. To Reed, there was something wanton in the disarray.

These days, of course, they probably all knew what was what, but Reed couldn't help but feel that there was also a certain innocence about them: a naive, carefree grace in the way they moved, and a casual freedom in their laughter and gestures. Life hadn't got to them yet; they hadn't felt its weight and seen the darkness at its core.

Mustn't get carried away, Reed told himself, with a smile. It was all very well to joke with Bill in the office about how sexy the schoolgirls who passed the window each day were, but it was positively unhealthy to mean it, or (God forbid!) attempt to do anything about it. He couldn't be turning into a dirty old man at thirty-five, could he? Sometimes the power and violence of his fantasies worried him, but perhaps everyone else had them too. It wasn't something you could talk about. He didn't really think he was abnormal; after all, he hadn't acted them out, and you couldn't be arrested for your fantasies, could you?

Where the hell was Francis? Reed peered out through the glass. Wind-blown rain washed across the huge plate windows and distorted the outside world. The scene looked like an impressionist painting. All detail was obliterated in favor of the overall mood: gray-glum and dreamlike.

Reed glanced at his watch again. After four o'clock. The only schoolchildren left now were the stragglers, the ones who lived nearby and didn't have to hurry for a bus. They sauntered over the bridge, shoving each other, playing tag, hopping and skipping over the cracks in the pavement, oblivious to the rain and the wind that drove it.

Francis ought to be here by now. Worried, Reed went over the arrangements again in his mind. He knew that he'd got the date right because he'd written it down in his appointment book. Reed had tried to call the previous evening to confirm, but no one had answered. If Francis had been trying to get in touch with him at work or at home, he would have been out of luck. Reed had been on the road for most of the past week, and Elsie, the receptionist, could hardly be trusted to get her own name right.

When five o'clock came and there was still no sign of Francis, Reed picked up his grip again and walked back down to the station. It was still raining, but not so fast, and the wind had dropped. The only train back home that night left Birmingham at nine-forty and didn't get to Carlisle until well after midnight. By then the local buses would have stopped running and he would have to get a taxi. Was it worth it?

There wasn't much alternative, really. A hotel would be too expensive. Still, the idea had its appeal: a warm room with a soft bed, shower, color television and maybe even a bar downstairs where he might meet a girl. He would just have to decide later. Anyway, if he did want to catch the train, he would have to take the eight-fifty from Redditch to get to Birmingham in time. That left three hours and fifty minutes to kill.

As he walked over the bridge and up toward the town center in the darkening evening, Reed noticed two schoolgirls walking in front of him. They must have been kept in detention, he thought, or perhaps they'd just finished games practice. No doubt they had to do that, even in the rain. One looked dumpy from behind, but her friend was a dream: long wavy hair tumbling messily over her shoulders; short skirt flicking over her long, slim thighs; white socks fallen around her ankles, leaving her shapely calves bare. Reed watched the tendons at the back of her knees flex and loosen as she walked and thought of her struggling beneath him, his hands on her soft throat. They turned down a side street and Reed carried on ahead, shaking off his fantasy.

Could Francis have got lumbered with taking detention or games? he wondered. Or perhaps he had passed by without even noticing Reed sheltering from the rain. He didn't know where Francis's school was, or even what it was called. Somehow, the subject had just never come up. Also, the village where he lived was about eight miles away from Redditch, and the local bus service was terrible. Still, he could phone. If Francis were home, he'd come out again and pick Reed up.

After phoning and getting no answer, Reed walked around town for a long time looking in shop windows and wondering about how to get out of the mess he was in. His grip weighed heavily in his hand. Finally he got hungry and ducked out of the light rain to the Tandoori Palace. It was still early, just after six, and the place was empty apart from a young couple absorbed in one another in a dim corner. Reed had the waiter's undivided attention. He ordered pakoras, tandoori, and dhal, and the food came quickly. It was also very good, and Reed ate too fast.

After the spiced tea, he took out his wallet to pay. He had some cash, but he had decided to have a pint or two, and he would have to take a taxi home from the station. Best hang on to the paper money. The waiter didn't seem to mind taking plastic, even for so small a sum, and Reed rewarded him with a generous tip. Next he tried Francis again, but the phone just rang and rang.

Outside, the streetlights reflected in oily puddles on the roads and pavements. After walking off his heartburn for half an hour, thoroughly soaked and out of breath, Reed ducked into the first pub he saw. The locals eyed him suspiciously at first, then ignored him and went back to their drinks.

"Pint of bitter, please," Reed said, rubbing his hands together. "In a sleeve glass, if you've got one."

"Sorry, sir," the landlord said, reaching for a mug. "The locals bring their own."

"Oh, very well."

"Nasty night."

"Yes," said Reed. "Very."

"From these parts?"

"No. Just passing through."

"Ah." The landlord passed over a brimming pint mug, took Reed's money, and went back to the conversation he'd been having with a round-faced man in a pinstripe suit. Reed took his drink over to a table and sat down.

Over the next hour and a half, he phoned Francis four more times, but still got no reply. He also changed pubs after each pint, but got very little in the way of a friendly greeting. Finally, at about twenty to nine, knowing he couldn't bear to wake up in such a miserable place even if he could afford a hotel, he went back to the station and took the train home.

Because of his intended visit to Francis, Reed hadn't planned anything for the weekend at home. The weather was miserable, anyway, so he spent most of his time indoors reading and watching television, or down at the local. He tried Francis's number a few more times, but still got no reply. He also phoned Camille, hoping that her warm, lithe body and her fondness for experiment might brighten up his Saturday night and Sunday morning, but all he got was her answering machine.

On Monday evening, just as he was about to go to bed after a long day catching up on boring paperwork, the phone rang. Grouchily, he picked up the receiver: "Yes?"

"Terry?"

"Yes."

"This is Francis."

"Where the hell—?"

"Did you come all the way down on Friday?"

"Of course I bloody well did. I thought we had an—"

"Oh God. Look, I'm sorry, mate, really I am. I tried to call. That woman at work—what's her name?"

"Elsie?"

"That's the one. She said she'd give you a message. I must admit she didn't sound as if she quite had her wits about her, but I'd no choice."

Reed softened a little. "What happened?"

"My mother. You know she's been ill for a long time?"

"Yes."

"Well, she died last Wednesday. I had to rush off back to Manchester. Look, I really am sorry, but you can see I couldn't do anything about it, can't you?"

"It's me who should be sorry," Reed said. "To hear about your mother, I mean."

"Yes, well, at least there'll be no more suffering for her. Maybe we could get together in a few weeks?"

"Sure. Just let me know when."

"All right. I've still got stuff to do, you know, things to organize. How about if I call you back in a couple of weeks?"

"Great, I'll look forward to it. Bye."

"Bye. And I'm sorry, Terry, really."

Reed put the phone down and went to bed. So that was it— the mystery solved.

The following evening, just after he'd arrived home from work, Reed heard a loud knock at his door. When he opened it, he saw two strangers standing there. At first he thought they were Jehovah's Witnesses—who else came to the door in pairs, wearing suits?—but these two didn't quite look the part. True, one did look a bit like a Bible salesman—chubby, with a cheerful, earnest expression on a face fringed by a neatly trimmed dark beard—but the other, painfully thin, with a long, pockmarked face, looked more like an undertaker, except for the way his sharp blue eyes glittered with intelligent suspicion.

"Mr. Reed? Mr. Terence J. Reed?" the cadaverous one said, in a deep, quiet voice, just the way Reed imagined a real under-taker would speak. And wasn't there a hint of the Midlands nasal quality in the way he slurred the vowels?

"Yes, I'm Terry Reed. What is it? What do you want?" Reed could already see, over their shoulders, his neighbors spying from their windows; little corners of white net-curtain twitched aside to give a clear view.

"We're police officers, sir. Mind if we come in for a moment?" They flashed their identity cards but put them away before Reed had time to see what was written there. He backed into the hallway, and they took their opportunity to enter. As soon as they had closed the door behind them, Reed noticed the one with the beard start glancing around him, taking everything in, while the other continued to hold Reed's gaze. Finally, Reed turned and led them into the living room. He felt some kind of signal pass between them behind his back.

"Nice place you've got," the thin one said, while the other prowled the room, picking up vases and looking inside, opening drawers an inch or two, then closing them again.

"Look, what is this?" Reed said. "Is he supposed to be poking through my things? I mean, do you have a search warrant or something?"

"Oh, don't mind him," the tall one said. "He's just like that. Insatiable curiosity. By the way, my name's Bentley, Detective Superintendent Bentley. My colleague over there goes by the name of Inspector Rodmoor. We're from the Midlands Regional Crime Squad." He looked to see Reed's reactions as he said this, but Reed tried to show no emotion at all.

"I still don't see what you want with me," he said.

"Just routine," said Bentley. "Mind if I sit down?"

"Be my guest."

Bentley sat in the rocker by the fireplace, and Reed sat opposite on the sofa. A mug of half-finished coffee stood between them on the glass-topped table, beside a couple of unpaid bills and the latest *Radio Times*.

"Would you like something to drink?" Reed offered.

Bentley shook his head.

"What about him?" Reed glanced over nervously toward Inspector Rodmoor, who was looking through his bookcase, pulling out volumes that caught his fancy and flipping through them.

Bentley folded his hands on his lap: "Just try to forget he's here."

But Reed couldn't. He kept flicking his eyes edgily from one to the other, always anxious about what Rodmoor was getting into next.

"Mr. Reed," Bentley went on, "were you in Redditch on the evening of November ninth? Last Friday, that was."

Reed put his hand to his brow, which was damp with sweat. "Let me think now . . . Yes, yes, I believe I was."

"Why?"

"What? Sorry . . . ?"

"I asked why. Why were you in Redditch? What was the purpose of your visit?"

He sounded like an immigration control officer at the airport, Reed thought. "I was there to meet an old university friend," he answered. "I've been going down for a weekend once a year or so ever since he moved there."

"And did you meet him?"

"As a matter of fact, no, I didn't." Reed explained the communications breakdown with Francis.

Bentley raised an eyebrow. Rodmoor rifled through the magazine rack by the fireplace.

"But you still went there?" Bentley persisted.

"Yes. I told you, I didn't know he'd be away. Look, do you mind telling me what this is about? I think I have a right to know."

Rodmoor fished a copy of *Mayfair* out of the magazine rack and held it up for Bentley to see. Bentley frowned and reached over for it. The cover showed a shapely blonde in skimpy pink lace panties and camisole, stockings and a suspender belt. She was on her knees on a sofa, and her round behind faced the viewer. Her face was also turned toward the camera, and she looked as if she'd just been licking her glossy red lips. The thin strap of the camisole had slipped over her upper arm.

"Nice," Bentley said. "Looks a bit young, though, don't you think?"

Reed shrugged. He felt embarrassed and didn't know what to say.

Bentley flipped through the rest of the magazine, pausing over the color spreads of naked women in fetching poses.

"It's not illegal you know," Reed burst out. "You can buy it in any news agent's shop. It's not pornography."

"That's a matter of opinion, isn't it, sir?" said Inspector Rodmoor, taking the magazine back from his boss and replacing it.

Bentley smiled. "Don't mind him, lad," he said. "He's a Methodist. Now where were we?"

Reed shook his head.

"Do you drive a car?" Bentley asked.

"No."

"Do you live here by yourself?"

"Yes."

"Girlfriends?"

"Some."

"But not to live with?"

"No."

"Magazines enough for you, eh?"

"Now just a minute—"

"Sorry," Bentley said, holding up his skeletal hand. "Pretty tasteless of me, that was. Out of line."

Why couldn't Reed quite believe the apology? He sensed very strongly that Bentley had made the remark on purpose to see how he would react. He hoped he'd passed the test. "You were going to tell me what all this was about . . ."

"Was I? Why don't you tell me about what you did in Redditch last Friday evening first. Inspector Rodmoor will join us here by the table and take notes. No hurry. Take your time."

And slowly, trying to remember all the details of that miserable, washed-out evening five days ago, Reed told them. At one point, Bentley asked him what he'd been wearing, and Inspector Rodmoor asked if they might have a look at his raincoat and grip. When Reed finished, the heavy silence stretched on for seconds. What were they thinking about? he wondered. Were they trying to make up their minds about him? What was he supposed to have done?

Finally, after they had asked him to go over one or two random points, Rodmoor closed his notebook and Bentley got to his feet: "That'll be all for now, sir."

"For now?"

"We might want to talk to you again. Don't know. Have to check up on a few points first. We'll just take the coat and grip

with us. If you don't mind, sir. Inspector Rodmoor will give you
a receipt. Be available, will you?"

In his confusion, Reed accepted the slip of paper from
Rodmoor and did nothing to stop them taking his things. "I'm
not planning on going anywhere, if that's what you mean."

Bentley smiled. He looked like an undertaker consoling the
bereaved. "Good. Well, we'll be off then." And they walked
toward the door.

"Aren't you going to tell me what it's all about?" Reed asked
again as he opened the door for them. They walked out onto
the path, and it was Inspector Rodmoor who turned and
frowned. "That's the funny thing about it, sir," he said, "that
you don't seem to know.'

"Believe me, I don't."

Rodmoor shook his head slowly. "Anybody would think you
don't read your papers." And they walked down the path to
their Rover.

Reed stood for a few moments watching the curtains opposite
twitch and wondering what on earth Rodmoor meant. Then he
realized that the newspapers had been delivered as usual the
past few days, so they must have been in with magazines in the
rack, but he had been too uninterested, too tired, or too busy
to read any of them. He often felt like that. News was, more
often than not, depressing, the last thing one needed on a wet
weekend in Carlisle. Quickly he shut the door on the gawking
neighbors and hurried toward the magazine rack.

He didn't have far to look. The item was on the front page of
yesterday's paper, under the headline, MIDLANDS MURDER SHOCK.
It read:

The quiet Midlands town of Redditch is still in shock today
over the brutal slaying of schoolgirl Debbie Harrison. Debbie, 15, failed to arrive home after a late hockey practice
on Friday evening. Police found her partially clad body in
an abandoned warehouse close to the town center early
Saturday morning. Detective Superintendent Bentley, in
charge of the investigation, told our reporter that police
are pursuing some positive leads. They would particularly
like to talk to anyone who was in the area of the bus station

and noticed a strange man hanging around the vicinity late that afternoon. Descriptions are vague so far, but the man was wearing a light tan raincoat and carrying a blue hold-all.

He read and reread the article in horror, but what was even worse than the words was the photograph that accompanied it. He couldn't be certain because it was a poor shot, but he thought it was the schoolgirl with the long wavy hair and the socks around her ankles, the one who had walked in front of him with her dumpy friend.

The most acceptable explanation of the police visit would be that they needed him as a possible witness, but the truth was that the "strange man hanging around the vicinity" wearing "a light tan raincoat" and carrying a "blue hold-all" was none other than himself, Terence J. Reed. But how did they know he'd been there?

The second time the police called, Reed was at work. They marched right into the office, brazen as brass, and asked him if he could spare some time to talk to them down at the station. Bill only looked on curiously, but Frank, the boss, was hardly able to hide his irritation. Reed wasn't his favorite employee, anyway; he hadn't been turning enough profit lately.

Nobody spoke during the journey, and when they got to the station, one of the local policemen pointed Bentley toward a free interview room. It was a bare place: gray metal desk, ashtray, three chairs. Bentley sat opposite Reed, and Inspector Rodmoor sat in a corner, out of his line of vision.

Bentley placed the buff folder he'd been carrying on the desk and smiled his funeral director's smile. "Just a few further points, Terry. Hope I don't have to keep you long."

"So do I," Reed said. "Look, I don't know what's going on, but shouldn't I call my lawyer or something?"

"Oh, I don't think so. It isn't as if we've charged you or anything. You're simply helping us with our inquiries, aren't you? Besides, do you actually have a solicitor? Most people don't."

Come to think of it, Reed didn't have one. He knew one,

though. Another old university friend had gone into law and
practiced nearby. Reed couldn't remember what he special-
ized in.

"Let me lay my cards on the table, as it were." Bentley said,
spreading his hands on the desk. "You admit you were in
Redditch last Friday evening to visit your friend. We've been in
touch with him, by the way, and he verifies your story. What
puzzles us is what you did between, say, four and eight-thirty.
A number of people saw you at various times, but there's at
least an hour or more here and there that we can't account
for."

"I've already told you what I did."

Bentley consulted the file he had set on the desk. "You ate at
roughly six o'clock, is that right?

"About then, yes."

"So you walked around Redditch in the rain between five and
six, and between six-thirty and seven? Hardly a pleasant aes-
thetic experience, I'd imagine."

"I told you, I was thinking things out. I looked in shops, got
lost a couple of times . . ."

"Did you happen to get lost in the vicinity of Simmons
Street?"

"I don't know the street names."

"Of course. Not much of a street, really, more an alley. It runs
by a number of disused warehouses—"

"Now wait a minute! If you're trying to tie me in to that girl's
murder, then you're way off beam. Perhaps I *had* better call a
solicitor, after all."

"Ah!" said Bentley, glancing over at Rodmoor. "So you *do*
read the papers?"

"I did. After you left. Of course I did."

"But not before?"

"I'd have known what you were on about, then, wouldn't I?
And while we're on the subject, how the hell did you find out I
was in Redditch that evening?"

"You used your Barclay Card in the Tandoori Palace," Bentley
said. "The waiter remembered you and looked up his records."

Reed slapped the desk. "There! That proves it! If I'd done

what you seem to be accusing me of, I'd hardly have been as daft as to leave my calling card, would I?"

Bentley shrugged. "Criminals make mistakes, just like everybody else. Otherwise we'd never catch any. And I'm not accusing you of anything at the moment. You can see our problem though, can't you? Your story sounds thin, very thin."

"I can't help that. It's the truth."

"What state would you say you were in when you went into the Tandoori Palace?"

"State?"

"Yes. Your condition."

Reed shrugged. "I was wet, I suppose. A bit fed up. I hadn't been able to get in touch with Francis. Hungry, too."

"Would you say you appeared agitated?"

"Not really, no."

"But someone who didn't know you might just assume that you were?"

"I don't know. Maybe. I was out of breath."

"Oh? Why?"

"Well I'd been walking around for a long time carrying my grip. It was quite heavy."

"Yes, of course. So you were wet and breathless when you ate in the restaurant. What about the pub you went into just after seven o'clock?"

"What about it?"

"Did you remain seated long?"

"I don't know what you mean."

"Did you just sit and sip your drink, have a nice rest after a heavy meal and a long walk?"

"Well, I had to go to the toilet, of course. And I tried phoning Francis a few more times."

"So you were up and down, a bit like a yo-yo, eh?"

"But I had a good reason! I was stranded. I desperately wanted to get in touch with my friend."

"Yes, of course. Cast your mind back a bit earlier in the afternoon. At about twenty past three, you asked a woman what time the schools came out."

"Yes. I . . . I couldn't remember. Francis is a teacher, so

naturally I wanted to know if I was early or late. It was starting to rain."

"But you'd visited him there before. You said so. He'd picked you up at the same place several times."

"I know. I just couldn't remember if it was three o'clock or four. I know it sounds silly, but it's true. Don't you ever forget little things like that?"

"So you asked the woman on the bridge? That *was* you?"

"Yes. Look, I'd hardly have done that, would I, if . . . I mean . . . like with the credit card. I'd hardly have advertised my intentions if I was going to . . . you know . . ."

Bentley raised a beetle black eyebrow. "Going to *what,* Terry?"

Reed ran his hands through his hair and rested his elbows on the desk. "It doesn't matter. This is absurd. I've done nothing. I'm innocent."

"Don't you find schoolgirls attractive?" Bentley went on in a soft voice. "After all, it would only be natural, wouldn't it? They can be real beauties at fifteen or sixteen, can't they? Proper little temptresses, some of them, I'll bet. Right prick-teasers. Just think about it—short skirts, bare legs, firm young tits. Doesn't it excite you, Terry? Don't you get hard just thinking about it?"

"No, it doesn't," Reed said tightly. "I'm not a pervert."

Bentley laughed. "Nobody's suggesting you are. It gets *me* going, I don't mind admitting. Perfectly normal, I'd say, to find a fifteen-year-old schoolgirl sexy. My Methodist Inspector might not agree, but you and I know different, Terry, don't we? All that sweet innocence wrapped up in a soft, desirable young body. Doesn't it just make your blood sing? And wouldn't it be easy to get a bit carried away if she resisted, put your hands around her throat . . . ?"

"No!" Reed said again, aware of his cheeks burning.

"What about those women in the magazine, Terry? The one we found at your house?"

"That's different."

"Don't tell me you buy it just for the stories."

"I didn't say that. I'm normal. I like looking at naked women, just like any other man."

"Some of them seemed very young to me."

"For Christ's sake, they're models. They get paid for posing like that. I told you before, that magazine's freely available. There's nothing illegal about it." Reed glanced over his shoulder at Rodmoor, who kept his head bent impassively over his notebook.

"And you like videos, too, don't you? We've had a little talk with Mr. Hakim in your corner shop. He told us about one video in particular you've rented lately. Soft porn, I suppose you'd call it. Nothing illegal, true, at least not yet, but a bit dodgy. I'd wonder about a bloke who watches stuff like that."

"It's a free country. I'm a normal single male. I have a right to watch whatever kind of videos I want."

"School's Out." Bentley said quietly. "A bit over the top, wouldn't you say?"

"But they weren't *real* schoolgirls. The lead was thirty if she was a day. Besides, I only rented it out of curiosity. I thought it might be a bit of a laugh."

"And was it?"

"I can't remember."

"But you see what I mean, don't you? It looks bad: the subject matter, the image. It all sounds a bit odd. Fishy."

"Well, it's not. I'm perfectly innocent, and that's the truth."

Bentley stood up abruptly and Rodmoor slipped out of the room. "You can go now," the Superintendent said. "It's been nice to have a little chat."

"That's it?"

"For the moment, yes."

"But don't leave town?"

Bentley laughed. "You really must give up those American cop shows. Though it's a wonder you find time to watch them with all those naughty videos you rent. They warp your sense of reality—cop shows and sex films. Life isn't like that at all."

"Thank you. I'll bear that in mind," Reed said. "I take it I *am* free to go?"

"Of course." Bentley gestured toward the door.

Reed left. He was shaking when he got out onto the wet, chilly street. Thank God the pubs were still open. He went into the first one he came to and ordered a double Scotch. Usually, he wasn't much of a spirits drinker, but these, he reminded himself as the fiery liquor warmed his belly, were unusual circumstances. He knew he should go back to work, but he couldn't face it: Bill's questions, Frank's obvious disapproval. No. He ordered another double. The first thing he did when he got into the house was tear up the copy of *Mayfair* and burn the pieces in the fireplace one by one. After that, he tore up his Video Club membership card and burned that too. Damn Hakim!

"Terence J. Reed, it is my duty to arrest you for the murder of Deborah Sue Harrison . . ."

Reed couldn't believe this was happening. Not to him. The world began to shimmer and fade before his eyes, and the next thing he knew Rodmoor was bent over him offering a glass of water, a benevolent smile on his Bible salesman's face.

The next few days were a nightmare. Reed was charged and held until his trial date could be set. There was no chance of bail, given the seriousness of his alleged crime. He had no money anyway, and no close family to support him. He had never felt so alone in his life as he did those long dark nights in the cell. Nothing terrible happened. None of the things he'd heard about in films and documentaries: he wasn't sodomized; nor was he forced to perform fellatio at knife-point; he wasn't even beaten up. Mostly he was left alone in the dark with his fears. He felt all the certainties of his life slip away from him, almost to the point where he wasn't even sure of the truth anymore: guilty or innocent? The more he proclaimed his innocence, the less people seemed to believe him. Had he done it? He might have done.

He felt like an inflatable doll, full of nothing but air, maneuvred into awkward positions by forces he could do nothing about. He had no control over his life anymore. Not only couldn't he come and go as he pleased, he couldn't even think for himself anymore. Solicitors and barristers and policemen did that for him. And in the cell, in the dark, everything seemed to close in on him and some nights he had to struggle for breath.

When the trial date finally arrived, Reed felt relief. At least he could breathe in the large, airy courtroom, and soon it would be all over, one way or another.

In the crowded court, Reed sat still as stone in the dock, steadily chewing the edges of his newly grown beard. He heard the evidence against him—all circumstantial, all convincing.

If the police surgeon had found traces of semen in the victim, an expert explained, then they could have tried for a genetic match with the defendant's DNA, and that would have settled Reed's guilt or innocence once and for all. But in this case it wasn't so easy: there had been no seminal fluid found in the dead girl. The forensics people speculated, from the state of her body, that the killer had tried to rape her, found he was impotent, and strangled her in his ensuing rage.

A woman called Maggie, with whom Reed had had a brief fling a year or so ago, was brought onto the stand. The defendant had been impotent with her, it was established, on several occasions toward the end of their relationship, and he had become angry about it more than once, using more and more violent means to achieve sexual satisfaction. Once he had gone so far as to put his hands around her throat.

Well, yes he had. He'd been worried. During the time with Maggie, he had been under a lot of stress at work, drinking too much as well, as he hadn't been able to get it up. So what? Happens to everyone. And she'd wanted it like that, too, the rough way. Putting his hands around her throat had been her idea, something she'd got from a kinky book she'd read, and he'd gone along with her because she told him it might cure his impotence. Now she made the whole sordid episode sound much worse than it had been. She also admitted she had been just eighteen at the time, as well, and, as he remembered, she'd said she was twenty-three.

Besides, he had been impotent and violent only with Maggie. They could have brought on any number of other women to testify to his gentleness and virility, though no doubt if they did, he thought, his promiscuity would count just as much against him. What did he have to do to appear as normal as he needed to be, as he had once thought he was?

The witnesses for the prosecution all arose to testify against Reed like the spirits from Virgil's world of the dead. Though they were still alive, they seemed more like spirits to him: insubstantial, unreal. The woman from the bridge identified him as the shifty-looking person who had asked her what time the schools came out; the Indian waiter and the landlord of the pub told how agitated Reed had looked and acted that evening; other people had spotted him in the street, apparently following the murdered girl and her friend. Mr. Hakim was there to tell the court what kind of videos Reed rented lately—including *School's Out*—and even Bill told how his colleague used to make remarks about the schoolgirls passing by: "You know, he'd get all excited about glimpsing a bit of black knicker when the wind blew their skirts up. It just seemed like a bit of a lark. I thought nothing of it at the time." Then he shrugged and gave Reed a pitying look. And as if all that weren't enough, there was Maggie, a shabby Dido, refusing to look at him as she told the court of the way he had abused and abandoned her.

Toward the end of the prosecution case, even Reed's barrister was beginning to look depressed. He did his best in cross-examination, but the damnedest thing was that they were all telling the truth, or their versions of it. Yes, Mr. Hakim admitted, other people had rented the same videos. Yes, he might have even watched some of them himself. But the fact remained that the man on trial was Terence J. Reed, and Reed had recently rented a video called *School's Out*, the kind of thing, ladies and gentlemen of the jury, that you wouldn't want to find your husbands or sons watching.

Reed could understand members of the victim's community appearing against him, and he could even comprehend Maggie's hurt pride. But why Hakim and Bill? What had he ever done to them? Had they never really liked him? It went on and on, a nightmare of distorted truth. Reed felt as if he had been set up in front of a funfair mirror, and all that the jurors could see was his warped and twisted reflection. I'm innocent, he kept telling himself as he gripped the rail, but his knuckles turned whiter and whiter and his voice grew fainter and fainter.

Hadn't Bill joined in the remarks about schoolgirls? Wasn't it all in the spirit of fun? Yes, of course. But Bill wasn't in the dock. It was Terence J. Reed who stood accused of killing an innocent fifteen-year-old schoolgirl. *He* had been in the right place at the right time, and *he* had passed remarks on the budding breasts and milky thighs of the girls who had crossed the road in front of their office every day.

Then, the morning before the defense case was about to open—Reed himself was set to go on the dock, and not at all sure by now what the truth was—a strange thing happened.

Bentley and Rodmoor came softly into the courtroom, tip-toed up to the judge, and began to whisper. Then the judge appeared to ask them questions. They nodded. Rodmoor looked in Reed's direction. After a few minutes of this, the two men took seats and the judge made a motion for the dismissal of all charges against the accused. Pandemonium broke out in court: reporters dashed for phones and the spectators' gallery buzzed with speculation. Amid it all, Terry Reed got to his feet, realized *what* had happened, if not *how,* and promptly collapsed.

Nervous exhaustion, the doctor said, and not surprising after the ordeal Reed had been through. Complete rest was the only cure.

When Reed felt well enough, a few days after the trial had ended in uproar, his solicitor dropped by to tell him what had happened. Apparently, another schoolgirl had been assaulted in the same area, only this one had proved more than a match for her attacker. She had fought tooth and nail to hang on to her life, and in doing so had managed to pick up a half brick and crack the man's skull with it. He hadn't been seriously injured, but he'd been unconscious long enough for the girl to get help. When he was arrested, the man had confessed to the murder of Debbie Harrison. He had known details not revealed in the papers. After a night-long interrogation, police officers had no doubt whatsoever that he was telling the truth. Which meant Reed couldn't possibly be guilty. Hence, motion for dismissal, end of trial. Reed was a free man again.

He stayed home for three weeks, hardly venturing out of the house except for food, and even then he always went further afield for it than Hakim's general store. His neighbors watched him walk by, their faces pinched with disapproval, as if he were some kind of monster in their midst. He almost expected them to get up a petition to force him out of his home.

During that time he heard not one word of apology from the undertaker and the Bible salesman; Francis still had "stuff to do . . . things to organize"; and Camille's answering machine seemed permanently switched on.

At night, Reed suffered claustrophobic nightmares of prison. He couldn't sleep well, and even the mild sleeping pills the doctor gave him didn't really help. The bags grew heavier and darker under his eyes. Some days he wandered the city in a dream, not knowing where he was going or, when he got there, how he had arrived.

The only thing that sustained him, the only pure, innocent, untarnished thing in his entire life, was when Debbie Harrison visited him in his dreams. She was alive then, just as she had been when he saw her for the first and only time, and he felt no desire to rob her of her innocence, only to partake of it himself. She smelled of apples in autumn, and everything they saw and did together became a source of pure wonder. When she smiled, his heart almost broke with joy.

At the end of the third week, Reed trimmed his beard, got out his suit, and went in to work. In the office, he was met with an embarrassed silence from Bill and a redundancy check from Frank, who thrust it at him without a word of explanation. Reed pocketed the check and left.

Every time he went into town, strangers stared at him in the street and whispered about him in pubs. Mothers held more tightly onto their daughters' hands when he passed them in the shopping centers. He seemed to have become quite a celebrity in his hometown. At first, he couldn't think why, then one day he plucked up the courage to visit the library and look up the newspapers that had been published during his trial.

What he found was total character annihilation, nothing less. When the headline about the capture of the real killer came out, it could have made no difference at all; the damage had already been done to Reed's reputation, and it was permanent. He might have been found innocent of the girl's murder, but he had been found guilty too, guilty of being a sick consumer of pornography, of being obsessed with young girls, unable to get it up without the aid of a struggle on the part of the female. None of it was true, of course, but somehow that didn't matter.

It had been made so. As it is written, so let it be. And to cap it all, his photograph had appeared almost every day, both with and without the beard. There could be very few people in England who would fail to recognize him in the street.

Reed stumbled outside into the hazy afternoon. It was warming up toward spring, but the air was moist and gray with rain so fine it was closer to mist. The pubs were still open, so he dropped by the nearest one and ordered a double Scotch. The other customers looked at him suspiciously as he sat hunched in his corner, eyes bloodshot and puffy from lack of sleep, gaze directed sharply inward.

Standing on the bridge in the misty rain an hour later, Reed couldn't remember making the actual decision to throw himself over the side, but he knew that was what he had to do. He couldn't even remember how he had ended up on this particular bridge, or the route he'd taken from the pub. He had thought, drinking his third double Scotch, that maybe he should go away and rebuild his life, perhaps abroad. But that didn't ring true as a solution. Life is what you have to live with, what you are, and now his life was what it had become, or what it had been turned into. It was what being in the wrong place at the wrong time had made it, and *that* was what he had to live with. The problem was, he couldn't live with it; therefore, he had to die.

He couldn't actually see the river below—everything was gray—but he knew it was there. The River Eden, it was called. Reed laughed harshly to himself. It wasn't his fault that the river that runs through Carlisle is called the Eden, he thought; it was just one of life's little ironies.

Twenty-five to four on a wet Wednesday afternoon. Nobody about. Now was as good a time as any.

Just as he was about to climb onto the parapet, a figure emerged from the mist. It was the first girl on her way home from school. Her gray pleated skirt swished around her long, slim legs, and her socks hung over her ankles. Under her green blazer, the misty rain had wet the top of her white blouse so much that it stuck to her chest. Reed gazed at her in awe. Her long blond hair had darkened and curled in the rain, sticking in strands over her cheeks. There were tears in his eyes. He moved away from the parapet.

As she neared him, she smiled shyly.

Innocence.

Reed stood before her in the mist and held his hands out, crying like a baby.

"Hello," he said.

CAROLYN WHEAT

GHOST STATION

Carolyn Wheat usually writes about a criminal lawyer named Cass Jameson, but here she introduces us to a new character, Sergeant Maureen Gallagher of New York City's transit police, whose problems extend far beyond the usual criminals lurking in dark subway tunnels. Here is a gripping portrait of a side of New York a tourist never sees, along with a strong new character we hope we'll be meeting again.

If there's one thing I can't stand, it's a woman drunk. The words burned my memory the way Irish whiskey used to burn my throat, only there was no pleasant haze of alcohol to follow. Just bitter heartburn pain.

It was my first night back on the job, back to being Sergeant Maureen Gallagher instead of "the patient." Wasn't it hard enough being a transit cop, hurtling beneath the streets of Manhattan on a subway train that should have been in the Transit Museum? Wasn't it enough that after four weeks of detox I felt empty instead of clean and sober? Did I *have* to have some rookie's casually cruel words ricocheting in my brain like a wild-card bullet?

Why couldn't I remember the good stuff? Why couldn't I think about O'Hara's beefy handshake, Greenspan's "Glad to see ya, Mo," Ianuzzo's smiling welcome? Why did I have to run the tape in my head of Manny Delgado asking Captain Lomax for a different partner?

"Hey, I got nothing against a lady sarge, Cap," he'd said. "Don't get me wrong. It's just that if there's one thing I can't stand . . ." Et cetera.

Lomax had done what any standup captain would—kicked Delgado's ass and told him the assignment stood. What he hadn't known was that I'd heard the words and couldn't erase them from my mind.

Even without Delgado, the night hadn't gotten off to a great start. Swinging in at midnight for a twelve-to-eight, I'd been greeted with the news that I was on Graffiti Patrol, the dirtiest, most mind-numbing assignment in the whole transit police duty roster. I was a sergeant, damn it, on my way to a gold shield, and I wasn't going to earn it dodging rats in tunnels or going after twelve-year-olds armed with spray paint.

Especially when the rest of the cop world, both under- and aboveground, was working overtime on the torch murders of homeless people. There'd been four human bonfires in the past six weeks, and the cops were determined there wouldn't be a fifth.

Was Lomax punishing me, or was this assignment his subtle way of easing my entry back into the world? Either way, I resented it. I wanted to be a real cop again, back with Sal Minucci, my old partner. He was assigned to the big one, in the thick of the action, where both of us belonged. I should have been with him. I was Anti-Crime, for God's sake, I should have been assigned—

Or should I? Did I really want to spend my work nights prowling New York's underground skid row, trying to get information from men and women too zonked out to take care of legs gone gangrenous, whose lives stretched from one bottle of Cool Breeze to another?

Hell, yes. If it would bring me one step closer to that gold shield, I'd interview all the devils in hell. On my day off.

If there's one thing I can't stand, it's a woman drunk.

What did Lomax think—that mingling with winos would topple me off the wagon? That I'd ask for a hit from some guy's short dog and pass out in the Bleecker Street station? Was that why he'd kept me off the big one and had me walking a rookie through routine Graffiti Patrol?

Was I getting paranoid, or was lack of alcohol rotting my brain?

Manny and I had gone to our respective locker rooms to suit up. Plain clothes—and I do mean plain. Long johns first; damp winter had a way of seeping down into the tunnels and into your very blood. Then a pair of denims the Goodwill would have turned down. Thick wool socks, fisherman's duck boots, a black turtleneck, and a photographer's vest with lots of pockets. A black knit hat pulled tight over my red hair.

Then the gear: flashlight, more important than a gun on this assignment, handcuffs, ticket book, radio, gun, knife. A slapper, an oversize blackjack, hidden in the rear pouch of the vest. They were against regulations; I'd get at least a command discipline if caught with it, but experience told me I'd rather have it than a gun going against a pack of kids.

I'd forgotten how heavy the stuff was; I felt like a telephone lineman.

I looked like a cat burglar.

Delgado and I met at the door. It was obvious he'd never done vandal duty before. His tan chinos were immaculate, and his hiking boots didn't look waterproof. His red plaid flannel shirt was neither warm enough nor the right dark color. With his Latin good looks, he would have been stunning in an L. L. Bean catalog, but after ten minutes in a subway tunnel, he'd pass for a chimney sweep.

"Where are we going?" he asked, his tone a shade short of sullen. And there was no respectful "Sergeant" at the end of the question, either. This boy needed a lesson in manners.

I took a malicious delight in describing our destination. "The Black Hole of Calcutta," I replied cheerfully, explaining that I meant the unused lower platform of the City Hall station downtown. The oldest, darkest, dankest spot in all Manhattan. If there were any subway alligators, they definitely lurked in the Black Hole.

The expression on Probationary Transit Police Officer Manuel Delgado's face was all I could have hoped for. I almost—but not quite—took pity on the kid when I added, "And after that, we'll try one or two of the ghost stations."

"Ghost stations?" Now he looked really worried. "What are those?"

This kid wasn't just a rookie; he was a suburbanite. Every New Yorker knew about ghost stations, abandoned platforms where trains no longer stopped. They were still lit, though, and showed up in the windows of passing trains like ghost towns on the prairie. They were ideal canvases for the aspiring artists of the underground city.

I explained on the subway, heading downtown. The car, which rattled under the city streets like a tin lizzie, was nearly riderless at 1:00 A.M. A typical Monday late tour.

The passengers were one Orthodox Jewish man falling asleep over his Hebrew Bible, two black women, both reading thick paperback romances, the obligatory pair of teenagers making out in the last seat, and an old Chinese woman.

I didn't want to look at Delgado. More than once I'd seen a fleeting smirk on his face when I glanced his way. It wasn't enough for insubordination; the best policy was to ignore it.

I let the rhythm of the subway car lull me into a litany of the AA slogans I was trying to work into my life: EASY DOES IT. KEEP IT SIMPLE, SWEETHEART. ONE DAY AT A TIME. I saw them in my mind the way they appeared on the walls at meetings, illuminated, like old Celtic manuscripts.

This night I had to take one hour at a time. Maybe even one minute at a time. My legs felt wobbly. I was a sailor too long from the sea. I'd lost my subway legs. I felt white and thin, as though I'd had several major organs removed.

Then the drunk got on. One of the black women got off, the other one looked up at the station sign and went back to her book, and the drunk got on.

If there's one thing I can't stand, it's a woman drunk.

ONE DAY AT A TIME. EASY DOES IT.

I stiffened. The last thing I wanted was to react in front of Delgado, but I couldn't help it. The sight of an obviously intoxicated man stumbling into our subway car brought the knowing smirk back to his face.

There was one at every AA meeting. No matter how nice the neighborhood, how well dressed most people attending the meeting were, there was always a drunk. A real drunk, still reeling, still reeking of cheap booze. My sponsor, Margie, said they were there for a reason, to let us middle-class, recovery-oriented types remember that "there but for the grace of God . . ."

I cringed whenever I saw them, especially if the object lesson for the day was a woman.

"Hey, kid," the drunk called out to Delgado, in a voice as inappropriately loud as a deaf man's, "how old are you?" The doors closed and the car lurched forward; the drunk all but fell into his seat.

"Old enough," Manny replied, flashing the polite smile a well-brought-up kid saves for his maiden aunt.

The undertone wasn't so pretty. Little sidelong glances at me that said, *See how nice I am to this old fart. See what a good boy I am. I like drunks, Sergeant Gallagher.*

To avoid my partner's face, I concentrated on the subway ads as though they contained all the wisdom of the Big Book. "Here's to birth defects," proclaimed a pregnant woman about to down a glass of beer. Two monks looked to heaven, thanking God in Spanish for the fine quality of their brandy.

Weren't there any signs on this damn train that didn't involve booze? Finally an ad I could smile at: the moon in black space; on it, someone had scrawled, "Alice Kramden was here, 1959."

My smile faded as I remembered Sal Minucci's raised fist, his Jackie Gleason growl. "One a these days, Gallagher, you're goin' to the moon. To the *moon!*"

It wasn't just the murder case I missed. It was Sal. The easy partnership of the man who'd put up with my hangovers, my depressions, my wild nights out with the boys.

"Y'know how old I am?" the drunk shouted, almost falling over in his seat. He righted himself. "Fifty-four in September," he announced, an expectant look on his face.

After a quick smirk in my direction, Manny gave the guy what he wanted. "You don't look it," he said. No trace of irony appeared on his Spanish altar boy's face. It was as though he'd never said the words that were eating into me like battery-acid AA coffee.

The sudden jab of anger that stabbed through me took me by surprise, especially since it wasn't directed at Delgado. *No, you don't look it.* I thought. *You look more like seventy.* White wisps of hair over a bright pink scalp. The face more than pink; a slab of raw calves' liver. Road maps of broken blood vessels on his nose and cheeks. Thin white arms and matchstick legs under too-big trousers. When he lifted his hand, ropy with bulging blue veins, it fluttered like a pennant in the breeze.

Like Uncle Paul's hands.

I turned away sharply. I couldn't look at the old guy anymore.

The constant visual digs Delgado kept throwing in my direction were nothing compared to the pain of looking at a man dying before my eyes. I didn't want to see blue eyes in that near-dead face. *As blue as the lakes of Killarney,* Uncle Paul used to say in his mock-Irish brogue.

I focused on the teenagers making out in the rear of the car. A couple of Spanish kids, wearing identical pink T-shirts and black leather jackets. If I stared at them long enough, would they stop groping and kissing, or would an audience spur their passion?

Uncle Paul. After Daddy left us, he was my special friend, and I was his best girl.

I squeezed my eyes shut, but the memories came anyway. The red bike Uncle Paul gave me for my tenth birthday. The first really big new thing, bought just for me, that I'd ever had. The best part was showing it off to cousin Tommy. For once I didn't need his hand-me-downs, or Aunt Bridget's clucking over me for being poor. *God bless the child who's got her own.*

I opened my eyes just as the Lex passed through the ghost station at Worth Street. Closed off to the public for maybe fifteen years, it seemed a mirage, dimly seen through the dirty windows of the subway car. Bright color on the white tile walls told me graffiti bombers had been there. A good place to check, but not until after City Hall. I owed Manny Delgado a trip to the Black Hole.

"Uh, Sergeant?"

I turned; a patronizing smile played on Delgado's lips. He'd apparently been trying to get my attention. "Sorry," I said, feigning a yawn. "Just a little tired."

Yeah, sure, his look remarked. "We're coming to Brooklyn Bridge. Shouldn't we get off the train?"

"Right." *Leave Uncle Paul where he belongs.*

At the Brooklyn Bridge stop, we climbed up the steps to the upper platform, showed our ID to the woman token clerk, and told her we were going into the tunnel toward City Hall. Then we went back downstairs, heading for the south end of the downtown platform.

As we were about to go past the gate marked NO UNAUTHOR-IZED PERSONNEL BEYOND THIS POINT, I looked back at the lighted platform, which made a crescent-shaped curve behind us. Almost in a mirror image, the old drunk was about to pass the forbidden gate and descend into the tunnel heading uptown.

He stepped carefully, holding on to the white, bathroom-tile walls, edging himself around the waist-high gate. He lowered himself down the stone steps the exact replica of the ones Manny and I were about to descend, then disappeared into the blackness.

I couldn't let him go. There were too many dangers in the subway, dangers beyond the torch killer everyone was on the hunt for. How many frozen bodies had I stumbled over on the catwalks between tunnels? How many huddled victims had been hit by trains as they lay in sodden sleep? And yet, I had to be careful. My friend Kathy Denzer had gone after a bum sleeping on the catwalk, only to have the man stab her in the arm for trying to save his life.

I couldn't let him go. Turning to Delgado, I said, "Let's save City Hall for later. I saw some graffiti at Worth Street on the way here. Let's check that out first."

He shrugged. At least he was being spared the Black Hole, his expression said.

Entering the tunnel's blackness, leaving behind the brightly lit world of sleepy riders, a tiny rush of adrenaline, like MSG after a Chinese dinner, coursed through my bloodstream. Part of it was pure reversion to childhood's fears. Hansel and Gretel. Snow White. Lost in dark woods, with enemies all around. In this case, rats. Their scuffling sent shivers up my spine as we balanced our way along the catwalk above the tracks.

The other part was elation. This was my job. I was good at it. I could put aside my fears and step boldly down into murky depths where few New Yorkers ever went.

Our flashlights shone dim as fireflies. I surveyed the gloomy underground world I'd spent my professional life in.

My imagination often took over in the tunnels. They became caves of doom. Or an evil wood, out of *Lord of the Rings*. The square columns holding up the tunnel roof were leafless trees, the constant trickle of foul water between the tracks a poisonous stream from which no one drank and lived.

Jones Beach. Uncle Paul's huge hand cradling my foot, then lifting me high in the air and flinging me backward, laughing with delight, into the cool water. Droplets clinging to his red beard, and Uncle Paul shaking them off into the sunlight like a wet Irish setter.

Me and Mo, we're the only true Gallaghers. The only red-heads. I got straight A's in English; nobody's grammar was safe from me—except Uncle Paul's.

I thought all men smelled like him: whiskey and tobacco.

As Manny and I plodded along the four-block tunnel between the live station and the dead one, we exchanged no words. The acrid stench of an old track fire filled my nostrils the way memories flooded my mind. Trying to push Uncle Paul away, I bent all my concentration on stepping carefully around the foul-smelling water, the burned debris I didn't want to identify.

I suspected Delgado's silence was due to fear; he wouldn't want a shaking voice to betray his tension. I knew how he felt. The first nighttime tunnel trek was a landmark in a young transit cop's life.

When the downtown express thundered past, we ducked into the coffin-sized alcoves set aside for transit workers. My heart pounded as the wind wake of the train pulled at my clothes; the fear of falling forward, landing under those relentless steel wheels, never left me, no matter how many times I stood in the well. I always thought of Anna Karenina; once in a while, in my drinking days, I'd wondered how it would feel to edge forward, to let the train's undertow pull me toward death.

I could never do it. I'd seen too much blood on the tracks.

Light at the end of the tunnel. The Worth Street station sent rays of hope into the spidery blackness. My step quickened; Delgado's pace matched mine. Soon we were almost running toward the light, like cavemen coming from the hunt to sit by the fire of safety.

We were almost at the edge of the platform when I motioned Delgado to stop. My hunger to bathe in the light was as great as his, but our post was in the shadows, watching.

A moment of panic. I'd lost the drunk. Had he fallen on the tracks, the electrified third rail roasting him like a pig at a barbecue? Not possible; we'd have heard, and smelled.

I had to admit, the graffiti painting wasn't a mindless scrawl.

It was a picture, full of color and life. Humanlike figures in bright primary shades, grass green, royal blue, orange, sun yellow, and carnation pink—colors unknown in the black-and-gray tunnels—stood in a line, waiting to go through a subway turnstile. Sexless, they were cookie-cutter replicas of one another, the only difference among them the color inside the black edges.

A rhythmic clicking sound made Delgado jump. "What the hell—?"

"Relax, Manny," I whispered. "It's the ball bearing in the spray-paint can. The vandals are here. As soon as the paint hits the tiles, we jump out and bust them."

Four rowdy teenagers, ranging in color from light brown to ebony, laughed raucously and punched one another with a theatrical style that said *We bad. We real bad.* They bounded up the steps from the other side of the platform and surveyed their artwork, playful as puppies, pointing out choice bits they had added to their mural.

It should have been simple. Two armed cops, with the advantage of surprise, against four kids armed with Day-Glo spray paint. Two things kept it from being simple: the drunk, wherever the hell he was, and the fact that one of the kids said, "Hey, bro, when Cool and Jo-Jo gettin' here?"

A very black kid with a nylon stocking on his head answered, "Jo-Jo be comin' with Pinto. Cool say he might be bringin' Slasher and T. P."

Great. Instead of two against four, it sounded like all the graffiti artists in New York City were planning a convention in the Worth Street ghost station.

"Sarge?" Delgado's voice was urgent. "We've gotta—"

"I know," I whispered back. "Get on the radio and call for backup."

Then I remembered. Worth Street was a dead spot. Lead in the ceiling above our heads turned our radios into worthless toys.

"Stop," I said wearily as Manny pulled the antenna up on his hand-held radio. "It won't work. You'll have to go back to Brooklyn Bridge. Alert Booth Robert two-twenty-one. Have them call Operations. Just ask for backup, don't make it a ten-thirteen." A 10-13 meant "officer in trouble," and I didn't want to be the sergeant who cried wolf.

"Try the radio along the way," I went on. "You never know when it will come to life. I'm not sure where the lead ends."

Watching Delgado trudge back along the catwalk, I felt lonely, helpless, and stupid. No one knew we'd gone to Worth Street instead of the Black Hole, and that was my fault.

"Hey," one of the kids called, pointing to a pile of old clothes in the corner of the platform, "what this dude be doin' in our crib?"

Dude? What dude? Then the old clothes began to rise; it was the drunk from the train. He was huddled into a fetal ball, hoping not to be noticed by the graffiti gang.

Nylon Stocking boogied over to the old drunk, sticking a finger in his ribs. "What you be doin' here, ol' man? Huh? Answer me."

A fat kid with a flat top walked over, sat down next to the drunk, reached into the old man's jacket pocket, and pulled out a half-empty pint bottle.

A lighter-skinned, thinner boy slapped the drunk around, first lifting him by the scruff of the neck, then laughing as he flopped back to the floor. The old guy tried to rise, only to be kicked in the ribs by Nylon Stocking.

The old guy was bleeding at the mouth. Fat Boy held the pint of booze aloft, teasing the drunk the way you tease a dog with a bone. The worst part was that the drunk was reaching for it, hands flapping wildly, begging. He'd have barked if they'd asked him to.

I was shaking, my stomach starting to heave. God, where was Manny? Where was my backup? I had to stop the kids before their friends got there, but I felt too sick to move. *If there's one thing I can't stand, it's a woman drunk.* It was as though every taunt, every kick, was aimed at me, not just at the old man.

I reached into my belt for my gun, then opened my vest's back pouch and pulled out the slapper. Ready to charge, I stopped cold when Nylon Stocking said, "Yo, y'all want to do him like we done the others?"

Fat Boy's face lit up. "Yeah," he agreed. "Feel like a cold night. We needs a little fire."

"You right, bro," the light-skinned kid chimed in. "I got the kerosene. Done took it from my momma heater."

"What he deserve, man," the fourth member of the gang said, his voice a low growl. "Comin' into our crib, pissin' on the art, smellin' up the place. This here *our* turf, dig?" He prodded the old man in the chest.

"I—I didn't mean nothing," the old man whimpered. "I just wanted a place to sleep."

Uncle Paul, sleeping on our couch when he was too drunk for Aunt Rose to put up with him. He was never too drunk for Mom to take him in. Never too drunk to give me one of his sweet Irish smiles and call me his best girl.

The light-skinned kid opened the bottle—ironically, it looked as if it once contained whiskey—and sprinkled the old man the way my mother sprinkled clothes before ironing them. Nylon Stocking pulled out a book of matches.

By the time Delgado came back, with or without backup, there'd be one more bonfire if I didn't do something. Fast.

Surprise was my only hope. Four of them, young and strong. One of me, out of shape and shaky.

I shot out a light. I cracked the bulb on the first shot. Target shooting was my best asset as a cop, and I used it to give the kids the impression they were surrounded.

The kids jumped away from the drunk, moving in all directions. "Shit," one said, "who shootin'?"

I shot out the second and last bulb. In the dark, I had the advantage. They wouldn't know, at least at first, that only one cop was coming after them.

"Let's book," another cried. "Ain't worth stayin' here to get shot."

I ran up the steps, onto the platform lit only by the moonlike rays from the other side of the tracks. Yelling "Stop, police," I waded into the kids, swinging my illegal slapper.

Thump into the ribs of the kid holding the kerosene bottle. He dropped it, clutching his chest and howling. I felt the breath whoosh out of him, heard the snap of rib cracking. I wheeled and slapped Nylon Stocking across the knee, earning another satisfying howl.

My breath came in gasps, curses pouring out of me. Blood

pounded in my temples, a thumping noise that sounded louder than the express train.

The advantage of surprise was over. The other two kids jumped me, one riding my back, the other going for my stomach with hard little fists. All I could see was a maddened teenage tornado circling me with blows. My arm felt light as I thrust my gun deep into the kid's stomach. He doubled, groaning.

It was like chugging beer at a cop racket. Every hit, every satisfying *whack* of blackjack against flesh made me hungry for the next. I whirled and socked. The kids kept coming, and I kept knocking them down like bowling pins.

The adrenaline rush was stupendous, filling me with elation. I was a real cop again. There was life after detox.

At last they stopped. Panting, I stood among the fallen, exhausted. My hair had escaped from my knit hat and hung in matted tangles over a face red-hot as a griddle.

I pulled out my cuffs and chained the kids together, wrist to wrist, wishing I had enough sets to do each individually. Together, even cuffed, they could overpower me. Especially since they were beginning to realize I was alone.

I felt weak, spent. As though I'd just made love.

I sat down on the platform, panting, my gun pointed at Nylon Stocking. "You have the right to remain silent," I began.

As I finished the last Miranda warning on the last kid, I heard the cavalry coming over the hill. Manny Delgado, with four reinforcements.

As the new officers took the collars, I motioned Manny aside, taking him to where the drunk lay sprawled in the corner, still shaking and whimpering.

"Do you smell anything?" I asked.

Manny wrinkled his nose. I looked down at the drunk.

A trickle of water seeped from underneath him; his crotch was soaked.

Uncle Paul, weaving his way home, singing off-key, stopping to take a piss under the lamppost. Nothing unusual in that, except that this time Julie Ann Mackinnon, my eighth-grade rival, watched from across the street. My cheeks burned as I recalled how she'd told the other kids what she'd seen, her hand cupped over her giggling mouth.

"Not that," I said, my tone sharp, my face reddening. "The kerosene. These kids are the torch killers. They were going to roast this guy. That's why I had to take them on alone."

Delgado's face registered the skepticism I'd seen lurking in his eyes all night. Could he trust me? He'd been suitably impressed at my chain gang of prisoners, but now I was talking about solving the crime that had every cop in the city on overtime.

"Look, just go back to Brooklyn Bridge and radio"—I was going to say Captain Lomax, when I thought better—"Sal Minucci in Anti-Crime. He'll want to have the guy's coat analyzed. And make sure somebody takes good care of that bottle." I pointed to the now-empty whiskey bottle the light-skinned boy had poured kerosene from.

"Isn't that his?" Manny indicated the drunk.

"No, his is a short dog," I said, then turned away as I realized the term was not widely known in nondrunk circles.

Just go, kid, I prayed. *Get the hell out of here before—*

He turned, following the backup officers with their chain gang. "And send for Emergency Medical for this guy," I added. "I'll stay here till they come."

I looked down at the drunk. His eyes were blue, a watery, no-color blue with all the life washed out of them. Uncle Paul's eyes.

Uncle Paul, blurry-faced and maudlin, too blitzed to care that I'd come home from school with a medal for the best English composition. I'd put my masterpiece by his chair, so he could read it after dinner. He spilled whiskey on it; the blue-black ink ran like tears and blotted out my carefully chosen words.

Uncle Paul, old, sick, and dying, just like this one. Living by that time more on the street than at home, though there were people who would take him in. His eyes more red than blue, his big frame wasted. I felt a sob rising, like death squeezing my lungs. I heaved, grabbing for air. My face was wet with tears I didn't recall shedding.

I hate you, Uncle Paul. I'll never be like you. Never.

I walked over to the drunk, still sprawled on the platform. I was a sleepwalker; my arm lifted itself. I jabbed the butt of my gun into old, thin ribs, feeling it bump against bone. It would be a baseball-size bruise. First a raw red-purple, then blue-violet, finally a sickly yellow-gray.

I lifted my foot, just high enough to land with a thud near the kidneys. The old drunk grunted, his mouth falling open. A drizzle of saliva fell to the ground. He put shaking hands to his face and squeezed his eyes shut. I lifted my foot again. I wanted to kick and kick and kick.

Uncle Paul, a frozen lump of meat found by some transit cop on the aboveground platform at 161st Street. The Yankee Stadium stop, where he took me when the Yanks played home games. We'd eat at the Yankee Tavern, me wolfing down a corned beef on rye and a cream soda, Uncle Paul putting away draft beer after draft beer.

Before he died, Uncle Paul had taken all the coins out of his pocket, stacking them in neat little piles beside him. Quarters, dimes, nickels, pennies. An inventory of his worldly goods.

I took a deep, shuddering breath, looked down at the sad old man I'd brutalized. A hot rush of shame washed over me.

I knelt down, gently moving the frail, blue-white hands away from the near-transparent face. The fear I saw in the liquid blue eyes sent a piercing ray of self-hatred through me.

If there's anything I can't stand, it's a woman drunk. Me too, Manny, I can't stand women drunks either.

The old man's lips trembled; tears filled his eyes and rolled down his thin cheeks. He shook his head from side to side, as though trying to wake himself from a bad dream.

"Why?" he asked, his voice a raven's croak.

"Because I loved you so much." The words weren't in my head anymore, they were slipping out into the silent, empty world of the ghost station. As though Uncle Paul weren't buried in Calvary Cemetery but could hear me with the ears of this old man who looked too damn much like him. "Because I wanted to be just like you. And I am." My voice broke. "I'm just like you, Uncle Paul. I'm a drunk." I put my head on my knee and sobbed like a child. All the shame of my drinking days welled up in my chest. The stupid things I'd said and done, the times I'd had to be taken home and put to bed, the times I'd thrown up in the street outside the bar. *If there's one thing I can't stand...*

"Oh, God, I wish I were dead."

The bony hand on mine felt like a talon. I started, then looked into the old man's watery eyes. I sat in the ghost station and saw in this stranger the ghost that had been my dying uncle.

"Why should you wish a thing like that?" the old man asked. His voice was clear, no booze-blurred slurring, no groping for words burned out of the brain by alcohol. "You're a young girl. You've got your whole life ahead of you."

My whole life. To be continued . . .

One day at a time. One night at a time.

When I got back to the District, changed out of my work clothes, showered, would there be a meeting waiting for me? Damn right; in the city that never sleeps, AA never sleeps either.

I reached over to the old man. My fingers brushed his silver stubble.

"I'm sorry, Uncle Paul," I said. "I'm sorry."

APPENDIX

THE YEARBOOK OF THE MYSTERY AND SUSPENSE STORY

THE YEAR'S BEST MYSTERY AND SUSPENSE NOVELS

Neil Albert, *The January Corpse* (Walker and Company)
Linda Barnes, *Steel Guitar* (Delacorte)
Lawrence Block, *A Dance at the Slaughterhouse* (Morrow)
Mary Higgins Clark, *Loves Music, Loves to Dance* (Simon & Schuster)
Max Allan Collins, *Stolen Away* (Bantam)
Patricia D. Cornwell, *Body of Evidence* (Scribners)
Barbara D'Amato, *Hard Tack* (Scribners)
Thomas D. Davis, *Suffer Little Children* (Walker and Company)
Len Deighton, *Mamista* (HarperCollins)
Pete Dexter, *Brotherly Love* (Random House)
Dick Francis, *Comeback* (Putnam)
J. F. Freedman, *Against the Wind* (Viking)
Elizabeth George, *A Suitable Vengeance* (Bantam)
Sue Grafton, *"H" Is for Homicide* (Henry Holt)
Michael Mewshaw, *True Crime* (Poseidon Press)
Marcia Muller, *Where Echoes Live* (Mysterious Press)
T. Jefferson Parker, *Pacific Beat* (St. Martin's Press)
Julie Smith, *The Axman's Jazz* (St. Martin's Press)
Jonathan Valin, *Second Chance* (Delacorte)
Barbara Vine, *King Solomon's Carpet* (Viking, London)

BIBLIOGRAPHY

I. Collections and Single Stories

1. Albert, T. M. *Tales of an Ulster Detective*. Bangor, N. Ireland: T. M. Albert Publications. Sixteen brief detective stories. (1989)
2. Brown, Fredric. *The Gibbering Night*. Hilo, Hawaii: Dennis McMillan Publications. Eighteenth volume of Brown's uncollected pulp writing, containing stories, contributions to trade journals, and a movie quiz.
3. ———. *The Pickled Punks*. Hilo, Hawaii: Dennis McMillan Publications. Nineteenth and final volume of Brown's uncollected pulp writing, containing stories, poems, contributions to trade journals, and a television script for "Alfred Hitchcock Presents."
4. Carr, John Dickson. *Fell and Foul Play*. New York: International Polygonics. Nine Dr. Fell stories and radio plays, two previously unpublished, plus five historical mysteries and the original uncut version of Carr's novella *The Third Bullet*. Edited and introduced by Douglas G. Greene.
5. ———. *Merrivale, March and Murder*. New York: International Polygonics. Two stories about Sir Henry Merrivale, nine about Colonel March, and seven others, including two stories and a radio play not previously collected. Edited and introduced by Douglas G. Greene.
6. Cassiday, Bruce. *Murder Game*. New York: Carroll & Graf. Three collected novelettes about Interpol's Inspector Birkby. The third story has no ending and a prize was offered for the best reader solution. Created by book packager Bill Adler.
7. Chesterton, G. K. *The Mask of Midas*. Trondheim, Norway: Classica. An English-language limited edition of the final Father Brown story, written shortly before Chesterton's death and published here for the first time.
8. Christie, Agatha. *Problem at Pollensa Bay*. London: HarperCollins. Eight stories, four new to British book pub-

lication and one, "The Harlequin Tea Set," which has not appeared in any previous Christie collection.

9. Collins, Max Allan. *Dying in the Post-War World*. Woodstock, VT: Countryman/Foul Play Press. Five stories and a new novella about private eye Nathan Heller.

10. Corris, Peter. *Man in the Shadows and Other Stories*. New York: Bantam. A short novel and six stories about Australian private eye Cliff Hardy, published for the first time in America.

11. Dahl, Roald. *The Collected Short Stories of Roald Dahl*. London: Michael Joseph. All fifty-one of Dahl's adult short stories, including two previously uncollected.

12. Davidson, Avram. *The Adventures of Doctor Eszterhazy*. Philadelphia: Owlswick Press. Thirteen mystery-fantasy tales, five previously collected in *The Inquiries of Doctor Eszterhazy* (1975). Foreword by Gene Wolfe, afterword by the author.

13. Ely, David. *Always Home and Other Stories*. New York: Donald I. Fine. A mixed collection of eighteen stories, two from *EQMM*, one new. Some are criminous.

14. Estleman, Loren D. *Eight Mile and Dequindre*. Eugene, OR: Mystery Scene Press/Pulphouse Publishing. A single Amos Walker story from *AHMM*, 1985. Part of a new series, Short Story Paperbacks. See also numbers 23, 26, 27, and 30 below.

15. Forsyth, Frederick. *The Deceiver*. New York: Bantam. Four novellas, with a brief framing story, about British Intelligence Chief Sam McCready.

16. Fraser, Antonia. *Jemima Shore at the Sunny Grave*. London: Bloomsbury. Nine stories from various sources, four about Jemima Shore.

17. Freemantle, Brian. *The Factory*. London: Century. Twelve linked stories about British Intelligence. (1990)

18. Gardner, Erle Stanley. *Honest Money and Other Short Novels*. New York: Carroll & Graf. Six novelettes from *Black Mask*, 1932–33, about Ken Corning, a forerunner of Perry Mason.

19. Gould, Philip. *The Eighth Continent: Tales of the Foreign Service*. Chapel Hill, NC: Algonquin Books. Three new

novelettes of intrigue about U.S. Information officer Charles McKay and his wife, Caroline.

20. Hickins, Michael. *The Actual Adventures of Michael Missing*. New York: Knopf. Eleven brief crime tales, some reprinted from a literary magazine, *The Quarterly*.

21. Himes, Chester. *The Collected Stories of Chester Himes*. New York: Thunder's Mouth Press. Sixty stories, 1933–78, including twenty-five published for the first time. About a third deal with crime and prison life. No detection.

22. Hoch, Edward D. *The Night My Friend*. Athens, OH: Ohio University Press. Twenty-two nonseries stories from the 1960s, mainly from *AHMM* and *The Saint Magazine*, one published for the first time in America. Edited and introduced by Francis M. Nevins, Jr.

23. ———. *The People of the Peacock*. Eugene, OR: Mystery Scene Press/Pulphouse Publishing. A single Captain Leopold novelette from *The Saint Magazine*, 1965. A Short Story Paperback.

24. ———. *The Spy Who Read Latin and Other Stories*. Helsinki: Eurographica. Five stories from *EQMM*, 1965–80, in an English-language limited edition.

25. Kaminsky, Stuart M. *Opening Shots*. Eugene, OR: Mystery Scene Press/Pulphouse Publishing. Eleven stories, one new, and a brief play. Part of a new series, Author's Choice Monthly. See also numbers 28 and 31 below.

26. Lutz, John. *Ride the Lightning*. Eugene, OR: Mystery Scene Press/Pulphouse Publishing. A single Edgar-winning short story from *AHMM*, 1985. A Short Story Paperback.

27. Maron, Margaret. *Lieutenant Harald and the "Treasure Island" Treasure*. Eugene, OR: Mystery Scene Press/Pulphouse Publishing. Two stories from *AHMM*, 1989–90. A Short Story Paperback.

28. Muller, Marcia. *Deceptions*. Eugene, OR: Mystery Scene Press/Pulphouse Publishing. Seven stories from various sources, 1982–90. Author's Choice Monthly.

29. Nolan, William F. *Blood Sky*. San Jose, CA: Deadline Publications. A limited-edition chapbook containing a single new short story, illustrated by the author. With a bibliog-

raphy of Nolan's horror/shock stories and an introduction by Joe R. Lansdale.

30. Pronzini, Bill. *Cat's-Paw*. Eugene, OR: Mystery Scene Press/ Pulphouse Publishing. Two "Nameless Detective" stories, 1983–88. A Short Story Paperback.

31. ———. *Stacked Deck*. Eugene, OR: Mystery Scene Press/ Pulphouse Publishing. Seven stories from various sources, 1967–91. Author's Choice Monthly.

32. Rendell, Ruth. *The Copper Peacock and Other Stories*. New York: Mysterious Press. Nine stories, eight from *EQMM* (including a Wexford mystery) and one from London's *Daily Telegraph*.

33. Stockbridge, Grant. *The Spider, Master of Men!* New York: Carroll & Graf. Two novellas from *The Spider Magazine*, 1940–43.

34. Thomson, June. *The Secret Files of Sherlock Holmes*. London: Constable. Seven new Holmes pastiches. (1990)

35. Thurber, James. *Thurber on Crime*. New York: Mysterious Press. Thirty-one stories and articles about crime, fictional and real. Edited by Robert Lopresti, foreword by Donald E. Westlake.

36. Wallace, Edgar. *Winning Colours: Selected Racing Writings of Edgar Wallace*. London Bellew. Twenty-two stories, many criminous, and thirty-five nonfiction pieces. Edited and introduced by John Welcome.

II. Anthologies

1. Adrian, Jack, ed. *Detective Stories from The Strand*. Oxford and New York: Oxford University Press. Twenty-five stories of mystery and detection from the *Strand Magazine*, 1903–48. Foreword by Julian Symons.

2. ———. *Strange Tales from The Strand*. Oxford and New York: Oxford University Press. Twenty-nine stories of mystery, horror, and the supernatural from the *Strand Magazine*, 1891–1950. A companion volume to number 1 above. Foreword by Julian Symons.

3. Ardai, Charles, ed. *Great Tales of Crime and Detection*.

New York: Galahad. Twenty-five stories, mainly from *EQMM* and *AHMM*. Introductions by Robert Bloch and John Lutz.

4. Bloch, Robert, ed. *Psycho-Paths*. New York: Tor Books. Seventeen new stories of psychopathic personalities, mainly criminous.

5. Chizmar, Richard, ed. *Cold Blood*. Shingletown, CA: Mark V. Ziesing. Twenty-five new mystery and horror stories, some fantasy.

6. Collings, Rex, ed. *A Body in the Library*. London: Bellew. Fourteen British mystery and suspense stories published before World War II.

7. ————. *Murder in the Vicarage: Classic Tales of Clerical Crime*. London: Bellew. Ten stories and excerpts from *The Mystery of Edwin Drood* by Charles Dickens.

8. Dalby, Richard, ed. *Crime for Christmas*. London: Michael O'Mara. Sixteen stories, three new.

9. ————. *Mystery for Christmas*. London: Michael O'Mara. Twenty-three stories, twelve new. Some crime, mainly fantasy. (1990)

10. Datlow, Ellen, ed. *A Whisper of Blood*. New York: Morrow. Eighteen stories, all but three new, on themes of mystery, horror, and vampirism. Mainly fantasy, a few criminous.

11. Gorman, Ed, ed. *Dark Crimes: Great Noir Fiction from the '40s to the '90s*. New York: Carroll & Graf. Two novels, by Gil Brewer and Peter Rabe, plus nineteen stories, two new. First of an annual series.

12. Gorman, Ed, and Martin H. Greenberg, eds. *Invitation to Murder*. Arlington Heights, IL: Dark Harvest. Eighteen new stories, some fantasy. Introduction by Bill Pronzini.

13. ————. *Solved*. New York: Carroll & Graf. Sixteen new stories and speculations in which mystery writers offer their solutions to unsolved crimes.

14. Greenberg, Martin H., and Ed Gorman, eds. *Cat Crimes*. New York: Donald I. Fine. Seventeen new mystery-suspense stories involving cats.

15. Hale, Hilary, ed. *Midwinter Mysteries 1*. London: Scribners. Nine stories in the first of a new anthology series, one previously published in *EQMM*.

16. Higgs, Mike, ed. *The Sexton Blake Detective Library*. Lon-

don: Hawk Books. Four novelettes and a comic strip, by various authors, about British sleuth Sexton Blake. The novelettes were first published in issues of *The Sexton Blake Library*, 1915. Introduction by Norman Wright.

17. Hoch, Edward D., ed. *The Year's Best Mystery and Suspense Stories 1991*. New York: Walker and Company. Thirteen of the best stories from 1990, with bibliography, necrology, and awards lists.

18. Jakubowski, Maxim, ed. *New Crimes 3*. London: Robinson. Eighteen new stories, two reprints, and a reprinted article.

19. Jordan, Cathleen, ed. *Alfred Hitchcock's Home Sweet Homicide*. New York: Walker and Company. Twelve stories from *AHMM*, 1966–90.

20. Keating, H. R. F., ed. *Crime Waves I*. London: Gollancz. Fourteen reprints and three new stories in the first of a new annual series from the Crime Writers' Association.

21. MacLeod, Charlotte, ed. *Christmas Stalkings*. New York: Mysterious Press. Thirteen new stories with Christmas themes.

22. Manguel, Alberto, ed. *Canadian Mystery Stories*. Toronto: Oxford University Press. Twenty stories, two new and three newly translated from the French-Canadian.

23. Manson, Cynthia, ed. *Murder at Christmas*. New York: Signet. Ten stories, mainly from *EQMM* and *AHMM*.

24. ———. *Mystery Cats*. New York: Signet. Sixteen stories, mainly from *EQMM* and *AHMM*.

25. ———. *Mystery for Halloween*. New York: Signet. Sixteen stories, mainly from *AHMM* and *EQMM*, some fantasy.

26. Olson, Paul F., and David B. Silva, eds. *Dead End: City Limits*. New York: St. Martin's Press. Seventeen new stories of "urban fear," mainly fantasy.

27. Paretsky, Sara, ed. *A Woman's Eye*. New York: Delacorte. Twenty-one new stories by women writers.

28. Peyton, Richard. *Sinister Gambits: Chess Stories of Murder and Mystery*. London: Souvenir Press. Eighteen stories, some fantasy.

29. Rejt, Maria, ed. *Winter's Crimes 23*. London: Macmillan. Eleven new stories by British writers.

30. Sellers, Peter, ed. *Cold Blood III*. Oakville, Ontario, Canada:

Mosaic Press. Sixteen new stories by Canadian writers.
(Listed in last year's volume but not available in the United
States until 1991. Listing repeated to avoid confusion with
number 5 above.)

31. Smith, Marie, ed. *More Ms. Murder*. London: Xanadu. Eighteen stories by women writers, mainly from *EQMM*.

32. Sullivan, Eleanor, ed. *Fifty Years of the Best from Ellery
Queen's Mystery Magazine*. New York: Carroll & Graf. An
anniversary volume containing fifty stories from *EQMM*,
1941–89. (British title: *Omnibus of Modern Crime Stories*)

33. ———. *Scarlet Letters: Tales of Adultery from Ellery
Queen's Mystery Magazine*. New York: Carroll & Graf. Sixteen stories, 1971–90.

34. Wallace, Marilyn, ed. *Sisters in Crime 4*. New York: Berkley.
Nineteen new stories and two reprints by women writers.

35. Zahava, Irene, ed. *The Fourth Womansleuth Anthology*.
Freedom, CA: The Crossing Press. Fifteen new stories by
women writers.

III. Nonfiction

1. Adey, Robert. *Locked Room Murders and Other Impossible
Crimes: A Comprehensive Bibliography*. Minneapolis and
San Francisco: Crossover Press. Revised and greatly ex-
panded American edition of a bibliography first published
in England in 1979, describing locked room and impossible
crime problems in 2,019 mystery novels and short stories.
Authors' solutions are summarized in a separate section at
the back of the book.

2. Bailey, Frankie Y. *Out of the Woodpile: Black Characters in
Crime and Detective Fiction*. Westport, Ct: Greenwood
Press. A study of black detectives and other black characters in crime fiction, with views of several of their creators
and a directory of relevant works of fiction, film, and
television.

3. Contento, William G., and Martin H. Greenberg. *Index to
Crime and Mystery Anthologies*. Boston: G. K. Hall. A title
and author index to some 1,031 anthologies, from 1875 to

the present, listing the complete contents of each volume as well as all anthology appearances for any given story. Introduction by Edward D. Hoch.

4. Green, Martin. *Seven Types of Adventure Tale*. University Park, PA: Penn State Press. A study of adventure stories from Dumas to Raymond Chandler.

5. Hillerman, Tony, and Ernie Bulow. *Talking Mysteries: A Conversation with Tony Hillerman*. Albuquerque: University of New Mexico Press. An interview, plus an essay and short story by Hillerman.

6. Huang, Jim, ed. *The Drood Review's 1991 Mystery Yearbook*. Boston: Crum Creek Press. An annual listing books published during 1990, together with awards, periodicals, mystery bookshops, and conventions.

7. Jakubowski, Maxim, ed. *100 Great Detectives*. New York: Carroll & Graf. Brief original essays on one hundred fictional sleuths, contributed by well-known mystery writers.

8. Keating, H. R. F. *The Writer's Library: Writing Crime Fiction*. New York: St. Martin's Press. Tips on writing and selling mysteries from the well-known British author.

9. Lewis, Margaret. *Ngaio Marsh: A Life*. London: Chatto & Windus. The first authorized biography of Roderick Alleyn's creator, based on interviews, letters, and notebooks. Photographs and bibliography.

10. McCauley, Michael J. *Jim Thompson: Sleep with the Devil*. New York: Mysterious Press. A biography of Thompson as seen through his novels.

11. Moffatt, June M., and Francis M. Nevins, Jr. *Edward D. Hoch Bibliography 1955–1991*. Van Nuys, CA: Southern California Institute for Fan Interests. A complete bibliography, introduced by Marvin Lachman.

12. Morley, Christopher. *The Standard Doyle Company: Christopher Morley on Sherlock Holmes*. New York: Fordham University Press. More than fifty essays and poems, with three brief fictions, about Holmes and the Baker Street Irregulars. Edited and introduced by Steven Rothman. (1990)

13. Paul, Robert S. *Whatever Happened to Sherlock Holmes? Detective Fiction, Popular Theology, and Society*. Carbon-

dale, IL: Southern Illinois University Press. The connections between theology and the popularity of detective fiction.

14. Redmond, Donald A. *Sherlock Holmes Among the Pirates; Copyright and Conan Doyle in America 1890–1930*. Westport, CT: Greenwood. A study of unauthorized publication of the Holmes stories. (1990)

15. Silverman, Kenneth. *Edgar A. Poe: Mournful and Never-Ending Remembrance*. New York: HarperCollins. A biography and psychological history.

16. Stafford, David. *The Silent Game: The Real World of Imaginary Spies*. Athens, GA: University of Georgia Press. Revised American edition of a study of twentieth-century espionage novelists (mainly British), first published in Canada in 1988.

17. Thorogood, Julia. *Margery Allingham: A Biography*. London: Heinemann. A life of the British mystery writer, creator of Albert Campion.

18. Waugh, Hillary. *Hillary Waugh's Guide to Mysteries and Mystery Writing*. Cincinnati: Writer's Digest Books. A history of the mystery, and a guide to writing it. Some chapters previously published.

19. Whiteman, Robin. *The Cadfael Companion: The World of Brother Cadfael*. London: Macdonald. A study of Ellis Peters's monastic sleuth and his medieval world, with an introduction by Peters.

20. Williams, John. *Into the Badlands*. London: Paladin/Grafton Books. A journey across America in 1989, interviewing some fifteen mystery and crime writers encountered along the way.

21. Wilt, David. *Hardboiled in Hollywood*. Bowling Green, OH: Bowling Green State University Popular Press. A study of five *Black Mask* writers and their work in films.

22. Wires, Richard. *John P. Marquand and Mr. Moto: Spy Adventures and Detective Films*. Muncie, IN: Ball State University Press. A study of the Mr. Moto novels and films.

23. Woolrich, Cornell. *Blues of a Lifetime: The Autobiography of Cornell Woolrich*. Bowling Green, OH: Bowling Green State University Popular Press. Five personal stories from Woolrich's life, edited by Mark T. Bassett.

AWARDS

Mystery Writers of America Edgar Awards

Best Novel: Lawrence Block, *A Dance at the Slaughterhouse* (Morrow)

Best First Novel: Peter Blauner, *Slow Motion Riot* (Morrow)

Best Original Paperback: Thomas Adcock, *Dark Maze* (Pocket Books)

Best Fact Crime: David Simon, *Homicide: A Year on the Killing Streets* (Houghton Mifflin)

Best Critical/Biographical: Kenneth Silverman, *Edgar A. Poe: Mournful and Never-Ending Remembrance* (HarperCollins)

Best Short Story: Wendy Hornsby, "Nine Sons" (*Sisters in Crime 4*, Berkley)

Best Young Adult: Theodore Taylor, *The Weirdo* (Harcourt Brace Jovanovich)

Best Juvenile: Betsy Byars, *Wanted . . . Mud Blossom* (Delacorte)

Best Episode in a Television Series: Gary Hopkins, "Poirot: The Lost Mine" (Dramatized by Michael Baker and David Renwick, *Mystery!*, PBS)

Best Television Feature or Miniseries: Bill Condon and Roy Johansen, "Murder 101" (TNT)

Best Motion Picture: Ted Tally, *The Silence of the Lambs*, based on Thomas Harris's novel (Orion)

Grandmaster: Elmore Leonard

Ellery Queen Award: Margaret Norton

Raven: Harold Q. Masur

Crime Writers Association (Britain)

Gold Dagger: Barbara Vine, *King Solomon's Carpet* (Viking, London)

Silver Dagger: Frances Fyfield, *Deep Sleep* (Heinemann)

John Creasey Memorial Award: Walter Mosley, *Devil in a Blue Dress* (Serpent's Tail)

Last Laugh Award: Mike Ripley, *Angels in Arms* (Collins)

'92 Award: Barbara Wilson, *Gaudi Afternoon* (Virago)

Gold Dagger for Nonfiction: John Bossy, *Giordano Bruno and the Embassy Affair* (Yale University Press)

CWA/Sunday Times Short Story Competition: Mary Arrigan, "The Song Went Up the Stair"

Diamond Dagger: Ruth Rendell

Crime Writers of Canada Arthur Ellis Awards (for 1990)

Best Novel: L. R. Wright, *A Chill Rain in January* (Macmillan, Toronto)

Best First Novel: Carsten Stroud, *Sniper's Moon* (Viking Penguin, Toronto)

Best Short Story: Peter Robinson, "Innocence" (*Cold Blood III*, Mosaic Press)

Best True Crime: Susan Mayse, *Ginger: The Life and Death of Albert Goodwin* (Harbour)

Best Genre Criticism/Reference: Donald A. Redmond, *Sherlock Holmes Among the Pirates; Copyright and Conan Doyle in America 1890–1930* (Greenwood, Westport CT)

Private Eye Writers of America Shamus Awards (for 1990)

Best P.I. Novel: Sue Grafton, *"G" Is for Gumshoe* (Holt)

Best Paperback P.I. Novel: W. Glenn Duncan, *Rafferty: Fatal Sisters* (Fawcett)

Best First P.I. Novel: Walter Mosley, *Devil in a Blue Dress* (Norton)

Best P.I. Short Story: Marcia Muller, "Final Resting Place" (*Justice for Hire*, Mysterious Press)

Lifetime Achievement: Roy Huggins

Bouchercon Anthony Awards (for 1990)

Best Novel: Sue Grafton, *"G" Is for Gumshoe* (Henry Holt)

Best First Novel: Patricia Cornwell, *Post Mortem* (Scribners)

Best Paperback Original (tie): Jim McCahery, *Grave Undertaking* (Knightsbridge) and Rochelle Krich, *Where's Mommy Now?* (Pinnacle)

Best Short Story: Susan Dunlap, "The Celestial Buffet" (*Sisters in Crime 2*, Berkley)

Best Movie: *Presumed Innocent* (Warner Brothers)

Best TV Series: *Mystery!* (PBS)
Lifetime Achievement: William Campbell Gault, William Link

Malice Domestic Agatha Awards (for 1990)

Best Novel: Nancy Pickard, *Bum Steer* (Pocket)
Best First Novel: Katherine Hall Page, *A Body in the Belfry* (St. Martin's)
Best Short Story: Joan Hess, "Too Much to Bare" (*Sisters in Crime 2*, Berkley)

NECROLOGY

1. Paul Brickhill (1916–91). Author of a single suspense novel, published in the U.S. as *War of Nerves* (1963).
2. Jess Carr (1930–90). Author of two mystery novels, beginning with *Moonshiners* (1979).
3. Mary Shura Craig (1923–91). Author of mystery novels and children's books as "M. S. Craig," "Mary Francis Craig," and "Meredith Hill." Elected president of Mystery Writers of America in 1990.
4. John Crosby (1912–91). Columnist and author of eight suspense novels, 1973–85.
5. Lillian Day (1893–91). Author of two mystery novels, starting with *Murder in Time* (1935), written in collaboration with her late husband, Norbert Lederer.
6. Theodore de la Torre-Bueno (1914–91). Short story writer and brother of mystery writer Lillian de la Torre.
7. Daniel B. Dodson (1918–91). Author of two mystery novels, including *The Man Who Ran Away* (1961).
8. Sumner Locke Elliott (1971–91). Australian-American author of several novels, at least two with crime elements, notably *Careful, He Might Hear You* (1962).
9. Elliot L. Gilbert (1930?–1991). College professor and specialist in Victorian and detective fiction. Edited a single anthology, *The World of Mystery Fiction* (1978), and authored two paperback mysteries.
10. Graham Greene (1904–91). Famed British author of twenty-four novels and fifty-two short stories, virtually all dealing with crime or intrigue to some degree. Among the most memorable, all filmed at least once, were *Orient Express* (1933), *This Gun For Hire* (1936), *Brighton Rock* (1938), *The Confidential Agent* (1939), *The Power and the Glory* (1940), *The Ministry of Fear* (1943), *The Heart of the Matter* (1948), *The Third Man* (1950), *The Quiet American* (1956), *Our Man in Havana* (1958), *The Honorary Consul* (1973), and *The Human Factor* (1978). Winner of the Grand Master Award from Mystery Writers of America.

11. A. B. Guthrie, Jr. (1901–91). Pulitzer Prize–winning author of historical westerns who also published five mystery novels, notably *Wild Pitch* (1973).

12. Ward Hawkins (1912–90). Pulp writer and contributor to *EQMM*, usually in collaboration with his late brother, John. The two authored a half-dozen mystery and adventure novels, 1940–58.

13. Howard Haycraft (1905–91). Well-known author of the most important early work of mystery scholarship, *Murder for Pleasure* (1941), editor of *The Art of the Mystery Story* (1946), and several anthologies of mystery fiction, all highly influential in the field. Past president of Mystery Writers of America.

14. Mary Ingate (1912–91). British author of four crime novels, starting with *The Sound of the Weir* (1974).

15. Leo Katcher (1911?–91). Novelist and screenwriter who authored five suspense novels, starting with *Hard Man* (1957).

16. Douglas Kiker (1930?–91). Television newsman who published a mystery novel, *Murder on Clam Pond*, in 1986.

17. Elliott Lewis (1917?–90). Radio mystery writer-producer who authored seven paperback private eye novels, starting with *Two Heads Are Better* (1980).

18. Malcolm Muggeridge (1903–90). Well-known British author of a single crime novel, *Affairs of the Heart* (1949).

19. James Atlee Phillips (1915–91). Author of twenty-three espionage thrillers about retired CIA agent Joe Fall, published mainly as by "Philip Atlee."

20. Douglas G. Shea (1910?–91). Short-story writer whose first mystery was published in *EQMM*, December 1976.

21. Benjamin Siegel (1914–91). Author of two mystery novels, beginning with *The Jurors* (1973).

22. Jimmy Starr (1904–90). Author of three mystery novels, notably *The Corpse Came C.O.D.* (1944).

23. Eleanor Sullivan (1928–91). *EQMM's* managing editor (1970–82) and editor (1982–91), also *AHMM's* editor (1976–81), and editor of numerous anthologies from the magazines. She published occasional fiction in both magazines, under her own name and as by "Julia DeHahn," "Lika

Van Ness," and "Ruth Graviros," receiving an Edgar nomination for a 1989 story under the latter name.

24. Thomas Tryon (1926–91). Actor and author of several novels, some criminous, including *The Other* (1971) and *Harvest Home* (1973).

25. John D. Voelker (1903–91). Author of the 1958 best-seller *Anatomy of a Murder*, published as by "Robert Traver."

26. Jean Francis Webb (1910–91). Author of eight mystery and gothic novels, one as by "Roberta Morrison," as well as numerous romance novels. Active in Mystery Writers of America.

HONOR ROLL

Abbreviations:
AHMM—Alfred Hitchcock's Mystery Magazine
EQMM—Ellery Queen's Mystery Magazine
(Starred stories are included in this volume. All dates are 1991.)

*Allyn, Doug, "Sleeper," *EQMM*, May
———, "Speed Demon," *EQMM*, October
Ardai, Charles, "The Investigation of Things," *AHMM*, February
Bankier, William, "The Ultimate Bummer," *EQMM*, March
———, "A Lot of Hurt Feelings," *EQMM*, June
Banks, Carolyn, "Counterpoint," *Penthouse Hot Talk*, March–April
Bell, Madison Smartt, "Cash Machine," *Story*, Spring
*Block, Lawrence, "A Blow for Freedom," *Playboy*, October
Burnham, Brenda Melton, "Ripples in the Stream," *AHMM*, December
Clark, Susan, "Serenade," *AHMM*, April
Collins, Barbara, "A Proper Burial," *Cat Crimes*
Collins, Lorraine, "Culture Shock," *EQMM*, June
Cross, Amanda, "Murder Without a Text," *A Woman's Eye*
*DuBois, Brendan, "My Brother's Night," *AHMM*, December
Fremlin, Celia, "Yellow Ken," *EQMM*, January
Gavrell, Kenneth, "Dead End on the Mountain," *AHMM*, February
Gordon, Alan, "The 730 Club," *AHMM*, October
Hoch, Edward D., "The Problem of the Blue Bicycle," *EQMM*, April
*———, "The Problem of the Grange Hall," *EQMM*, Mid-December
*Hornsby, Wendy, "Nine Sons," *Sisters in Crime 4*
Howard, Clark, "When the Rain Forest Burned," *EQMM*, March
———, "Dark Conception," *EQMM*, October
Hughes, Dorothy B., "That Summer at Quichiquois," *A Woman's Eye*

Jordan, Robert P., "Murder Off Blackstone Street," *AHMM*, November

*Kaminsky, Stuart M., "Punishment," *The Armchair Detective*, Summer

Kellerman, Faye, "Discards," *A Woman's Eye*

Lamburn, Nell, "Jimmy's Day," *EQMM*, March

Layefsky, Virginia, "This Place Belongs to You," *EQMM*, January

Limón, Martin, "The Woman from Hamhung," *AHMM*, July

*Lovesey, Peter, "The Crime of Miss Oyster Brown," *EQMM*, May

———, "Ginger's Waterloo," *Cat Crimes*

Lowe, William T., "So Long, Lana Turner," *AHMM*, February

Mackay, Scott, "The Orphan," *EQMM*, October

*Malzberg, Barry N., "Folly for Three," *A Whisper of Blood*

Maron, Margaret, "Lieutenant Harald and the Impossible Gun," *Sisters in Crime 4*

McGonegal, Richard F., "Probable Cause," *AHMM*, January

———, "Suitable for Framing," *AHMM*, September

Muller, Marcia, "Benny's Space," *A Woman's Eye*

Natsuki, Shizuko, "Divine Punishment," *EQMM*, March

Nielsen, Helen, "The One," *EQMM*, November

North, John, "Out of Bounds," *Cold Blood III*

Olson, Donald, "The Bigamist," *EQMM*, June

Pachter, Josh, "The Ivory Beast," *Gathering*, Summer

Paris, Jack, "Bush Fever," *Cold Blood III*

Petrin, Jas. R., "Man on the Roof," *Cold Blood III*

Pickard, Nancy, "The Dead Past," *Invitation to Murder*

Plews, Sara, "Blind Date," *Cold Blood III*

Powell, James, "The Tamerlane Crutch," *Cold Blood III*

———, "Winter Hiatus," *EQMM*, October

*Pronzini, Bill, "La Bellazza delle Bellezze," *Invitation to Murder*

———. "Souls Burning," *Dark Crimes*

*Rendell, Ruth, "Mother's Help," *The Copper Peacock and Other Stories*

Resnicow, Herbert, "A Few Strokes for Mitzi," *Nassau Review '91*

Robinson, Gregor, "Partners," *Cold Blood III*

*Robinson, Peter, "Innocence," *Cold Blood III*

Sellers, Peter, "This One's Trouble," *AHMM*, July

Shwartz, Susan, "Dreaming in Black and White," *Psycho-Paths*

Skarky, Jerry F., "The Symbolic Method," *AHMM*, April
Slesar, Henry, "What do I do about Dora?" *AHMM*, Mid-December
Stodghill, Dick, "Deadly Money," *AHMM*, November
Turnbull, Peter, "Because You're a Cop," *EQMM*, October
Wasylyk, Stephen, "Jump Start," *AHMM*, August
———, "Confession," *AHMM*, October
Watts, Timothy, "The Haircut," *EQMM*, April
*Wheat, Carolyn, "Ghost Station," *A Woman's Eye*
Yorke, Margaret, "Widow's Might," *EQMM*, October